The Book

of

April

Vol. 2 of the

Rowan Branch Trilogy

Pam Collins

The Book of April

Book cover and design by Pam Collins

Printed in the United States of America
The Troy Book Makers • Troy, New York • thetroybookmakers.com

To order additional copies of this title,
contact your favorite local bookstore
or visit www.shoptbmbooks.com

ISBN: 978-1-61468-784-9

For the beautiful heretics

Contents

Prologue – Betrayal..6

Chapter 1 – A Second Chance................................14

Chapter 2 – A Perilous Journey...............................28

Chapter 3 – Behind the Falls...................................39

Chapter 4 – Sirona's Despair..................................53

Chapter 5 – At the Hedge and Hearth....................67

Chapter 6 – The White Spring................................85

Chapter 7 – A Page Turns....................................103

Chapter 8 – Crumbs..117

Chapter 9 – The Circle Widens...........................129

Chapter 10 – The Red Notebook........................149

Chapter 11 – The Way Forward.........................159

Chapter 12 – Of Bees and Trees.........................178

Chapter 13 – Return to Glastonbury...............200

Chapter 14 – Bargains Fulfilled........................220

Chapter 15 – The Space Between...................231

Chapter 16 – The Wizard Awakens...............247

Chapter 17 – New Blood................................259

Chapter 18 – Ascent.......................................277

Chapter 19 – Sacred Alchemy.......................295

Epilogue 322

The Characters..327

Prologue

Betrayal

Somerset, England
Present Day

It was painfully clear to Abernathy Whitestone that escape was out of the question. Even had he been willing to bear the disgrace of walking away from his promise, of turning his back on this imposing collection of hooded and secretive men, and walking (if his legs would even manage to obey his will) out of the room, there was some...power...emanating from Vas that not only kept him rooted, but was pulling at his brain, as though his skull had been surgically incised and cold, grasping instruments inserted to pull out his memories as one might pluck feathers from a bird.

*Alright, alright...*he pushed into his thoughts...*I will give you what I promised.* But would he tell it all? The pain in his head intensified. *Of course...I will omit nothing...*

"I'm not entirely sure why I agreed to meet them," Whitestone began at long last, struggling to keep his voice steady. "At first, I was quite dismissive of them, but the tale the women brought to me..."

At the word *women* there was a murmur among the assemblage and a hiss of robes shifting that sent a chill down Whitestone's already sweating back.

*Continue...*the voice in his head demanded.

"...the tale they brought to me was impossible to ignore. They..." he was careful to keep the word *women* off his lips..."were convinced that one of them had some kind of connection to Merlin and furthermore that there was a curse involved."

Another rustle of robes. Whitestone was nearly overwhelmed by the image of black vipers slithering at his feet, surrounding him, hungry. That he had any ability at all to speak was a miracle, but the *thing* that was inside his head drove him on.

"As an Arthurian scholar, they believed, I could perhaps help them unravel their mystery. I demurred, but one of them was particularly persuasive, and drew on my...interest...and...."

Here Whitestone stumbled. What really did happen that day? Somehow, he had gone from half-asleep and dismissive to wide awake and eager. Some power had pulled him from his seat and sent him to his library, a disarray of all manner of manuscripts which he'd long ago given up keeping in any kind of order. And yet, a sliver of memory opened up and his hand lit upon a volume he had never considered very significant, but now...now...

"I remembered the writings of a nun around 900 AD, how she'd written about visions she'd had of Merlin...." His throat tightened, terrified of the predatory atmosphere in the room. Why had he not thought this through? Why had he not been more aware of the effect his story would have on the Society? The mere mention of a nun and Merlin in the same sentence was sure to bring down the wrath of this assembly, even if he was only the messenger. And yet now, the feeling of slithering annoyance had changed. Now there was a stillness that was even more terrifying....

CONTINUE the voice in his head demanded.

"...visions...that...Merlin had had a... daughter."

Perhaps he had passed out. Perhaps there were snakes after all and he had been bitten and now lay dying, for everything had changed. He was bathed in a white light -- not a comforting one, but a light that obliterated everything, including it seemed, his will. He heard himself speaking as though from far away, continuing his story, helpless to do anything us.

"The women were stunned by the news," he felt himself rush on. "One of them said, '*not of his soul, then, but of his blood*'. We spoke of Merlin's enchantment in the Forest of Broceliande and how perhaps he could be freed. The thought excited me. To have the object of my life's study returned to this world was beyond my wildest imaginings. What was fact and what fiction, what the fruits of our imaginings or a legend of earlier times so compelling as to survive through the ages? The thought of having those answers at last was intoxicating. After all, the legends say that he and Arthur would someday return. Wondrous should this day exist in my lifetime.

"They left saying little more," Abernathy rushed on, "but I remember suggesting they go to Merlin's cave in Cornwall, though I had no idea what they would find there beyond sea and stone. I was caught up in my own longings. But sometime later when one of them returned to tell me the unimaginable, that they had indeed found the cave in the forest where Merlin had been ensorcelled and, furthermore, believed they had been successful in releasing his spirit...my own spirit trembled. What could this mean? I was overwhelmed with a sense of the unnatural, of inappropriate meddling in the proper order. It was then that I contacted this Society."

With that, Whitestone's head dropped to his chest, then, as though waking, he raised it up again to find that his vision had cleared and the room had returned to relative normalcy.

At his elbow, Ignatius Vas asked with a fake, oily politeness, "And, Professor Whitestone, what were the names of these...*women?"*

"The...difficult one was called Sirona," Whitestone answered, hesitating to give them Raina's name.

"And the other?" the leader pressed.

That pain behind his eyes again.

"Raina," Whitestone said in a whisper.

"I'm sorry, louder please?"

"RAINA," Whitestone nearly shouted, forcing the name out of himself, too distressed to notice that among the hooded men, one raised his head slightly at the name.

"Thank you, Professor. Now if you please, could you provide us with their last names? That is, after all," Vas said, his hands playing obscenely across his robes, "what you came here for."

"I don't know their last names. I'm sorry, but I don't," Whitestone said, pleadingly, but the pain in his head return with a ferocity. "*I DON'T.* I would tell you if I knew, but I don't."

Again, Whitestone failed to see a slight movement among the men, but at that moment the pain ceased.

"We thank you for your tale," the High Priest said, his tone changing dramatically. Now it was all business, the cajoling tone gone, as it was clear that Whitestone would soon be as well. "It was good of you to come to us. Now it is best that you go about your business and forget this day."

A cloaked figure slipped from the shadows and, taking Abernathy Whitestone's arm led him decisively from the chamber and out into the light of day, a light which seemed to clear his mind, wiping away the memory of the last few hours. It was a fine spring day. He would return to his rooms knowing that he had done his duty, but not exactly sure how. No matter. He could rest easy. Return to his books. Imagine himself a mage in the employ of a king, who, lacking in cunning was adored by the people and much in need of the assistance of scholarly wisdom.

Inside the hall, there was a flurry of cloaks and scraping of chairs as the assemblage began to disperse, assured by their esteemed leader that each would be contacted individually and given whatever task was required of them in the face of this news. One lingered, however, until the hall was empty and the High Priest gone from the dais. When he was certain there was no one around, he left by the door reserved for the eerie and reclusive Ignatius Vas, and made his way down the narrow corridor to the heavy oaken door he knew to be the entrance to the High Priest's chambers. Three short knocks, a pause, and then two more. He waited, then repeated the coded knock. When the door opened, Malcolm Holtz entered, certain that his news would be well received.

"Brother Malcolm, all the way here from the States," Vas intoned, barely looking up from where he stood at an elegantly carved table, his heavily ringed hand tracing down the page of a large tome. When the man who had opened the door put a hand out to keep Malcolm from entering any further into the room, Vas waved him back. "I believe Brother Malcolm has some important information for us. Otherwise, why would he be so brazen as to come to our chambers without invite?" So saying, Vas raised his head and bored his eyes into Malcolm's.

"Your Eminence," Malcolm said, with a slight bow of his head, mustering a tone of reverence which wasn't entirely sincere, resenting, as he did, groveling before anyone, much less accepting the implication that Vas himself hadn't signaled his visitation.

"Well, speak then," and with a single flick of his wrist sent his servant from the room and motioned Malcolm forward, but not to a seat. The two men stood face to face, Vas having moved just enough to block Malcolm's view of the book he'd been perusing.

"It's about the women mentioned by the professor, or rather, one of the women," Malcolm said, trying to weight his words with the import he believed they carried.

"Yes, yes, go on..."

"The woman he called Raina...I...know of her. Her last name is Quinn and she's from the States."

"How can you be sure of that?"

"It....adds up." Malcolm had no intention of sharing his private life with this self-important man by revealing that Raina was his ex-wife, but he was fairly certain that it was indeed *his* Raina who had been involved in this business. It is what brought him to England and to this meeting of the Society, having gleaned from snooping in April's correspondence that her mother had been involved in some kind of witchery in Glastonbury, and perhaps April as well.

"You're relatively new to our Society, are you not Brother Malcolm?" the elder man said, almost accusingly.

"I am, Your Eminence, but no less devoted to your cause. Women's witchery must be rooted out at whatever cost, and certainly this business of Merlin's soul..."

"I doubt very much that we have to worry about *Merlin's soul*, though I do not doubt Whitestone's tale. Quite likely, these women did indeed travel to some cave in France and believe in their deranged little brains that they freed the soul of a mighty wizard – who'd been ensorcelled for 1500 years no less," Vas let out a gravelly chuckle. "Not only do I not believe that's possible, I question whether an ancient wizard, even had he existed, would have had a soul at all. But," he continued, smoothing his vestments, "the story is well suited to sounding the alarm. Imagine...legend's most powerful wizard's soul loose in our present world. It will do well to unify the masses in our favor." That horrid chuckle again. "Even the professor himself was terrified at the thought. Why else would he have brought the news to us?

"No, Brother Malcolm, my concern is much more...nuanced." The High Priest turned his back to Malcolm as he spoke, moving back to the book on the table and caressing its pages. "My concern is this level of heretical behavior on behalf of a gaggle of women. It's one thing to parade around Glastonbury dressed as fairies and whatnot, but the intensity of this enterprise and the motivation for it needs investigating. And this woman Raina is from America you say?"

"She is."

"As are you, yes?"

"Yes."

"And do you know where she resides?"

Malcolm hesitated. "Yes."

"Then if you are as devoted as you say, you will return to your native land and spy on this woman. Gather what information you can, gain a surety that she is indeed the right person, and keep us informed." Vas waved his hand as though dismissing Malcolm, but Malcolm chose to ignore the gesture.

"This other woman," Malcolm risked what Vas would surely see as prying, but hadn't he earned the right to know more? "Do we know anything of her?"

The High Priest wheeled on Malcolm. "You have your orders, Brother Malcolm. Play your part and leave the rest to me."

Malcolm nodded and turned to leave, heaving open the heavy door and, risking a tiny act of passive aggression, left it open as he made his way down the hall and out of the sacred temple of the Society for the Preservation of Heaven, leaving Ignatius Vas alone in his ostentatious chambers to ponder the day's revelations. As he did so, unseen by any save perhaps his butler, Vas let a half-smile ooze from his lips as he leaned over the open tome once again and rested his finger under a single name...*Sirona.*

Chapter 1

A Second Chance

Wales
Circa 500 AD

The sound of hoofbeats thrumming their way into the pre-dawn hush was enough to startle Abertha into full wakefulness as she crept from the bedroom to the kitchen, careful not to disturb her husband's restless slumber. But the sudden wail of a babe sent her flying to the door. Hand on the latch, she paused, steadying herself against the wave of memory that threatened to crush her barely mended heart. *Not again,* she pleaded with fate. Or was it *still?* Deep inside, Abertha knew that nothing really ends, finally and completely. Life was not full of endings and beginnings, only change, alteration, transmutation. Life was a spiral dance, things coming around and around again, never quite the same, never free of the influence, the choices, of the past. Even before opening the door, she knew what she would find.

Still, the sight of the raven dark hair, the startling green eyes, too full of knowing for a babe, made her catch her breath and twisted her heart.

"Oh Annwyl," she cried aloud as she swooped the babe into her arms and held it fiercely against her breast, as though it might fly away if not securely tethered. Knowing full well she would find only an empty yard, nevertheless, she stepped off the porch and searched into every inch of the familiar landscape for the presence of her beloved Annwyl, all the while feeling the baby's heartbeat against her own. But despite the rising light, there was no sign of the daughter she had raised, and loved, and sent away.

Defeated, Abertha returned to the cottage, feeling all her unshed tears threaten a deluge. When they came, they soaked the baby's swaddling, as though the simple cloth could absorb Abertha's anguish, promising a redemption the woman was not yet ready to accept as her right to claim. Still, as her swollen heart emptied into the silence of the morning, Abertha knew she had been given a second chance, and that whatever Annwyl's fate, there was enough love and trust left in her to choose Abertha to care for the best part of her. And – dare she hope – so long as Annwyl knew where her baby was, there was a thread, gossamer thin though it might be, between the two women. No stranger to such fragility, on that thread Abertha did indeed hang her hopes.

Gently laying the babe on the kitchen table, Abertha began to unwind the swaddling – slowly, reverently, imagining it had been Annwyl's beloved hands that had touched it last. When a copper coin clattered against the aged wood, it took Abertha a minute to make sense of it. Then it came to her. That fateful day of Annwyl's sixteenth birthday when she had innocently sent her daughter to her friend Nesta, the herbalist, for lavender honey. She had given her three coppers, one of which, it appeared, now lay upon her kitchen table. She recognized the mark, proof, if she needed it, that it was indeed Annwyl, and not a proxy, who had left the babe.

But the coin begged a question. What had happened that day? Annwyl had dutifully returned with the honey, for which she must then have paid the full price, unless Nesta had discounted the item. Yet Annwyl had not returned the coin, nor told the story. And, there was the awkward tension between Annwyl and the guests that night – most particularly the herbalist. As Abertha thought back to that night, she remembered the fear that had come over her, the way the tension sat in the room like a coiled snake, confirming her suspicions that the powers Annwyl had inherited had ceased their latency, had awakened in her and demanded a trial which, on that day of her sixteenth birthday, Annwyl had, in some unseemly way, exercised while on her errand.

Now Abertha picked up the coin and, with her left hand on the babe's chest, held the mystery copper tightly between the thumb and second finger of her other hand and waited for the vision, calling on her own long unused powers. The babe stirred slightly under her hand, but Abertha kept her mind focused on the coin.

Annwyl's face, darkened, almost unrecognizable, handing the herbalist two coins. The herbalist's face, a somnambulant mask, handing Annwyl a jar in return. Then, a single copper, buried among the roots of an oak.

The babe whimpered, bringing Abertha back to the kitchen and her waking memory of that day. So, her suspicions had not been unfounded. Annwyl had learned to use the power of manipulating the will of others – power inherited from her wizard father. Merlin. Oh Merlin. Are not all the traps that bind us of our own making after all?

Gazing down at the babe, Abertha brushed the midnight hair from an alabaster forehead, then ran her finger down the side of the precious, unspoiled face, lingering on the tiny lips, so innocent and yet so full of potential power she could almost feel it quiver at her touch.

I failed you once, dear one, her heart spoke. *I cannot promise I will not fail you again, but if I do it will not be for want of trying. But do you have any idea what you ask of me? So long buried, what paltry power I am heir to, so painfully excised from my being and my behavior, yet not from my soul it would seem. Such things can never be erased, only ignored or denied – and done so at our peril, I now realize. Whatever ill fate I thought I was avoiding by hiding from my own birthright, only manifested itself in the pain you've endured. How I long to know what has happened to you since you left us, but no coin can tell me that, nor would I ask it of this babe, whether it holds those memories or not.*

And yet, was she not on the verge of doing so? Let the babe be innocent as long as it can be, she thought as she returned to the task of freeing the infant from its tear-soaked bindings to see that it was, as expected, a girl child. Merlin's granddaughter. The persistence of his lineage, lying here in all her vulnerability on this humble kitchen table, centerpiece of the humble life Abertha had chosen for herself – chosen, in denial and flight from her own ancient beginnings.

Derwen had not yet risen, nor did she expect him to. As though losing Annwyl hadn't been heartache enough, Abertha had as good as lost her husband as well. On the day that Annwyl rode out of their yard, clinging to Merlin's back, Derwen's spirit left him, as though Annwyl had packed it in her bag along with what few belongings she had taken from her life with the two of them.

He had taken to his bed that very night and had barely left it since, leaving Abertha to take on his chores in addition to her own. She had struggled to keep their homestead from falling to ruin, but friends had helped, and she was a stronger woman than she had let on. So, she managed. But what she had not managed well was the loss of Derwen's companionship – his gentle ways, his generosity, his care with animals and the land, and his endearing devotion to Abertha and their household. They still shared the same bed, but only out of necessity. The only other bed in their small cottage was the one Annwyl had slept in – emotionally off-limits to both of them. So night after night Abertha would lay next to her love, although it was more like lying next to a corpse, praying that perhaps tonight would be the night he would wake out of his despair and rejoin the living – and her. And day after day she would rise to life, to honor the blessing of it and do what needed to be done, while Derwen wasted away, unmovable and unmoved.

Now, she held the babe wrapped in her best shawl, as she stood on the threshold of Annwyl's room, imagining it inhabited by another child, and wondering if the child's presence would be the thing that could reanimate her husband. It had to. She couldn't imagine taking on the care of this precious being without his help, nor could she imagine Derwen turning his back on parenting the daughter of the young woman he had loved so fiercely. How would she continue to cling to any faith in humanity at all if still he would not rise?

Turning away from Annwyl's room and the vision of a new child growing there, Abertha moved toward the room where Derwen languished, but stopped just short of the door, suddenly terrified of his rejection. It was not characteristic of Abertha to balk at difficult things, but at this moment she couldn't help herself. Her knees threatened to buckle. The child she held was no mirage nor were the events of the morning a dream. Enough for her to come to terms with before entering head first into Derwen's despair. How to approach this required some thought and a bolstering of her resources.

By mid-morning, Abertha had determined to visit Nesta. Their friendship had deepened since the departure of Annwyl. Though Abertha longed to share the truth of Annwyl's parentage with Nesta, she nevertheless maintained the same story with her as she had given out to anyone who asked – that Annwyl's true father, a nameless member of Arthur's court, had come to claim his daughter once she had come of age. But though it was never discussed, Abertha sensed in Nesta an awareness that there was more to be said, though it never would be. Now, desperate for the support Derwen seemed unable to provide, Abertha would turn to Nesta whom she was certain would willingly share in whatever Abertha was comfortable revealing without pressing for more.

That something significant had happened between Annwyl and Nesta on the day of Annwyl's sixteenth birthday, Abertha had always sensed. But the true nature of it had been shrouded in mystery until Abertha had held the coin. Exactly what Nesta understood of the exchange, Abertha didn't know, nor would she ask her, for to do so would risk giving away the secret of Annwyl's parentage – a secret that Abertha determined must be maintained at all costs. But that Nesta would know immediately that the babe was Annwyl's, of that Abertha was certain. And yet, equally certain was she that Nesta would support Abertha in a tale that claimed the babe was delivered anonymously – a tale that would be readily accepted by the community given the reputation Abertha and Derwen enjoyed as loving and generous folk.

At Nesta's door, Abertha paused before knocking. What a fine line she would have to walk, being as honest with her friend as she dared, but not succumbing to the urge to unburden herself of everything that had so ravaged her heart to hold onto all these years. *Oh Derwen, how I long for your return from despair,* she thought. But she could not curse him. He was, after all, just a simple and loving man, not heir to the blood of the old folk as she was. No matter that she had turned her back on it, one cannot deny one's blood, and it was that connection, after all, that had led Merlin to trust her with his child. No, she could not blame Derwen. Rather she should blame herself for asking him to take on the rearing of what would inevitably be a child beyond his ken.

Nesta's door opened before Abertha had raised her hand. Wordlessly, Nesta moved aside to admit her friend and usher her to a seat. An aromatic tea arrived at

Abertha's elbow before her weight was fully released to the chair. Still wordlessly, Abertha handed the babe to Nesta. Gently lifting the corner of Abertha's shawl from the baby's face, Nesta let out a sigh and a single word.

"Annwyl."

"Before dawn this very morning," Abertha whispered, though there was no one but the two to hear. "I saw no one, but I have reason to believe – or I feel it in my heart – that it was Annwyl herself who left her."

Again, silence consumed the two women as they contemplated the fate of the young woman they had toasted not so very long ago. So full of hope for her, so complacent in the belief that her life, while not perfect, would certainly not evolve into abandoning a child before she had even fully tasted womanhood. Relieved for the moment of the burden of the child, Abertha fell prey to a fathomless grief for the daughter she had raised and loved so deeply. What suffering had she endured in these past months? Nesta's own tears fell freely as her friend keened her grief in the safety of their friendship.

When at last Abertha could raise her head, it was Nesta who spoke first.

"This will be our shared burden. You needn't feel you must undertake this alone. We will raise her together."

Abertha nodded in assent and gratitude.

"I would not have anyone but us know that it is Annwyl's child. To admit such..."

"Of course," Nesta reassured her. "The babe appeared on your doorstep, that is all. No one will care to pry further. And, should one day Annwyl return..."

"Oh, Nesta. Such a hope will tear me apart! Not an hour will pass that I don't cast my eyes to the road, my heart quickening at the possibility of her return. How would I give the babe all the love and attention she deserves if my eyes are perpetually cast in outward glance? No. That is a hope I must bury deep if I am to continue to live fully in the demands of the present." And bury it she would, or so she believed, but that which is buried can always be exhumed.

At that, Abertha held her tongue, choosing not to voice what she also feared, that Annwyl had the capacity to walk away from love without a backward glance. That she had made the impossible decision of giving up her child likely meant that she had already cut the child from her heart. Then again, Annwyl herself had been abandoned, her mother dead at her birth, her father unwilling to gather her to him, giving her instead to Abertha and Derwen to raise, ill-fated as that turned out to be. No. Unlikely that Annwyl would ever return.

"And Derwen?" Nesta asked, as gently as she could.

"The same. I'm not sure how to share this with him. Obviously, I must eventually, but I have no idea how he'll take it – if he'll even respond to it. What if it drives him even deeper into his despair? If it leads him to imagine what Annwyl has gone through..."

"Somehow, we must get him to focus on the child, on her needs, appeal to his protective instincts. Has he not responded at all to the latest concoctions I've prepared?" Nesta asked, already sensing the answer.

"Only a little," Abertha sighed. "He's eating a bit better, thanks me for my ministrations, but then turns his face away again and falls into the dark place that is now his home."

"You mustn't give up hope, Abertha. Time has its ways and who knows what hope this child brings? Life is suffering, but each new child brings the innocence of a fresh start. Let us turn our love for Annwyl into a devotion to this child and a commitment to her well-being and healthy life. She is the piece of Annwyl that we *do* have."

And the continuation of a line I question the worth of, Abertha thought. *But perhaps that is not for me to judge. It is as it is. It is not for me to question the role in it which fate has given me, but to carry it out with a willing heart.*

That evening, after preparing a meal for herself, she settled the babe in Annwyl's room and went to Derwen with bread and cheese and a tea steeped of a new concoction Nesta had made that afternoon. As she sat beside the bed, encouraging Derwen to eat, she chatted about her day as she always did, struggling as she did so to keep her emotions out of her voice. She spoke of the trivialities of life, a visit to her friend, a mended dress, a new shirt for Derwen she had finally finished. Was that a glimmer of interest she saw in his eyes or was it just her own vain hope she saw reflected there? At least he drank all his tea, though his hands shook as he did so. When he finally shrunk down again into the womb of the bed, Abertha found herself overwhelmed with a pity for him she had not let herself feel for a long time. As she brushed the steel gray hair away from his face, she felt his soul reach out to her, pleading for help she didn't know how to give. She bent to kiss him and lingered with her lips against his skin as though she could transfer some of her life force into him. Then, with a sigh, she straightened and left the room.

As she stoked the fire, she heard the babe begin to fuss. This wasn't going to be easy, she thought. Perhaps she was too old to care for a babe again. Retrieving the child from Annwyl's room, she returned to the fireside and sank into her rocker. Peering into the babe's emerald eyes Abertha fell into an odd state, as though she was some mythic being and the babe was pure, unformed energy, waiting for the story that would give her shape and meaning. With the babe lovingly cradled in her arms, Abertha began her tale.

"Dear one," she said, running her hand across the babe's cheek, "let me tell you a story...your story. For good or ill, you are the continuation of a very special line, one that stretches back to an earlier time, when the Old Ways were alive in the land and in people's hearts. The people from which you come knew the land, this land, as intimately as they knew their own skin. We (and that I say "we" you will soon understand), belonged to the land and knew our place in it. In return, the land gave us all we needed. The best life was a simple one full of joy and celebration, and a true heart full of gratitude and reverence for the sacredness of all living things."

Abertha drew the babe to her face and set a lingering kiss upon her tiny nose. Amazing how much the human heart can hold, she thought, feeling the memories evoked by her story and the love she felt for the babe combine in an ethereal alchemy that brought tears to her eyes. But her tale had only just begun, and so she drew breath and continued.

"Among the people, there were those who held the wisdom of the folk, their history, their dreams. They were the poets, the doctors, the philosophers. Your grandfather was such a one. In fact, your grandfather was a prince among his kind. He had many names but history will remember him as "Merlin." I say "had" because it has been carried on the wind that he has met his doom at the hands of the enchantress Nimue. For, wise as Merlin was, he was still a man, still subject to the call of the heart and the demands of our earthly bodies.

"It was his humanness that resulted in you, dear one of the emerald eyes. You see, Nimue was not the only one to enchant him, though she was the most treacherous. There was another. A kind and loving woman, beautiful beyond all imagining, with such a generous heart it was impossible to refuse her. Had she chosen to, she could have commanded every soul who knew her to do her bidding, but the only thing greater than her beauty was her compassion and fierce respect for the sovereignty of each and all."

Here Abertha paused, overcome by the memory. Unperturbed by the delay, the babe stared up at Abertha, fixing her with eyes the color of spring leaves touched by the sun, reminding the storyteller that it is the present that counts – that is, after all, all we have of the past.

"And so," Abertha said, "she hid the power of her beauty in the only way she knew how, by feigning a simple mind. For the most part her ruse worked, until Merlin came along. The piercing eye of the greatest wizard in the land could see beyond her disguise. He who could sense the dragons roiling beneath the land where King Vortigern strove to build his Keep, saw your grandmother for what she was – not just a loving and gentle woman, but one whose wisdom rivalled his own, though she had no will to exercise that wisdom against others.

"Perhaps it was the joy of being recognized for what she was, for realizing that there was no fooling Merlin, that encouraged her to let her full being shine forth for him and him alone. As for Merlin, he was caught in the whirlwind of feminine beauty, goodness, and intellect at its apex in one person. But Merlin lived to serve Arthur and his kingly dream of peace, unity, and justice throughout the land, whereas your grandmother was compelled to maintain her cloak of ignorance with everyone save Merlin. The complexities of their relationship took their toll.

"You would ask me how it is that I know of all this," Abertha said, smiling down at the babe as though she had, indeed, asked. "There was a time when Merlin and I were friends, sharing as we did the ancestry of the old ones. But whereas Merlin chose to be a king-maker, I fled from the weight of wisdom and leadership. I wanted only to live a simple life. Merlin and I fought bitterly. He accused me of betraying not just my ancestors but the very soul of the land. His accusations wounded me deeply, all the more so because I sensed he was right. So I turned my own self-doubt on him, and imagined I hated him. I cast him as a self-serving, manipulating villain. Nevertheless, when your grandmother fell into madness under the strain of her life and died giving birth to your mother, it was me to whom Merlin turned to care for the child, your mother, who I named Annwyl."

At that, Abertha's voice caught in her throat. Her eyes misted and through her tears, the face of the babe melded into that of its mother. As she had done all those years before, it was the baby, Annwyl, that Abertha now held, clinging to her as Derwen drove their cart through the falling snow and whispering forest to this very house. Remembering that night and all the days of love and worry that came after, she clung to the babe like a life-line until she could bring herself back to the present. But before she could return to her story, she heard a footfall behind her. Derwen was making his way, shakily, to the chair across from her.

"Has Annwyl returned?" he asked, his voice barely audible, his body little more than a stick propped upright.

Calling on all her strength, she struggled to reflect the nonchalance with which Derwen had returned, after sixteen years, to his place by the hearth. "No my love, Annwyl has not returned, but a piece of her has. And you," she queried, despite her fear that what she saw before her was no more than a dream that her words would dispel, "have you returned to me at last?"

Chapter 2

A Perilous Journey

Derwen had all but fallen into the chair across from Abertha – his chair, so agonizingly vacant all these months. Now his body was dwarfed by it, a painful diminishment of a hard-working, big-hearted man. But here he was at last, upright and sitting with her by the hearth. Hope crept into Abertha's heart on tip-toe. It was a beginning; the rest would surely follow.

"I heard you speaking..." Derwen said, barely audible, but his words hit Abertha as though she had been struck. Since Derwen had taken to his bed, Abertha had gone about her domestic business in silence. The only time she spoke was at Derwen's bedside where, nightly, she dutifully, if uselessly, recounted the day's events. Other than that, she had not spoken in these rooms, nor did she ever have any company that got much past the doorway, except for her friend Nesta. This aspect of the diminishment of her life now hit her full force, releasing a gale of unstoppable tears.

"Don't cry my love, our Annwyl has returned," Derwen croaked, holding out trembling arms as though he would hold the babe.

Abertha moved to where Derwen sat, and gently placed the babe in his arms, folding them around the precious bundle while keeping her own in place to secure the child, wrestling with when and how to bring Derwen into the present. But Abertha was a realist and either Derwen would deal with the truth or he wouldn't. There was no future in putting out anything other. Before Abertha could speak, however, out of the fog of his caged brain, Derwen found a thread and followed it to its conclusion.

"But this can't be Annwyl, can it?" he asked the room in general. "She was a young woman when...but this babe, so like her...Abertha..." he pleaded, looking up at her.

Tightening her grip on Derwen's arms and the child within them, Abertha took a deep breath. "No, my dear. This is not Annwyl as you well know. But I have reason to believe that it is her child. It seems that fate has given us a second chance."

Then, making a plea of her own, she continued, "My love. You must come back to me. I cannot do this alone." And though she *could* have, *would* have if necessity had demanded it, she ardently preferred not to, and so her need of him was the story she told both herself and the withered man before her. *Let this story be the road he travels to return to me...and the babe. Let this be the story he lives into.*

Over the next few weeks, both Derwen and the child grew strong in Abertha's care. She fed them abundantly and spoke with them gently, but without coddling. Both were expected to take on their responsibilities as they were able, the babe to coo and smile, Derwen to tend to his chores as his growing strength allowed. In her younger days, this was her way, and she managed it with energy and grace. But now, life had taken its toll, and when at last she fell into bed each night, she was more than a little grateful to release the taut attention she applied to her charges throughout the day. Even with Nesta's herbs and her help with the child, Abertha was well aware that she was working beyond what was comfortable and appropriate for her age. She prayed that Derwen would attain full recovery before she gave out. And there was the other thing – the journey she had decided she must take. A journey that must happen soon, while she was still able and, moreover, while her courage held.

The day came sooner rather than later. The westering sun had poked a finger of light into their kitchen, turning everything a soothing amber. Derwen was sitting at the table, speaking of trifles to the babe in his arms while Abertha ladled stew into bowls.

"I've fixed the cart and checked all the tack for the horse," he said, reporting on the day's work as was his wont.

"So I saw," Abertha said, cheerfully, despite her rising tension at what she was about to say.

"You've done well, keeping the horse well-fed and groomed..." Derwen said, somewhat sheepishly. He had always admired Abertha's steadfastness. He suspected there was little she couldn't do, but he was still ashamed of his fall into despair and the way it had left her without the partner he hoped she depended on. For Abertha's part, she made a study of keeping any blame of him from her words or demeanor, but she couldn't do much about the self-blame he refused to relinquish.

"My dearest," she began, her heartbeat loud in her ears, "it is good you've put the wagon in order. I must take a trip."

"Oh? Something you need for the wee one?"

She could dissemble until their bowls were empty and the sun was finished for the day, but what was the point?

"I need to go North to the Berwyn Mountains...to Pistyll Rhaeadr..."

"Ach, no! That's miles from here. Our horse will never make it." Had she lost her mind?

"She will. I'll take my time..." Abertha said, trying to sound much more confident than she was.

"What *I*? You can't be dreaming you'll go alone..." Derwen was beside himself.

"You know you won't be allowed behind the falls..." Abertha said apologetically, looking at her husband with a mixture of pity and appreciation, this common man who was brave enough to marry a woman of the faire folk. Many years had passed in good companionship, leaving the trials of their youth behind them, or so she thought. To bring it up now seemed cruel and unnecessary. But that was the truth of it. One can't hide from who they are. Sooner or later our roots will yank at us, make themselves known, especially when there are new generations connected to them.

Derwen sat staring at the babe. It was some time before he spoke.

"It's because of her isn't it? But why now? You kept Annwyl from them, why is this babe any different?"

Abertha shifted in her seat. How to explain? She barely understood it herself, and yet it was a pull she could not ignore.

"She is yet another generation. They deserve to know." The explanation was incomplete and Abertha knew it. "To tell you the truth, my love, I barely know why myself, but I know as sure as I'm sitting here with you that it must be done. To ignore the call would eventually undo me, which would spread to you...and the babe."

"They will want her. Are you willing to give her up?"

"Never. Perhaps..." but Abertha's voice caught in her throat. No matter. They both knew what she was thinking – that Annwyl would one day return looking for her daughter whom she had given to them in trust. The babe in Derwen's arms was proof that Annwyl well knew of their love for her...and trusted to it, despite her leaving – a link, as frail as a strand of web, but a link nonetheless.

"To return to them is risky in more ways than one," Derwen said, still not ready to give in. Not on this. "They could take the babe by force...and take you as well."

"I don't think so. They are who they are, but they're not cruel. And their power is waning. They're being sought out by the emissaries of the new religion. I would imagine they're very careful about what they do."

"All the more reason they may want new blood..." Derwen was grasping at straws.

"Perhaps I won't even find them. Perhaps they've abandoned the Falls, although I doubt it. If anything, it is their last stronghold."

The amber rays of the westering sun had turned a feeble gray. Derwen rose to light the candles and stoke the fire. As he handed the babe to Abertha they both knew the debate was over. But Abertha would not go alone, especially as she planned to take the babe with her. Derwen would accompany her as far as he was able, then Abertha would make her way along the secret path to the place of her people behind the Falls. The journey was fraught with every kind of danger imaginable, but if Abertha was sure that to stay put would be worse, Derwen would defer to her wisdom. If he could see Abertha's own power re-emerging in her, he did not let on. He would hold fast to the covenant between them and believe that whatever his wife was experiencing was not of her own choosing. As he always had, (or almost always), he would serve her. To do otherwise was unthinkable. It would bring him no joy.

A storm kept them housebound for two days, delaying their journey and raising Abertha's anxiety until it plagued her like the sound of a poorly tuned fiddle. The rain slashed against the house and the wind rattled the door like some mythical beast demanding entry. Despite herself, Abertha hated such storms. As stout as she believed her little house to be, when nature raged as it was doing now, she wondered what they would do if all their hard work had not been enough –if the timbers would not hold. But if she worried the babe would sense her anxiety and become inconsolable, she needn't have. If anything, the babe seemed soothed by the storm, sucking the edge of her blanket in infant bliss, dreaming whatever wee ones dream, leaving the adults to worry about earthly things.

While the babe slept, Abertha directed her jitters into baking cakes for the journey – sweet cakes, cheese cakes, breads enriched with whatever greens she could find. There would be more than enough to sustain them on the road ahead. For Derwen, however, with venturing out a near impossibility, he was at loose ends. To counter Abertha's fear he might relapse, Derwen's good wife was a wonder at finding little things for him to do – preparations for the journey; things to put right before they left; helping her fetch things she could have easily, and perhaps more efficiently, gotten for herself.

When at last the rain ceased and the wind had worn itself out, they were well ready to take their leave. Hitching the horse to the well-provisioned wagon, they pulled out of the yard before full light to make the most of the day. They had packed carefully, in a way that did not advertise the extent of their supplies. Likewise, they wore their most battered clothing to be as invisible and uninviting as possible. Their food was wrapped tightly in a clean blanket, then over-lain with a cloth that had been in the barn and was no stranger to sheep dung. What coin they had, they hid on their persons, Abertha tucking the coin from the babe's swaddling close to her heart – a talisman against harm. Lastly, Derwen stashed a cudgel where he could easily reach it from his perch on the wagon. It wasn't pleasurable to think about encountering bandits on the road, but better to be prepared than surprised.

The first day out passed pleasantly, the sun warmed their faces, a slight breeze brought them the myriad scents of the countryside. A shred of excitement nudged aside some of Abertha's anxiety. It was good, after all, to be on the road, not that she needed adventure at her age, but the memory of adventure was sweet. Abertha let it play in her mind as she rocked with the motion of the cart.

As the light waned, they felt safe enough to pass the night under the stars. Making camp by some sheltering rocks, they built a small fire and filled themselves with Abertha's delicious cakes, made even tastier by the circumstances of having spent the day outdoors. The babe was an easy traveler, alternating between sleep and wide-eyed wonder as the shadows of tree limbs and winged things played across her face. After their repast, it was agreed that Abertha would sleep in the wagon with the babe, while Derwen slept by the fire. The last thing Abertha remembered was the half-moon caught in the branches that bent protectively over their little camp.

Bird song woke them well before the sun managed to climb over the horizon to chase away the mist of dawn. Wandering into the verge of the woods to relieve herself, Abertha was delighted to find a little stream. Making her way to it, she knelt to take and sip and rinse her face, then called to Derwen to join her and bring the babe. Dipping the corner of her shawl into the stream, she gently washed the babe's face and hands, all the while marveling at the infant's beauty and easy disposition.

"I'd have myself a dip if you don't mind," Derwen said, eyeing the water as though it was pure gold.

Laughing, Abertha assented.

"Have your bath then," she said. "I'll go back to the wagon and keep a lookout. But mind you don't dally...." She needn't have said more. They both knew they'd been lucky so far. One did not travel the open road without one eye on the margins, on the lookout for reavers and rakes.

Derwen returned soon enough, smiling from ear to ear, his wet hair slicked back. For a moment Abertha saw in him the young man who had so thoroughly captured her heart that she had left her people to be with him. The irony was not lost on her that now, after all these years, here she was, risking life and limb to return to those people and with Derwen at her side. She could have gotten lost in thoughts about all they had faced and survived as a couple, but if today was to be anything like yesterday, she'd rather let the day take her – relish it for its beauty, persistence, and powers of rejuvenation.

But no sooner had they pulled out onto the road than they were met by a band of three rough-looking men on horseback, blocking their way. As Abertha tightened her grip on Annwyl's daughter, she felt Derwen shift beside her, pulling himself up straighter.

"Good day gentlemen," he said, not a quiver in his voice. "I hope you'll find no quarrel with a poor family on the road, looking for work."

Leaning to one side, as though to get a better look at the wagon's contents, the man in the middle said, "I see no household goods. Do you travel with naught but your own skin?"

Despite the derisive laughter, Derwen kept his backbone ramrod straight as he spun the tale he hoped would save their necks.

"Aye. Nothing left from the fire. A poorly placed candle has taken all we own."

"A pitiable tale, that," said another, kicking his horse into a walk that brought him to Abertha's side of the cart.

"A babe! My, my. Perhaps this woman is not as old as she looks. Might have some fun left in her yet."

Derwen felt Abertha flinch, but risked putting a hand on her arm. *Not now woman,* he hoped his touch would convey. *Best hold that tongue of yours for now at least.* Whether or not his unspoken plea found its mark, Abertha did indeed hold her tongue. For a moment all was still...unbearably still...as though fate was deciding what would happen next. Then the man dismounted as his companions drew closer to the wagon. With false gallantry, the brigand made a slight bow to Abertha and held out his hand.

"Why don't you pass that babe of yours off to yon gentleman and step down here so I can get a better look at ye."

"Go along," Derwen whispered to his wife, reaching for the babe, and as he did so, surreptitiously nudged the cudgel toward her. But as soon as the babe was out of Abertha's arms, it let out a piercing wail that seemed to echo through the forest. The man at Abertha's side let out a curse and grabbed for her arm as though to pull her from the wagon. Another wail, this time enough to sting their ears. Then from the forest came a rushing of wings and branches, leaves flying into their faces and branches breaking from the trees, whipping against the horses and their riders as they fell. As though some hidden door had opened, a swarm of ravens blackened the sky and, as one terrifying cloud of wrath, descended on the ruffians, pecking and clawing, blinding them with midnight wings.

"GO," Abertha shouted as she snatched the wailing babe from Derwen's arms. Derwen whipped the horse into motion, cut around the riders and drove hard until the clatter of the attacking birds was no more than a gentle rustle and the babe had settled into Abertha's arms, once again serene.

As their hearts slowed, it was Derwen who broke the silence.

"The forest will protect its own," he said. "Proof sure enough that the wee one we carry is Merlin's granddaughter."

But Abertha could not speak, could not affirm Derwen's words, not that she needed to. They both knew the truth of what they had seen. Lifting the babe to her lips, she kissed its brow and whispered a prayer of gratitude into its wisp of hair. And then she knew why she was making this journey, taking this child to her people, *her* people. On her own, she knew she hadn't the wisdom she needed to properly care for this precious child, this repository of the old ways.

And why was she, Abertha – the one who had turned her back on her people – why was she the one to whom this task had fallen? She had failed Annwyl, a weight she carried in her heart that she could barely manage. Now this. Merlin's powers not diminished, but it would seem, amplified, while Merlin himself lay enchanted, immobilized by his own foolhardiness, if the tales were to be believed. The simple life – that's what she had hoped for. A simple life with a good-hearted man, rooted to the land, living out their days doing no harm. Now she saw that she had been a fool to think she could turn her back on her birthright, escape the demands of her rightful station. Was fate really that clever? That inescapable?

Chapter 3

Behind the Falls

They arrived at the Goat and Gull just before sunset, road-weary, but safe. Derwen saw to it that their horse was well cared for and readied for the rest of the journey. The cart would stay with Derwen at the Inn while Abertha rode with the child into the mountains along the hidden road to the Falls. Derwen protested with every fiber of his being but not a word left his lips; he knew the futility of anything he might say. No circumstance existed that would allow Derwen behind the Falls. Indeed, if he were to try to go with Abertha, the magic that protected her homeland would likely obscure the way for both of them.

The little family was welcome at the Inn, but not without odd glances from this one and that. Abertha wanted to believe that the tell-tale signs of her lineage had been altered by time, undetectable by anyone except her kin, but on that point, she was mistaken. There were tells, especially for these people who lived so close to the misty veil. Not fair folk themselves, nevertheless they lived in awe of the Fey, respected them, and knew the tales of the common folk who once lived side by side with the Fey, until the people of the cross came and proclaimed themselves sole arbiters of the sacred. Perhaps what had saved the Fey in these parts was the ruggedness of the landscape. There were more hospitable places to build towns and churches, to draw people into the new ways, and so the mountain folk were freer to live out their fierce loyalty to the Fey and the other denizens of the place. That loyalty persisted through the generations even as the fair folk drifted away higher into the mountains, leaving behind what they could for the people who lived within sight of the mystical falls of Pistyll Rhaeadr.

And so, yes, they watched and they wondered at this strange family, but most of all the child, who, when anyone could get a good look, bore the visage of the wise ones, plain as day.

For their part, Abertha and Derwen did their best to eat their stew with restraint (despite their ravenous hunger) while chatting amiably with those who came to wish them well, hoping for a bit of news from the road, and perhaps a slip of the tongue regarding their business there, of which none would ask directly. To do so was not their way, of course, and for it Derwen and Abertha were grateful. In return, Abertha was as generous with the child as she dared be, letting folks coo at her and gently touch her here and there. The babe drew people to her, as though she was a sacred relic, lost but now returned. They looked upon her with more delight than even the most darling baby commands. It was as though something about her struck a note in them that had been silent for so long, they had nearly forgotten its sound. Yet here it was. Sweet and resonant, perfectly tuned to the ever-present sound of falling water.

It was a pleasant evening. The fire and ale warmed them inside and out; the good company consoled them. The eventual sleep, coming gently and naturally, restored them.

At first light, Abertha crept to the stables. No point in waking Derwen, nor was there any point in long good-byes, entreaties or warnings. By now, they both knew what had to be done. With the babe strapped securely to her breast, Abertha mounted their horse and led it into the mountains along a trail only she could see.

At the edge of the waterfall she paused, the sound and smell of water threatening to drown her in reverie. She had loved this place – but she had loved Derwen more. Now, the freedom of childhood bubbled up from wherever our memories are stored and kept her rooted, holding still to hold on as we sometimes do coming out of a sweet dream we don't want to leave. But the horse was restless and the memory faded, so she made her way behind the veil, where the hoofbeats echoed off the stone walls and mist bathed her face and hands. She could see no guards as she approached the Keep, but she knew they were there. Would they challenge her? Remember her? Or was she somehow expected?

She was met at the gate, warders appearing as from nowhere. Silently, they led her horse away and ushered her into the great hall. Once comfortably seated, they bowed to her respectfully and left her to contemplate the silence and beauty of her surroundings. This she had forgotten, or had it changed? She had remembered the hall being more richly appointed, but then, youth sees with more impressionable eyes. Still, as she remembered it, there were the tiny lights everywhere, their source a mystery.

"Daughter, you have come."

Before her stood her mother, aged but still the beautiful and imposing Ysbail, leaning on the arm of Abertha's youngest sister, Snow, who, though she was barely more than a toddler when Abertha left, was instantly recognizable by her violet eyes and snow-white hair, white even at birth. Abertha stood and dropped a slight curtsey meant for them both.

"And you have brought us a surprise I see," Ysbail continued. Abertha's heartbeat quickened, beating hard against the infant so tightly bound to her. Suddenly, she wished she hadn't come. What was she thinking? These powerful women. Abertha was nothing to them. Years ago she'd arrogantly renounced her right to their care and respect. Now, voluntarily, she was putting herself at their mercy.

"Shall we go to the inner rooms?" her sister asked, though it was hardly a question. Abertha moved to stand at her mother's side, terrified. But to her surprise, Ysbail wove her arm into Abertha's and leaned into her.

"I never thought to see you again, my daughter. Whatever news you bring, good or ill, the joy of having you here will sustain me."

Together they walked into the inner rooms of the Keep, the rooms Abertha remembered all too well. Here she had played, grown from a child to a young woman, and finally torn herself away.

Once her mother was seated, Snow moved to Abertha.

"Let's get this gift unwrapped, shall we?" she said as she began to gently unwind the binding cloth from the babe. Abertha let Snow take the child and with a glance between them, assented to her handing the child to their mother who held her tenderly, but gazed at her with a look that Abertha found unreadable.

Exactly, Abertha thought. *This child is a blessing, as are all children, but what does her existence mean of Annwyl's life? How best to care for her child, keep her safe, both from others and herself?* Abertha had no answers and, in truth, the questions had deepened during the journey, whispered from the depths of the woods, the vastness of the world.

"I assume this is Annwyl's child?" Ysbail asked, not taking her eyes from the babe.

"We believe so...there have been signs...."

"But you don't know for sure?"

Abertha's shoulder's drooped. So much to share with her mother, so little energy to do it. She should have come so much sooner...

"She was left on the doorstep before dawn. I only heard a rider galloping out of the yard, but I felt...I'm sure it was Annwyl." And there was the matter of the coin, and the encounter on the road...

Ysbail ran her finger around the babe's face, outlined her eyes and mouth, smoothed her hair. "She is truly Fey. Of that I am sure."

Only then did Ysbail look up from the child and fix Abertha with her eyes. Unjudging, curious, the steady gaze of a Fey seeking the truth.

"Tell me of Annwyl..." she said.

Abertha could do nothing other than assent, telling all, from the day the midwife handed the child to Abertha to the day her dear Annwyl rode away from their cottage, clinging to Merlin's cloak. As she recited her tale, food and drink appeared, the fire was stoked, and the light in the room warmed to an amber glow that held the women safe in sacred space and time.

How Ysbail and Snow were reacting she had no idea. She was lost in memories and the realization of the importance of what she was doing. Until now, the events of which she spoke had been known to only a few, but in this telling, they would become part of the tribe's history. Snow would re-tell the story of Merlin's daughter, embellish it, and send it on its way through time and generations.

When at last Abertha had finished, she sat with her head down, tears dropping onto her hands. She had failed so piteously. She saw that now.

"You did your best..." Ysbail said gently as she reached to lift her daughter's chin.

"Why did Merlin leave her with us instead of you?" Abertha asked, the pain of her failure making her voice shrill, pleading.

Ysbail sighed. "I believe he honestly had no idea what she was...what she would become. Merlin was such a loner. He rarely sought council, and certainly not on this. He saw only his love for Carys and the magic that sparked between them. That a child would come from the union was far from his mind.

"And then there is the issue of the new religion. When at last he had to come to terms with a child, he may well have thought she'd be safer in the world of men. There may have been some logic to that, and yet, obviously, the powers of the old ways will not be denied – will not just disappear even if left unattended."

And there it was, the gentle rebuke that Abertha knew had to come sooner or later. What of her own powers? She had turned her back on them. Had they withered from disuse? The question hung in the air, unspoken – for now.

"So my daughter," Ysbail continued, "what are your plans for this child?"

"I came here determined to keep her and ask only a blessing," Abertha said, her intentions becoming clear to herself only now. "Now I see things differently. Perhaps it was even her will more than mine that brought me here. If you would have her here with you, I will assent to that." Abertha's eye strayed to Snow, sitting so quietly, so reverently beside her mother. Snow's eyes were gleaming, hungry even, revealing that she was eager to have the babe among them. With that thought came another. Derwen. The babe had brought him back to life. How would he respond if she returned to the Inn without her? Abertha's heart ripped. Here she was, a crone in her own right but still needing the council of her mother. For the moment, she abandoned all control, like letting out a breath that had been held too long.

"We would have happily taken Annwyl had we been asked, but we weren't," Ysbail said.

"Now, our circumstances have become more critical in these years since Annwyl's birth. If the Roman religion was a threat then, now we are under siege. The new order is determined to annihilate us, that they have made clear. How to respond? At this point, fighting back is not an option. Our enemies are much more bloodthirsty than we, as we have learned. Such violence is not our way. To engage in it, even to save our lives, would destroy our souls – a much more precious commodity than this earth-walk."

Ysbail seemed to weary as she spoke, and now Snow's attention was wholly on her mother as she drew the strength to carry on. "We are in hiding now and will soon seek an even more distant refuge, in the hopes that one day we can return. Our future, however, is uncertain. To take a babe into that uncertainty seems unfair and unwise. But in you there is an alternative. Keep the child that she may hide in plain sight. In that way she will keep the bloodline intact. Diluted, but flowing still in the midst of our enemies, undetectable."

Abertha saw the logic in Ysbail's argument, with one concern. "What of the powers and their destructive influence on Annwyl? I would not have the babe suffer as her mother did."

Ysbail smiled at her daughter, a sad but hopeful look. "We were caught unprepared for poor Annwyl's experience, but now we are aware. You, my daughter, will use your own wisdom and experience to teach her – not to use them and make herself visible, but to shelter them, wrap them in love and store them away...as you have. Who better to do that than you?"

"I'm not sure..." Abertha stammered.

"None of us are. We are in unknown territory, but isn't that the way of life?" Ysbail's face broke into a wan smile. "But in you, Abertha, love is boundless. I see that now. With love and wisdom you will find a way, and do your best."

Ysbail rose with some difficulty, but determination still flashed through her demeanor. "Now, Snow will take you to your room where you can refresh and rest. Tonight we will bless the child, and for that I have much to prepare."

Ysbail kissed the babe before handing her back to Abertha, then held them both in a long embrace before leaving the room.

Abertha awoke well rested. The babe lay near her in a beautifully carved cradle, cozy on a bed of sheepskin and dressed in a gown of gossamer threads, with a circlet of violet flowers on her tiny head. As Abertha stirred, the baby turned its head to her and smiled as though it knew exactly what was going on.

"Sweet babe," Abertha said, "you have come into your own. And now I realize, we have never named you..."

"With your leave, she will be named tonight." It was Snow. She'd entered the room as soundlessly as her name implied and now stood at Abertha's bedside holding a stunning multicolored gown – its threads shimmered and danced as she held it out for Abertha to see.

"Oh yes, this is to be quite the night," Snow said, reading Abertha's face.

"I will look silly in that," Abertha said, not unkindly. "I'm much too old for such bright colors."

"On the contrary, sister," Snow said, a huge grin on her face, perhaps enjoying her sister's discomfort just a bit. "As the babe is dressed in white for purity and innocence, you have earned, in all your life's challenges, the right to wear every color of nature."

"Humph," was about all Abertha could manage.

The hall was ablaze with both earthly and otherworldly light. The decorations were the people themselves, dressed stunningly in all shades, accessorized in flowers and leaves, artfully woven and plaited into their hair, their clothes. On a dais at the far end of the hall sat the Queen of the Fey, veiled and surrounded by her Company, both men and women, among whom sat Ysbail. Love and pride swelled in Abertha's chest, seasoned with a touch of regret. Perhaps she had been wrong in her youthful rejection of the Way. Yes, her people were powerful, and some of their actions could be questioned, especially by one who was not privy to the larger context. But they were never evil, never hurtful without cause, and above all, as Ysbail had said, never bloodthirsty. The Fey would never decimate an entire village.

Had Annwyl been raised here...

"Come sister, you must run the gauntlet. All must see the babe and bless her. Hold fast, I am at your side."

Snow took Abertha's arm and led her along the line of those gathered. As Abertha moved among them, she felt the walls of the Keep melt away, leaving her among the trees, the rocks, the animals and streams. Each person seemed a part of the natural tableau – this one foxlike, that one a dew drop. And as each touched the child, a bit of their being transferred to her, until she held the essence of all that is part of the living world.

As if in a dream, Abertha felt herself led to the dais where the Queen rose and descended the steps to stand before her. With no word spoken, Abertha handed the babe to the Queen who kissed her, whispered something into her ear, then held her aloft.

In a voice like a flowing stream, the Queen pronounced, "Let this child be recognized and loved as one of us. Would that we could hold her close and take joy in her growing and learning, but given the times, we have chosen to send her into the world of humankind, a hidden gem, an invisible vehicle to carry the Way forward into the unknown and distant future." Then the Queen lowered the child, held her out to the assembly and asked,

"Who names this child?"

Abertha couldn't have spoken if she'd wished to. Snow at her side was a blessed crutch as the weighty significance of the ceremony dawned on Abertha with a force she was unprepared to handle. Helpless, Abertha looked to her mother, but Ysbail failed to acknowledge the glance, for whatever reasons Abertha could not imagine. Would no one name the babe? Abertha's heart tightened in her chest. Surely...

"As I believe I am kin, I wish to claim the honor."

A man stepped from the crowd, wrinkled and grey, but not without an enduring vitality and an air of deserved honor. At the Queen's gesture, he approached the dais and placed a weathered hand upon the babe's brow.

"Of beauty she will have abundance, that is clear. No need for a name that claims what is already hers. Rather I would give her a name that speaks to her promise, that being victory for the Old Ways. For that, I name her Buddug."

Abertha stifled a wince. *Buddug ("bee-thig")* was not a pretty name. For her part, she would have named her something simple and common, a flower perhaps. "Buddug" seemed to place too much expectation on such a wee one...and she who was to raise her. Who was this man to claim this right? But the Queen appeared satisfied, pleased even. She kissed Buddug's brow, nose and lips, and then before handing her back to Abertha, spoke to the child in a voice loud enough to be heard throughout the mountains and beyond.

"Buddug, I bless you and charge you with the memory of this day. You and all those who come from you are the hope of this fair but troubled world. Hear this," and now the Queen lifted her face. "The day will come when humankind tire of the useless belief in false gods and turn again to the Earth, the true Life-Giver. When that day comes the descendants of this child, Buddug, will lead humankind back to the true Way, as stewards of the Earth and all its Beings. May it be so."

A murmur arose from the crowd, the sound of wind in the trees, falling water, dancing leaves. In her own heart Abertha felt both the sadness and hope of what the future held for her people. Her people. They *were* her people and she would always be a part of them. In this moment, the ache and confusion of her separation began to heal. She had chosen to live among the non-Fey – not a banishment, but now she saw, a preparation for what lay ahead. Each had their role to play. Hers was to foster and guide this special child – Merlin's granddaughter – so that the wisdom and power of the old ways might find a path through the ages. She pulled Buddug tightly to herself and left the hall on the benevolent winds of her people's love.

Back in her room, Abertha placed Buddug in her cradle and let her mind replay the events of the evening. Who was the man who had come forward? What did he know of Annwyl's birth? And what of Derwen? Poor Derwen alone at the Inn, almost forgotten in the intensity of her return to the Falls. He had figured in none of this, and yet she knew he would love Buddug with all his heart. Love. That was the key, the light that revealed the way forward....

The tea at her bedside was sweet and soothing. She should have suspected it, but she drank it mindlessly and fell asleep before the dregs had cooled.

The following morning, Ysbail and Snow walked Abertha to the gates where Snow lovingly tied Buddug to Abertha's breast with a glistening cloth. Secured to her horse was a pack of gifts, all of which Abertha tried to refuse.

"They'll just be thief bait on the road," she had protested, but Ysbail assured her they were spell-protected. They would not attract but rather repel anyone for whom they were not intended. And there was the matter of the fancy dress she had worn at the ceremony. Ardently, she pleaded to leave it behind.

"Where would I wear such finery on the farm?"

"It is part of the story," Snow had insisted. "Put it in a chest against the day it will be of some use."

And so they had laden her with blessings, both spoken and tangible, making the leave-taking even harder than it already was. She longed to get to know Snow better, this younger sister so full of life, and perhaps one better suited to raising Buddug. And Ysbail. She feared her mother was nearing her end, and wondered if she'd have the strength for the long journey that had been hinted at in their talks. So this was the price she paid for her decision all those years ago. Where was the fairy draft that would ease *this* pain?

Before she took the reins of her horse, she turned to the women one last time.

"Who was the man who named the babe?"

Ysbail hesitated, but a direct question deserves a direct answer. Especially this one.

"He was to be your betrothed, before you...made a different choice."

"*My betrothed!* But he said he was kin to Buddug..."

"He is the brother of Carys, Annwyl's mother," Ysbail said, regretting what she knew this would cost Abertha to know.

"Then why didn't he...?"

"It was Merlin's choice and, as we've already surmised, Merlin believed her to be safer with...the non-Fey. But now you see, you have been a part of this since the beginning." Ysbail put her boney hand on Abertha's face. "Go with the blessing of the earth and sky my beloved daughter, and do not regret your decisions. What point in second-guessing them now? Perhaps your actions were exactly the right ones, for here we are and who would have knowingly missed the joy of these past few days?"

If Abertha didn't leave now, she never would. A lingering hug for her mother and sister and off she went, back behind the Falls and out into the world of humankind and all that awaited her, not the least of which would be to tell Derwen of what had passed here, while keeping the importance of his role going forward clear and indisputable. Just the first of all the challenges she faced. But as she rode down the enchanted path, she couldn't help but wonder how things might have been different.

Chapter 4

Sirona's Despair

Somerset, England
The Present

Tuttle's Time Emporium looked as it always did, as though time could not touch it. Ironic, perhaps, given that its entire inventory was devoted to all things *time.* The same equanimity could not, however, be applied to Sirona as she approached the charming little shop. The bright green and gold of its exterior was contradicted by Sirona's dark and restive visage. A passerby would have thought the woman was suffering from serious sleep deprivation or some crushing disease. But there was no one to see her as she slipped into the shop.

"Ah, the charming Lady Sirona," Tuttle called out before he had cast a proper glance at his visitor. But as she advanced, he could see her ravaged look and grew immediately concerned. Sirona was not one for moods. He'd never known anyone so cool in any circumstance, so willing to face down a threat. He scuttled from behind the counter and met her half-way down the aisle, grasping her hands as though he might pull her up from whatever she was drowning in.

"Oh my dear Sirona...what is it?"

Sirona fixed Tuttle with wild eyes.

"I must go back. You must get me back."

Few knew Tuttle as anything more than a humble clock-maker, able to repair even the oldest timepiece. And those few who knew otherwise, of which Sirona was one, would never so blatantly even hint at his adventures in time. That Sirona had so forgotten herself in this regard, was evidence that her distressed state was serious – perhaps more serious than Tuttle was equipped to deal with, but here she was, so he must do his best.

Tuttle turned the sign on the door to "closed" and ushered Sirona into the tiny apartment at the back of the store. Dare he take the time to put the kettle on, or did this call for immediate intervention? He decided on the latter and, eschewing the kitchen, ushered Sirona to a comfortable chair in his modest sitting room, then pulled another chair up close to her.

"Tell me my Lady, what is it that troubles you?"

Sirona was near tears. "I want to go back. I must go back. Perhaps I could warn him..."

Tuttle sighed. *She knows better than this,* he thought. Even if he could send her back, to disrupt history like that was unthinkable.

"You are speaking of Merlin, I presume," he said, stalling for time. He couldn't bear to give her the flat "no" that was the only possible response to her request – at least not yet. Best to get her to talk it out, to come to the inevitable answer on her own.

"To be so trapped like that for so long!" Sirona wailed. "When we were in the cave, Raina felt his presence. It nearly undid her. And as she moaned, connecting with him as she did, I heard his own voice, his dear voice, mixed with hers...and in such agony! Oh, Tuttle, where does such cruelty as Nimue's come from, to trap another being in suspension between life and death?"

Tuttle could not answer her. In all his travels throughout time he had seen unspeakable evil everywhere and still he hadn't an explanation for it – at least not one he could live with.

"But you were successful in releasing his soul at last, were you not?" he offered.

"So we think. And hopefully, that will be a boon to humanity, but my soul aches for *him*, the man, and the time when we lived together in a world we understood – at least better than I do this one. Merlin and Morgan le Fay, rooted in the power of earth-wisdom...."

"Sirona," Tuttle leaned closer to her. "You know that even then the old ways were fading. Rome's military might, aligned with the new religion as it was, was no match for the innocence of the indigenous culture of which you speak. Going back would only put your soul through all that pain again. Better we move forward from our present time, armed with what we can remember of the ancient ways. Is that not why you worked so hard to release Merlin's spirit? To bring it back into "circulation" as it were?"

"Yes, of course," the exhaustion was evident in Sirona's voice, "but being in the cave awoke something in me that is yearning...crying out ages of anguish. I feel like I'm being undone by it," she finished, defeated.

Tuttle was more than a little concerned for his friend. A blessing, yes, to have consciousness of one's past lives, but also, as it now appeared, a weighty burden. If anyone could handle such knowledge, it would be Sirona. Yet here she was, reduced to pleading for something she knew was against the laws of nature. It was time to stop dissembling.

"Sirona," Tuttle began, moving his chair closer to her, "dear Lady Sirona, you know what you ask is not possible. Even if I could send you back, I wouldn't. No good would come of it."

Tuttle waited with bated breath, but there was only silence from his guest. The sound of dozens of ticking clocks oozed into the apartment from the shop, a stark reminder that time moved on inexorably, regardless of human need. But the ticking was not in unison, the cacophony a reminder that time moves differently depending on perspective, circumstance, disposition. *And experience* thought Tuttle. His adventures in time travel had left him prone to a kind of motion sickness. There were times when he felt like he was in two time-streams at once, one moving at a different rate than the other. Keeping his balance in such circumstances was tricky business. Not unlike the ability to connect with one's past lives, he imagined. Is one here or there? This person or that? He hated to think of Sirona feeling that kind of displacement. Everyone who knew her depended on her stability, her confidence, her easy laughter – and Tuttle was no exception.

When at last she spoke, Tuttle jumped at the sound, lost as he was in his own thoughts.

"If I cannot travel through time, then I must at least travel to France in *this* time, return to the cave and stand in the presence of whatever is left of my friend, " she said, her shoulders slumped in defeat, her dark eyes full of agony.

"And what do you hope to find there?" Tuttle asked as gently as he could. "With Merlin's spirit released what would remain with any hint of life in it?"

"I have no idea, but I must do something to satisfy this...craving...that's tearing at me. It can't, it won't, be ignored."

Perhaps Tuttle should have thought a bit more before opening his mouth. Or perhaps he had been infected with Sirona's urgency, for he made the offer with uncharacteristic incaution.

"Then give me a week before you go. While I cannot send you physically through time, I think I can make a concoction that will let you *see through* time, using your soul's history as your vehicle. But I caution you, visit only one past life. To do more might well crash your mind. You are too precious, my Lady, to lose."

At that, Sirona lifted her dark eyes to Tuttle. "Then that will have to do. If I cannot change the past, at least I may be able to make some peace with it."

"One more caution," Tuttle insisted. "Do not become obsessed with the past. Even if we could go back and think we're changing something, we could never know for sure what the results of our actions might be. For all we know, what had happened *must* happen and will find its way despite our efforts. What matters, what *is*, is the present. This is where we are and this is what we can rightly influence. You have released Merlin's spirit into the world. Now, whatever good that will bring needs to be nourished.

You are key to that, Sirona. We learn from the past so that we can act in the present."

Tuttle took Sirona's hands and helped her from the chair.

"Return a week from today and I will have your tincture ready. That will give you time to prepare for the journey."

"You are a dear," Sirona said with a sad smile. "I can see it in your eyes that you worry for me. Do not."

"I know. I understand being compelled. But...if you change your mind..."

"I won't," she said, and squeezing his hands as she let them go, turned to leave.

Niall was having none of it.

"You cannot be serious! We were lucky to find the cave the first time, to perform the ritual and return without incident. Why tempt fate?"

"But you see how I am, or at least you see some of it," Sirona protested. "I'm being called...compelled..."

"Does it not occur to you that the compulsion you feel might be of evil intent? You said you thought you felt Nimue's spirit in the cave. If she still haunts the place is it too much to think that she – her spirit – might be plotting some kind of revenge for undoing her enchantment?"

Niall was more than a little distressed at Sirona's determination. For his part, he was eternally grateful that they had released Merlin's spirit that day in the cave – if indeed they had – without further incident. That is to say without any kind of magical retribution. Then again, he did not have one foot in the fairy realm as Sirona did. He was fully unburdened by magic as far as he could tell, his past lives a mystery he was content to let be. That he was drawn to Sirona like a moth to fairy lights was enough to contend with. And while being her lover presented challenges, he'd so far been able to survive, he'd never seen her this agitated. Most likely, he would not be able to dissuade her, but that thought didn't keep him from trying.

"Perhaps you're misreading it," he offered, ignoring her raised eyebrow and plunging on. "Perhaps you're missing April and Raina. Might it be time to make a trip to the States, to spend time with your brother, Art, and reconnect with your companions? Perhaps they need you. It was hard for all of you when they left."

"I won't disagree that I miss them sorely. And I will soon make the trip to Aries Lake. But I must do this first. Niall, I do respect your concern, I do, but this kind of call cannot be ignored. If Nimue is lying in wait, ignoring her might have worse complications than meeting her head on. Perhaps she *is* plotting some kind of revenge. If that is so, it is my responsibility to address it. Surely, you see that, my love." Sirona reached out to Niall with a loving touch. Such a long-suffering soul. She knew what his love for her cost him, but she couldn't change what she was or what she saw her role in this life to be.

"Then we will go together," Niall said, giving in as he knew he would. "And let me see if Percy is willing to join us. He was instrumental in finding the cave before. Hopefully he will be so again...and," Niall added as an afterthought, "three's a good number for such endeavors."

"I should go alone..." Sirona said, but in truth, she would appreciate the support of the two men. In fact, she had a suspicion that their energy had been an important piece of the ritual, guarding the cave as they had. She had felt their caring surrounding her, Raina and April as they had ventured inward, into the darkness and uncertainty that awaited them. The men were the women's safety net – their tether to the present, the blessed mundanity of the non-mystical world.

Niall waited patiently. He knew Sirona would respect his need to go with her, to be there for her if she needed him. For all that he gave her, that was her part of their covenant. Independent as she was, she would accept his desire to care and protect.

Except for Tuttle's tincture, the three had set out with little preparation, armed only with intent. Sirona, however, had done her own kind of preparation to steady her mind and arouse her sense of her past lives, urging a unity of purpose, but always being careful to root herself in her present state, as Tuttle had advised.

"Do not let yourself get lost in the persona of a past life. That would be as dangerous as being lost in time itself," he had warned. "Give yourself a grounding word or phrase that will return you from wherever the visioning takes you, back to your present self, in your present time, lest you become a time zombie." Tuttle had smiled when he said it, but Sirona knew that such a horrific fate was more than a little possible.

Once in the forest, Sirona saw that little had changed since their last, fateful visit. The threads she had previously tied to branches to mark their way as they sought the cave were still there, allowing the three to follow them to the clearing. A wave of deja vu swept over her as they stood face to face with the cave entrance, despite its being obscured by the branches they had so carefully placed to hide it from others. And now here she was again, at the site of Merlin's entrapment. Even had they been successful in releasing his spirit, the body of her precious friend still existed, in some altered form, woven into the life of the tree into which Nimue had ensorcelled him. Sirona stifled a cry. It had been for Merlin that she was yearning – a soul-longing that had persisted for untold ages. And still it burned.

Niall and Percy cleared away the brush from the cave entrance while Sirona took herself a little way off, swallowed the time tincture as Tuttle had instructed and rehearsed her mantra for returning from the visioning. She had planned to go directly to Morgan le Fay, the soul experience that spoke most clearly to her and the one that would resonate with Merlin's, though if that would have any effect now that his soul was released, she had no idea. It would also resonate with Nimue which was both Sirona's hope and fear. Was she strong enough to engage Nimue's spirit, and urge it into the light – heal whatever wound had led the gifted enchantress to give Merlin such a tormented death and curse his offspring?

This was so much less than what she had hoped for when she first visited Tuttle. She had desired to travel back and be with Merlin in both body and spirit. Perhaps to warn him, but at least to be in his presence, to tell him of the future – this lost and possibly doomed epoch. Now, she realized, she had lost that thread. She had no idea what she had hoped to do here, only that she needed to be again in whatever presence was left of the great mage.

As Sirona emerged from the forest, she saw that Niall and Percy were standing guard at the cave entrance, waiting patiently for her to complete whatever preparations she had deemed necessary. As she approached, they looked at her with affectionate concern.

"It's not too late to change your mind," Niall said, a hint of panic in his voice.

Percy squirmed where he stood, his beautiful face creased with dark memory. "After all this time, I still feel Nimue's presence, her seemingly bottomless rage. The soul of Merlin's owl still carries within me the torment she subjected him to. Whether embodied or in spirit, Nimue is no one to tangle with. I urge you to reconsider, Sirona."

Dear Percy, Sirona thought. This beautiful avian creature, this evolution of the soul of Merlin's owl. Did he not long for Merlin as she did? If so, he must understand her present need. A quick kiss on his cheek, then she turned and strode to the cave entrance.

Memory was her light. As though on a tether, she was drawn deep into the cave, to the unnatural tree that was Merlin's living crypt. At its base she crumbled, fully awash in despair. Crying out, she wept from the depths of her being. *Oh Merlin, protector of the old ways, friend to the dark Morgan le Fay. You and I, standing amid the sacred stones, sensing the danger of the new religion set on casting men's eyes to the cold heavens and away from the living earth. How I long to stand by you again, flesh and blood, together in that sacred, legendary time.*

Would her tears never stop? Would she cry until her body turned to dust, become ashes scattered across the cave floor? Such a dissolution – she longed for it. But would it stop the pain or would her soul carry it out into the world to plague yet another with endless torment?

That final thought brought her up short. This torment was hers to bear. What a violation it would be of her soul's intent – that of a healer – to abdicate her responsibility in this life.

Is this your message to me then, dear friend?

Sirona reached out her hand to caress the rough bark which was all that remained of her friend, but as she did so a spark stung her mind and cast her back in time.

As Morgan le Fay, she stood in Arthur's court. There was Merlin, at Arthur's side, as was his wont. And Nimue, barely a woman, as blond and innocent as Morgan was dark and weighted with the obligations of her station. Seeing how Nimue lurked in the shadows, it was clear that the young woman was not a significant player in Arthur's grand narrative...at least, not yet.

It was a particularly festive night in Court. Lancelot had returned from some grand adventure, his magnificence filling the great hall as though the sun had been brought inside. The love and admiration Lancelot inspired was palpable among the assembly, and Morgan was not immune to it. It was hard not to fall in love with this gifted knight. He was the living embodiment of human perfection. And in his virtuous radiance, Arthur was in rare form as he always was when Lancelot was at court, a mood Morgan loved to see on him. Too often, Arthur struggled with the perpetual challenges of maintaining a just and united kingdom, but in Lancelot's presence, anything seemed possible. And so the crown sat more lightly on the good king's head this night and soon the seats at the Round Table were vacated as the dancing began.

But before she could enter into the merriment, a cloud passed over the scene and Sirona saw as with Morgan's eyes. Behind all the joy and admiration lurked the specter of jealousy, like a tiny finger of dread snaking through the room. Some instinct drew Morgan's attention back to Nimue, still in the shadows. Morgan was torn between joining the dancing and going to the young woman, to bring her into the light, to befriend her. In that moment, she realized she never had. All her love and attention had been on Arthur and Merlin. Never had she paid this young woman any mind, assuming she'd find her own way. She was certainly pretty enough. All on her own, she would soon be the envy of all. No need for Morgan to concern herself with her. But Sirona's double vision saw the flaw in that thinking. We're not meant to traverse the challenges of life alone, without a soul friend. When that space is left vacant, the emptiness howls in the darkness, inviting all manner of beings who prowl, hungry, ready to feed on another's life force.

Turning her back on the merriment, Morgan began to make her way to Nimue, but paused when she saw that a man was at the ear of the young woman. Not just any man, but one of those so-called priests of the new religion that Arthur, in his magnanimity, tolerated at court, albeit against Morgan's advice. Instinctively Morgan disliked them, distrusted the severity and joylessness that seemed to be their creed. Moreover, their worship of a tortured prophet made her blood run cold. She suspected it was the torture more than the prophet that they valued. In her dreams she would sometimes see her beloved Merlin hung on one of the over-sized crosses they all wore...the device on which the sacred was executed.

Morgan pulled herself into the shadows, as close to Nimue and the monk as she dared venture. Unable to hear their conversation, she nevertheless read the expressions on their faces – the monk red-faced and insistent, Nimue's features moving from listless to energized, a nod here and there, and then a terrifying look of malicious intent that nearly stopped Morgan's heart. Before she could pull herself together, she saw Nimue make her way toward Merlin where he sat, while the monk disappeared into the shadows, erasing all evidence of his presence.

Morgan was on the verge of intervening to warn Merlin, when suddenly, the vision melted into nothingness and Sirona was again kneeling in the impenetrable dark of the cave, exhausted by the tears, the vision, the revelation she had just witnessed. So. Nimue, in her innocence, had been infected by the purveyors of the new religion, and weaponized against Merlin who, as Sirona well knew, was the sworn enemy of the Roman agenda. It all made sense now. But what had they promised Nimue? What was powerful enough to draw her away from her own kind, her own ancestral ways? Could Morgan have intervened if she'd befriended the young woman sooner?

No matter now. Nothing she could do but learn from her mistakes. And how many lifetimes does it take to finally get it right? Her thoughts went to April, the young woman who had come into her present life. "April" had been her grounding word if she'd needed it. Perhaps, without her consciously calling on it, it had been her anchor all along.

Sirona had lost all sense of time. Now she thought of Percy and Niall, faithfully keeping watch. Likely they were beginning to worry. As she put her hand on the cave floor to push herself to her feet, she felt something sharp. In the darkness, she curled her fingers around it, stood, and, turning to the light coming from the entrance, made her way back to the present.

Chapter 5

At the Hedge and Hearth

Aries Lake, USA
Present

"Very clever of you to build a pottery studio for *me* at *your* house." Raina had said, barely disguising her thrill at what Art had created while she was off in Glastonbury.

"I didn't want to presume, either that you really *wanted* a studio, or that I could start putting nails in your house and knocking out walls," Art had countered.

"Disingenuous."

"Do you think so?" Art had asked, his eyes twinkling. Raina had been away for longer than he would have wanted, but the separation was necessary, and it had given him enough time to redesign the back part of his cottage into an airy, sunlit studio. And Raina was right – he was pretty sure she would love it.

"You've caught me out," he had said, gallantly admitting his guilt. "The truth is, a reliable party rather insisted that you get a studio..."

"Sirona," Raina had surmised.

"And April, too, actually. Your daughter was adamant. It is true though that I wasn't inclined to start building something onto your cottage without your permission – to acquire which would have of course ruined the surprise. But is it really so bad that it brings you to me on a regular basis?"

Of course it wasn't, and Raina had answered him by curling into his arms, delighting in the feel of him, the scent of him. She had missed him sorely during those months away and now she was sure he had felt the same.

That was weeks ago, the very first day of her arrival back in the States. Since then, hardly a day had gone by that she hadn't spent time at the wheel, wet clay up to her elbows, often smudged on her nose or chin. The shelves Art had built along the interior walls were already full of her work, which Art found compellingly beautiful, but she was never satisfied. She'd claimed she was searching for the perfect marriage between form and design but so far, at least in her eyes, she had yet to find it. And so it was that Art had found her working away on a beautiful sunny morning even before breakfast.

"If you're going to keep coming here so early in the day you might as well move in," Art said, having entered the studio but keeping a respectful distance from the mud-slinging spin of the wheel. Raina knew he meant it. He'd hinted at it before, but she always slid away from the topic. As much as she couldn't get enough of this wonderful man, there was something about her little cottage – her mother's cottage – that she treasured. More than it being her only connection to a mother she had barely known, there was a special quality to it that just felt so right, so comforting. And there were still mysteries there to be unraveled. She was sure of it.

Now Raina stopped the wheel and, her hands still on the pot beneath them, smiled up at this man she had grown to love more deeply than anyone except her precious daughter, April.

"I hope I'm not disturbing you," she offered, knowing full well that there was little she could do to disturb this easy-going man.

"Not at all. More likely I'm disturbing you. If I can pull you out of here, I have somewhere I'd like to take you today," Art said.

"Oh? Where?" Raina began, but then, knowing what Art would say, said it for him. "Let me guess...it's a surprise."

"Yes, of course," he replied, flashing his most disarming smile.

Art had already made a hearty breakfast which Raina gobbled up with satisfaction. After a shower and clean clothes, she re-appeared at his house as ready as she could be for one of his can't-tell-you-until-we-get-there road trips. Just in case, she'd donned one of what April teasingly called her "hippie skirts" and a light blouse. The day was warm for early spring and, once she was away from the gravitational pull of her studio, she was glad to be out and about.

The open windows tossed her hair around, but she let it fly. The air was too sweet to hide from. Raina had learned early on that Art rarely took the highway, preferring instead the twists and turns of country roads – a habit that often left Raina queasy, but if she closed her eyes and turned her head to the sun, she'd survive the trip.

When at last Art pulled off the road into a small gravel parking lot, what met Raina's gaze chased away her discomfort in an instant. There, amid a profusion of flowers and leaves, like a maid resting in her garden, was a darling little house with a sign over the door that read "The Hedge and Hearth Reading Room." The house smiled out of a facade of wooden siding painted a buttery yellow, with pleasing green trim that wavered in the sunlight, catching the play of light and wind as did the proliferation of flora that clung to the sides of the building like adoring friends. The door, a delicious cinnamon color, was split, like the old Dutch doors, though why one would peek in the upper part only and not wish to enter by means of the full door, one could only guess.

Raina turned to Art, her mouth hanging open despite herself.

"Cute, isn't it?" he said, smiling his most impish smile. This time he had her but good.

"It looks like the kind of house I used to draw as a kid. Part house, part face," Raina finally managed.

"I think most kids have drawn houses like this – an archetype of warmth and safety," Art suggested.

"Well, technically, it's a bunga..."

"So, are we going to discuss architecture, or are we going in?" Art said, grabbing Raina's hand and leading her up the porch steps.

As he opened the door and stood back to let her in, she heard the sound of exceptionally musical chimes, but saw no evidence of them. Immediately, the delicious smell of books filled her head. Scattered around the room in artful and friendly arrangements were comfortable chairs and small tables amid shelves and shelves of books – more than seemed possible from the looks of the outside. More than half of the chairs were populated with readers. Some looked up as the newcomers entered; others remained glued to their books. As Raina glanced around the room, something struck her as odd about the people there. It reminded her of the Imbolc party she had attended with Sirona, where everyone was dressed as some kind of animal or mythical being, but these people were not in costume at all. Still, there was just a hint of some non-human quality to them. And certainly the young lady who had looked up when they entered and held Raina's gaze just a bit too long, seemed...fairy-like.

But Art was gently leading her to a large desk in the center of the room at which sat a beautiful woman with straight, jet black hair and ruddy skin. From her hair floated a single feather, and from her ears hung exquisite adornments of strung beads and porcupine quills. As Art approached the desk, the woman stood up and gave him the slightest bow.

"Welcome Arthur," she said. "You've come at last."

"Lily, good to see you. I'd like to introduce you to my...friend...Raina."

At that, there was a stir from the assembled readers. If Raina heard it, she gave no sign.

"Welcome," Lily said, warmly enough, but only her eyes were smiling, and that just barely.

Then, turning back to Art, Lily said, "I assume you'd like the key?"

"If you please," Art said, waiting patiently as Lily pulled out a drawer and rummaged for said key. When she handed it to Art, she did so by cupping his hand with her empty one, as though making sure the key was transferred without incident. Art accepted the key, closing his hand around it protectively while the two stood, still connected for a few moments longer. To Raina, it looked as though some kind of ritual was being completed. Then it was Art's turn to nod to Lily.

"Take all the time you need," Lily said, looking at Raina as she let go of Art's hands.

Disoriented by the strange atmosphere, Raina tried to say the expected "thank you" but Art had already put his arm around her shoulders, steering her toward a bookcase in the back of the room. There he slid his hand expertly beneath a shelf then stood back as the bookcase slid to the right, revealing a small door into which Art fit the treasured key. Raina saw nothing but darkness until Art found another hidden switch that flooded the room with a gentle glow. A windowless, hidden room. Raina wondered what treasure or treasures must be present to justify such secrecy.

The lamplight revealed beautiful tapestries, one on each of the four walls, each depicting a different aspect of nature: sea life, four-leggeds, plants, and birds. What she did not notice was that in each picture a tiny human was hidden in among the creatures. In the center of the small space was a table with two chairs and on the table sat a single large book.

"Have a seat, Raina," Art said. "I've been dying to show you this."

As Raina sat, Art took the chair across from her and sat watching her expectantly.

"*Well Prayers*," she read on the brown leather cover of the tome.

"Go head," Art urged. "Open it."

The book was over-sized, like a sacred manuscript. Without even knowing what was inside, she opened it reverently and began to read. Page after page she read, her eyes filling up and her vision blurring, but she wiped the tears away and read on and on, until she remembered that Art was sitting across from her. When she finally looked up at him, she was shocked to see that tears were streaming down *his* face as well.

"Oh my word," she managed to say. "Is this what I think it is?"

"It is indeed," he answered, his voice breaking slightly. "The experiences of folks who have been to the Well."

The Well on the hill and the day that changed everything. A bit lost on an exploratory hike, she had stumbled upon a seemingly simple puddle beneath a tree which turned out to be anything but. Her experience there had brought her to her knees and driven her, shaken and confused, to Art's house. Then just a neighbor – a new friend – she poured out her story to him and his sister Sirona and got more than she'd bargained for. In explaining to her that she had found a sacred well, they included their own story, even more mind-spinning than the notion of holy wells in the hills around Aries Lake. That story revealed that the siblings embodied the reincarnated souls of King Arthur and Morgan le Fay – and moreover, that they suspected that she,

Raina, was in some way connected to Merlin's soul – for which they had been ardently seeking. That was the beginning of it all and nothing had been the same since.

"Beautiful poetry, is it not?" Art's voice broke into her reverie.

"Uncannily so," Raina said in a whisper, drawn through all that had transpired since that pivotal day and back into the Hedge and Hearth.

"Some of it is almost like...song," she said, so much less of a stranger to mystical experiences than she had been months before. "Not words at all," she continued, "but sounds...I don't understand how that can be, but..." Raina trailed off, returning her gaze to the book and smoothing her hand over it, barely touching it, like one might caress a child so as not to wake them from slumber.

"When you're ready, you can add your own piece. The book is waiting for it," Art said, with something in his voice Raina had not heard before.

"I could never..." she stammered.

"But you must...and you will," Art gently insisted. "All who have been to the well are drawn to share their experience here, in this book. To archive it if you will. Now that you know it exists, it will pull you and draw the right song out of you."

"I feel full to bursting...there's so much here and it's so beautiful, beyond anything I can imagine," Raina was talking to herself as much as to Art. "I need time to process this. May I come back again?"

"As often as you like," Art said, now a bit more like himself. "You are now one of the people to whom this belongs."

Raina closed the book reverently, then stood on shaky legs. As they left the room and returned the bookshelf to its proper place, Raina was taken aback to see that all the folks who had been reading when she and Art had arrived, were now standing in a semi-circle, effectively blocking the way. Raina panicked. Had Art let her see something she shouldn't have? She felt the heat rise in her face and her heartbeat quicken, but at that moment Lily stood out from the crowd.

"They're wondering if you would be so kind as to tell them your story," she explained.

"*My* story?" Raina asked. Did they want an account of her experience at the well, here, on the spot? But how could she share that with even a fraction of the elegance she had just witnessed?

"You are the one who released Merlin's spirit, are you not?" Lily asked, fixing Raina with her dark eyes.

Raina looked at Art in a panic. Was this happening? How did they know? And why these people? But Art smiled at her, beaming with admiration.

"It's ok. They can know. You are a hero and heroes must be prepared to tell their tale. It goes with the territory."

"You could have warned me..." Raina said under her breath, more than a little put out.

"I never would have gotten you here," Art said, smiling his most disarming grin. "After all you've been through, a little story telling should be a breeze. I think you'll enjoy it once you get into it."

Raina turned from Art to again face the expectant crowd. As though someone had flipped a switch, for a brief moment she saw all manner of plant and animal standing before her, but on two legs, all looking at her as a friend, a relative even. Just as quickly the vision passed, but the friendly demeanor of her audience remained.

"Ok then, but I'll need to sit."

She was taken upstairs, to an area clearly arranged for performance. They sat her in a high-backed chair then clustered around her, most in chairs, but some on the floor at her feet like children. Then as one they turned their strange faces to her, some resting their chins on their hands, and waited for her to begin.

But begin where, she wondered? So much to tell. So many revelations eventually leading to that fateful day in Brittany.

"It wasn't me alone," she began, because that was the thought uppermost in her mind. Not her alone at all. At that, all the faces of those involved smiled out at her from memory. How dear they all were. "Just tell the story, Raina," they seemed to say from their familiar visages. "Just tell *our* story."

"There were five of us," she said, "Sirona, Sirona's friend Niall, a...man...called Percy, my daughter April, and myself. Armed with the knowledge and support of so many others, we headed from Glastonbury to Brittany and the Paimpont Forest where Merlin is reputed to be buried. But it was not to that site that we ventured, but rather to a different one our collective wisdom led us to – a hidden cave deep in the oldest part of the Forest of Broceliande..."

Raina went on to tell about the ritual the three women performed in the cave as the men stood guard outside. She spoke of the thousand-year-old cauldron they used to mix the elements they had brought, the invocation Raina spoke, the words coming to her only at the last minute, and how April finished it when she faltered. Then, the swirling mist from the cauldron, what they believed was Merlin's soul rising out of it and into the darkness above them, and finally the cauldron shattering and dissolving into the earth. What she did not share was Sirona's spontaneous plea to Nimue's spirit, if it was present in the cave at all. Nor did she try to put into words what she, Raina, had felt upon entering the cave – the anguish of Merlin's being, trapped, half living, half dead, in the body of a tree for nearly two thousand years.

At the end of her tale there was a long silence, until a burly man with a rumbling voice spoke.

"And you believe you were successful?"

"We think so," Raina answered honestly, "though we can't be entirely sure. There were some signs, or what we thought were signs, but how can anyone be sure of such things?"

"We've felt a change here," the fairy-girl spoke up. "Ever so slight, like a cool breeze after the rain."

"For me, I've felt a sliver of hope enter my heart," another said.

Raina sat astonished. All the way from Brittany to here in the States? Could it be that releasing Merlin's spirit, if they had indeed done so, could have such a wide-ranging effect? And yet, wasn't that their hope?

Lily spoke next.

"There are many here who were on the brink of despair, convinced that humankind was impenitent, unredeemable, and that we had missed our last chance to recover the health of our planet. Merlin's soul was more than the soul of just one man. It was a powerful spirit of interconnection with the earth that was taken out of circulation, if you will, for nearly two millennia – far too long. Its release, if released it has been, may have come too late, or it may have come just in time. At the very least, perhaps even the belief that it is free may be enough to embolden similarly inclined spirits to rise up and fight for the Mother."

At that, Raina's audience rose one by one and moved toward her – not crowding her but clearly wanting to share space with her. A murmur of approval surrounded Raina and gestures of appreciation brought her to her feet. She longed for Sirona and April to be here with her – to see and feel this, for Raina ardently believed that she was the least important person in whatever success they had achieved that day in the forest. But she would accept this gratitude on their behalf, and strengthen her pledge to support her friend and her daughter in whatever was to come next.

Then Art was at her side and the people pulled away, but the threads of connection were not broken. At the door, Lily took the key from Art with the same ritual gestures as she had given it, then turned to Raina, her dark eyes now glistening with friendship.

"You are always welcome here. We see who you are, what you have been. We honor that and are here to support you, to teach you what we know, and to join you if need be. We are a part of your destiny."

As Art pulled his car away from the Hedge and Hearth, Raina sat in stunned silence. Art let her sit until he sensed that she was ready to talk.

"So, go ahead. Ask me," he opened.

"Ask you what? Where do I start? You tell me," Raina rejoined.

"I don't want to presume..."

"Presume away. Anything you tell me will help me make sense of what happened back there," Raina said, trying to keep the tinge of anger out of her voice that always seemed to appear when Art was being cagey.

Then she relented. "Ok, tell me about those people. You will think me mad but at a certain point, for just a moment, they all looked like animals or...plants...or something. You know how such visions scare the crap out of me, even now, even after all I've been through."

"Fear not, oh sensitive one," Art assured her. "You are not going mad. Your intuitive nature was spot on. All of those people are host to souls that were once such as you describe. Most people have no memory of the past lives of their souls...don't really *want* to know and so embrace a new birth as a clean slate. Others, to varying degrees, find ways to see and hang onto those past lives. You know that is true for Sirona and me. Sirona, as you know, is fierce about it. The same is true for all the folks you saw in the Hedge and Hearth. They purposely cling to their animal natures and for those who can see it, those natures peek out from time to time."

"What motivates them to do so?" Raina asked.

"The truth of it. Most of us probably house souls that have been in beings other than humans at some time or another. We are, after all, connected to everything through spirit, or energy if you will. For some, like those who so admired you today, those connections are precious. They prove the truth of our interconnectedness and it fulfills a longing we all have but don't understand the root of – the longing to be in communion with all that is."

"Merlin..." Raina began.

"...knew this, yes," Art replied. "Was this. From whence come the stories of his ability to shape-shift do you think? He was adept at getting in touch with the animal nature of his past soul-lives and with those of others as well."

"Hence their obvious reverence for Merlin," Raina said, the pieces starting to fit.

"Yes," Art agreed, "and others like him. Merlin was not the only such being, but he was an exceptionally powerful one. And the fact that his story has persisted for hundreds of years, however mutated, speaks to that."

Suddenly Raina felt her whole body heat up like someone was holding a torch too close. A realization hit her with a force she could barely withstand.

"That's why I could see them..." she barely managed to utter. "Because I am of Merlin's blood."

"Bingo. Now you're getting it." Art was trying to keep things light, but was well aware of what Raina must be going through. It was a lot to take in.

"I don't want this..." Raina said, the old fear of madness rising in her.

"You don't have a choice, my love, and you know it." Art had a way of slipping seamlessly from light-heartedness to the gentle sternness of his own kingly past.

"You felt it in the cave, you saw the power of it today. It will only threaten you if you try to run from it, deny it. Embrace it and you will learn its joys."

"But the responsibility..." Raina protested.

"A piece of cake for you, Raina. You take on the responsibility for the well-being of everyone you care about, and that without the awareness of your power and the knowledge to use it." Art suddenly pulled to the side of the road, stopped the car, and swiveled to face Raina his features more intense than Raina had ever seen them.

"Do you not realize that you are a modern-day expression of Druidic wisdom? You are a gift to the world. That doesn't mean you have to go on tour or shout it from the roof-tops. I won't let you. Your place is here with me, with the lake, the Well. We will protect you...love you fiercely if only you will let us. Whatever you are meant to do will reveal itself and we will handle that as it comes. For now, the most important thing is for you to be comfortable with what you are and together we will explore how to let that shine. And there is April. She has the same powers as you. She is the next generation of their expression. As you have always done, you are here to help her grow into them."

Raina saw the plea in Art's eyes and realized with a start that his ability to see her potential and his desire to help her live into it had been there from the very beginning. Even before they learned of her ancestral connection to Merlin, he had seen something in her he wasn't going to let go of. Art Fisher, inheritor of the spirit that had once animated the great King Arthur, recognized his beloved mentor despite the journey of the ages. Whether it was spirit or DNA, he sensed the presence of the wizard and wasn't going to relinquish it. All that their ancient souls had accomplished so long ago, but could not finish...what could they do now with this second chance?

For her part, all Raina knew for certain was that she loved this man from head to toe, and from the 5th century AD to the present shadow-threatened age if that was the reality of it. Whether she could handle these uncanny powers or not, not a drop of her wished to be quit of this man. And she trusted him. Implicitly.

She reached out to touch his dear face. So be it then.

"Let's get back on the road," she said. "Let's get home."

There's nothing more beautiful than a willow tree in a strong wind, Raina thought as she sat on Art's porch, still in pajamas, legs pulled up, hands wrapped around her coffee cup. It was a beautiful morning, already warm with a strong wind, white caps on the lake and the soothing sound of waves rolling the pebbles along the shore. Raina loved days like this, when the wind made everything dance. And this morning that included her heart.

Art hadn't even had to ask her to stay; it just evolved naturally from the day's events. Once home from the Hedge and Hearth, they had talked more about her awakening powers. Raina's misgivings about her inheritance as the scion of Merlin melted in the presence of Art's calm assurances that such powers were not only a gift, but a missing piece in the fabric of the modern world, and one that urgently needed to be returned, activated, and celebrated.

Dinner, wine, more talk, and the drift to Art's bed flowed together as naturally as morning glories reach toward the heavens. There was no hesitancy, no shyness. The two had been moving inexorably toward this communion since the day Art came to help move Raina from her office – like a prince rescuing her from her tower, Raina thought.

The prince, the king, benevolent and devoted to the well-being of the land and his people – such was the essence of Art's soul life that sang out in all its majesty as the two made love. Not the dominance of a king greedy for wealth and power, but the generous nature of a true sovereign who uses his station to lift up and protect others. Arthur the King – no wonder his story has persisted through the ages and the promise of his return been the hope of so many. And last night he was all hers – and she, his.

And here she was, awake and facing a new day while he slept on. Unusual. Typically it was Art knocking on her door, anxious to take her on some adventure before she was barely awake. But not today. Today she was alive in the world as she could never remember being, happy to let her love sleep while she practiced being in what felt like a new skin, a new mind...a new world.

Raina watched the willow branches flow, back and forth, giving form to the invisible wind, like long hair underwater, or birds gathering in a murmuration. Interesting how nature's forms repeat over and over, in all manner of being, and yet never get old, never fail to thrill, always fresh, as though happening for the first time. Like

Art and her last night. A repeated form, and yet, for Raina, every bit of it brand new.

Chapter 6

The White Spring

Late April was early for swimming, but the lake beckoned irresistibly. The days had been unseasonably warm, and the sun glistened daily across its rippled surface. Since moving to her mother's cottage the previous winter, Raina had been longing to take a plunge. Now, with her eyes full of the iridescent green of spring and the promise of the coming summer alive in the wind, she could wait no longer. She would have gone in with or without Art's company, but the two of them had been nearly inseparable since their trip to the Hedge and Hearth. Today would be no exception. And, truth be told, Art was as eager to immerse himself as was Raina.

Raina's chest constricted as she threw herself forward into the icy waters. Like a defense against the cold, she took a few strokes, then stopped and looked back for Art, still only in up to his knees. The devil in her urged her to splash his cowardly form, shivering in the shallows, but how could she be so mean to a man who was so dear to her? Instead, she settled for a gentle taunt.

"It won't get any warmer with you standing there..."

"Give me time woman, give me time," he fired back through chattering teeth.

"Well, I'm not staying in here forever..."

But he was already underwater, stroking toward her. He came up gasping, smiling, full of the mischief she'd come to love about him. Together they swam through the barely thawed water until they could feel it pulling the warmth from their blood. Enough is enough. Once on shore, the slight chill of the air had no effect on their numbed skin, but the sun felt glorious. Art was vigorously toweling his wet hair when he suddenly stopped in mid-rub.

"Something's wrong," he said. "I can feel it."

"Just like that?" Raina asked. What could possibly invade the calm of this splendid morning?

"I think it's Sirona," he answered over his shoulder as he strode back to the cottage.

By the time Raina caught up with him, he was already at the computer, reading an email. Over his shoulder Raina read,

Art,

I'll cut to the chase. Sirona is not doing well. She has been depressed for some time, almost ever since Raina and April left, but it's taken a concerning turn. She insisted on returning to Brittany, to Nimue's cave, but you must know, she did so against the advice of Percy and myself. But you know your sister -- there was no stopping her. As before, Percy and I guarded the entrance. She wasn't in there long, perhaps ten minutes at best, and when she came out, she seemed ok, though she wasn't prepared to speak of what went on inside. We returned home, thinking she had accomplished what she wished, but she still wasn't herself and after a few days she took to her bed and no amount of coaxing could bring her around. We've tried everything but though we get her to eat barely enough to keep her alive, we can get nothing else out of her.

Rowan came and stayed with her for three days, giving her teas, chanting, whispering...whatever else that magical being had in her toolbox. When Rowan finally emerged from Sirona's chambers, she told

us that Sirona was soul-sick, stuck, and perhaps under the malevolent influence of Nimue's spirit which, it must be said, was my fear from the beginning. After trying everything she could think of to break through and bring Sirona back to the present, Rowan had to admit defeat. Her only advice to us at that point was that we should get Sirona out of Glastonbury and into your care, and the companionship of Raina and April. I hate to see her go, but I must conclude at this point that I am no help to her here and I believe Rowan is correct. The atmosphere here is too charged, too full of magic of all kinds. The trouble now is that Sirona is in no shape to travel alone...

"I'll go get her," Raina said before getting to Niall's conclusion. "I'll book a flight today. Tell him I'm coming!" Raina's voice was quivering and tears were pooling on her lids. Just the thought of Sirona so incapacitated made Raina feel that perhaps the earth was about to stop turning. "Tell him, *tell him*," she said again, panic rising in her voice, "I'm packing now."

Art caught her arm and drew her to him.

"You would leave me now?" Art asked, uncharacteristically possessive.

Half turning to him, she nearly shouted, "It's your *sister!* Sirona needs me!"

"And you she will have, and me and the lake and April. Everything we have to give is hers, but Niall or Percy could bring her to us. The thought of you leaving again..." Art could not finish, nor did he need to. Raina well knew what he was feeling. The thought of leaving Art was piercing, but Sirona's need threatened to pull her heart right out of her chest if she did not follow where it was leading. The two stood a moment in tortured silence, doing their best to absorb the blow of painful choices.

Finally, Raina collected herself enough to speak calmly. "If Rowan says she needs us, then the sooner at least one of us is with her, the better."

"Must you always be so smart?" Art said, with the saddest smile Raina had ever seen on any human being. "Actually, knowing my sister, it is quite possible that neither Niall nor Percy could rouse her enough to get her on a plane. I hate to admit it, but if anyone can call Sirona into herself, it's you. And... you are a creature of *this* world. Rowan's diagnosis suggests that a break from *her* world will be part of Sirona's cure. Only you can bring that to her." Art drew a tortured breath. "Go pack. I'll write back to Niall and book the first flight I find."

Raina nodded, and began to leave, but Art caught her arm again.

"But promise me you won't stay away one second longer than necessary, do you hear me?" Art looked about to say more, but caught himself. Raina looked deeply into her lover's face. Was there a vulnerability there that had not been there before? Was her king not as invincible as she believed? Indeed, as she had come to depend on? Was this the shadow side of a love as deep as they had found, that the very object of your love was weakened by the love itself? Her mind recoiled from the thought. She wanted to believe that Art's love for her made him stronger, just as his love had done for her. The last thing she'd want would be for her love to weaken him in any way – for her sake as much as his. She put her hand up to his still-damp hair and ruffled it as she kissed him.

"For everyone's sake, I will return here with our beloved Sirona as soon as possible. And take no care for my comfort – book whatever is the soonest flight you can find."

The return to Glastonbury was more charged with emotion than Raina had anticipated.

As the Tor came into view Raina was brought back to the night of the ritual on its peak, twelve women calling upon Spirit to guide them in their quest to release Merlin. Raina had ascended the hill still somewhat of a skeptic and descended it trembling with the power she felt there and the indisputable truth that Spirit or the Goddess had spoken to each of the twelve women in turn, offering guidance for their quest, as enigmatic as some of it was. And there was also the realization that the quest required the involvement of April, whom she would have given her life to keep safe. But Rowan and even Sirona had insisted that Spirit's reference to a young woman clearly pointed to April. How could it be that this daughter with whom she had finally been reunited after all these years was now to be put in the middle of a dangerous quest, surrounded by uncertainty, sorcery and half-guessed-at ritual?

Raina ran her hand through her hair, as though to push away the overwhelming and conflicting emotions of that time...not so long ago as all that. April was safely back in the States, finishing her last semester of college, and she and Art were settling into a life for themselves. Only Sirona seemed to be suffering some consequence of their mission. Sirona. Even now, Raina could not imagine her friend as anything other than completely and totally self-possessed.

Surely, it couldn't be as bad as Niall had made out. Nevertheless, Raina quickened her pace and soon found herself at Sirona's apartment.

Niall was at the door before she could knock.

"Raina, bless you," Niall said, grabbing at her bag and pulling it across the threshold. There were no pleasantries, no "How was your trip?" or "Can I get you something to drink?" only an unmistakable urgency in Niall's red-rimmed eyes and bird-like movements.

"Come," was all he said, as he led her through the familiar outer rooms and into Sirona's bed chamber.

A gasp came from Raina despite herself. She was totally unprepared for what she saw. Instead of her beautiful, raven-haired, vivacious friend, there on the bed lay a skeleton with a thin layer of skin barely covering her bones. Her glossy black hair had turned to soot, grey streaks running through it like ash. But for the moment, Raina was spared the sight of the sunken eyes and the broken spirit that stared out of them. Whether Sirona had heard their approach or not, she had not turned her head toward the door, but continued to stare out into the empty sky outside her window.

Biting her lip, Raina looked at Niall as though for some suggestion as to how to proceed, but Niall only shrugged, then nodded toward the form on the bed, apparently unable to speak. Perhaps Raina's presence had re-opened the wound Niall had been living with for weeks.

Gathering herself as best she could, she walked to her friend's bedside and sat on the edge of it, reaching out a trembling hand to touch the shriveled skin of Sirona's cheek.

"Dear one, I am here." Raina whispered. For a long moment, Raina was afraid her friend would not respond, but then Sirona turned her head slowly and fixed her empty eyes upon the newcomer.

"Raina?" she croaked.

Fighting revulsion, willing herself to see the friend she remembered beneath the woman who now, it seemed, lay dying, Raina found her voice.

"Yes, sister of my heart. It's Raina. I'm here..."

Whether Sirona smiled or grimaced, Raina could not say, so emaciated was the face that had turned to her. But it was a small something, anyway, upon which Raina would build some hope.

Over the next few weeks, Sirona responded slowly to Raina's ministrations, but respond she did. Each day she would eat a bit more, and when she wasn't sleeping Raina would read to her or make stories out of their adventures together, beginning each one with "Remember the time when...." If Raina had thought that she would fly into Glastonbury, pack a bag for Sirona then fly out again, she was mistaken. It would take time to get Sirona strong enough to even think of making the trip. The letter to Art was painful to write...*not sure when she will be strong enough to travel....* It didn't take a magic mirror to imagine the disappointment on his face when he read those words. She only hoped that telling him of Sirona's slow but obvious progress would soften the blow.

Then came the day when the old Sirona peeked out from behind the death mask. Her voice little more than a croak, she asked, "What of Art...and you?"

The sudden abundance of color in Raina's face contrasted sharply with the pale visage of her friend. Raina would have preferred to share the story of her growing relationship with Art later, when Sirona was closer to her old self, unsure exactly how Sirona would take the news of it. But how could she ignore this first sign of an interest in life from her patient?

"We...we have grown...close," Raina stammered.

"How close?" from the wounded raven on the bed.

"Close." Raina repeated, thinking perhaps Sirona, in her weakness, would ask no more.

"*That* close?" And suddenly, there was a spark in those dark eyes. Raina caught it and laughed aloud. She grabbed her friend's hand and put it to her lips.

"Yes, *that close*." And for the rest of the afternoon, Raina told the tale of everything that had happened between her and Art since her return to the States: the pottery studio, the trip to the Hedge and Hearth, the polar plunge and the love making. Periodically, Sirona would squeeze her friend's hand, or make little sounds of delight. And all the while, the recognition grew in Sirona's eyes, and a smudge of color returned to her cheeks.

On the day that Sirona got out of bed and shuffled to the kitchen for breakfast, Niall handed Raina a folded piece of paper. Opening it, Raina read:

Take her to the White Spring

-- *Rowan*

After Sirona returned to her bed, Raina left her to her nap and slipped out to question Niall.

"What is the White Spring?"

"It's the companion to the Red Spring, of which you know from the Chalice Well Gardens," Niall explained. "They both come out of the Tor, but the White Spring is underground, and white from calcite deposits. Many go there for healing. Sirona knows it well, but I think she's given up much faith in even the sacred waters of the Tor to heal her malaise. Still, you can try...when she's strong enough. You can make an appointment to see it outside of regular visiting hours so that she'll have privacy."

Raina flicked the paper against her palm. "Why didn't Rowan suggest this earlier, before I came?"

"I think she wanted you here...that you had something to do with the success of such a venture." Niall looked at Raina pleadingly. Clearly, it had been their hope all along that Raina would be the one to come to Sirona.

On the day that Niall drove the two women to the White Spring Temple on Well House Lane, Raina had risen early, full of an agitation she had no name for, no sense of what caused it. There was much to be thankful for. Sirona was getting stronger every day and when Raina mentioned the Spring, Sirona readily agreed to the plan. If all went well both Raina and Niall agreed that they could begin planning the trip to the States – back home, to the lake and Art. As much as she revered Glastonbury and was grateful for all she had learned there, her heart was back with Art. Perhaps that was the source of the agitation she felt...that perhaps the visit to the Spring would somehow work against Sirona's healing. But how could it? Sirona was content – perhaps even eager – to go. Maybe it was something about the Spring itself, the fact that it was underground, that troubled Raina. The Chalice Well was all sunshine and gardens. Raina had felt limitless in its presence. But the way Niall had described the Temple of the White Spring, built literally under the Tor, made Raina uneasy. *No cellphones or cameras,* he had explained, *only candlelight and hushed voices.* It all sounded a bit too...*interior*...for Raina's taste.

No matter. Rowan had felt the White Spring would help Sirona's healing, so Raina would put on a good face and swallowed her unease.

But the moment they stepped inside the temple Raina's unease pooled in the pit of her stomach. The air was damp and lit only by candles flickering from all the natural ledges of the cavern. When their eyes had adjusted to the dim light, Raina led Sirona to the edge of the healing pool, helped her kneel, then, fighting a wave of nausea, backed away to give Sirona some space.

The sound of dripping water filled Raina's ears as though it was a torrent. Unable to do otherwise, she sat on the damp stone floor and wrapped her arms around herself, hoping to steady the quivering feeling that was taking her over. But the feeling only intensified, as though her insides were churning, trying to burst from her limp body. Just on the verge of crying out, Raina fell into a swoon and in a dream-state imagined herself another being entirely. A cloaked figure, with a knotted beard, steel-gray eyes, and bent from the burden of wisdom. Merlin. The Spring had called to him, called him up from the DNA she carried, and shared, with the great Mage. He was at home here, his being resonated with every aspect of the cavernous temple, his soul flowed in and out of his body – her body – as though it was part of the calcite-tinged waters.

Not so Raina. She felt she was being torn apart. She had felt the part of her that was Merlin's lineage before, but never like this. Never had that ancestral energy come so alive, so into itself, disregarding all that had gone beyond it. There was nothing she could do but tolerate it and hope it would somehow abate. But when she heard a splash from the pool, she forced herself to turn toward Sirona, only to find her friend face down in four feet of water.

"No!" she cried, and when her legs failed to move, she pulled herself across the damp floor to the edge of the pool, and somehow managed to pull herself in. Where was the guardian that supposedly stood in the shadows, there to assist them?

Raina reached for Sirona and grabbing her garment managed to pull her face up, praying she had not gotten to her too late. How she wished she had listened to her earlier misgivings. Never had she imagined that her friend had agreed so readily to the outing because she saw it as a way to end her torment. But as Raina added her own tears to the sacred stream, Sirona gasped and sat up. Hardly registering her relief, or the fact that her own physical discomfort had left her, Raina struggled to find her feet and pull Sirona upright. Holding each other, they stumbled from the pool, drenched and trembling. Speech seemed out of the question as they made their way through the darkness toward the door.

The light of day was too bright for their eyes and so they did not see Niall running toward them, panic written all over him.

"My God! What happened in there..." Niall, seeing them soaked and trembling, choked on his own words, having the same thought as Raina. Not Sirona. Please not Sirona. Of all people to consider taking her own life, and in a sacred pool at that. It was more than he could conceive and still keep his wits about him.

As he hustled the women into the car Sirona whispered, "Take me home."

"That's where we're going, love. Just hang on," Niall said through the quiver in his voice as he struggled to navigate the narrow lanes of Glastonbury more quickly than was wise.

"No, I mean *home."*

Well before Niall had pulled up to Sirona's apartment, Raina saw that there was a cloaked figure sitting on the porch. Her pulse quickened. After what had happened at the White Spring, she was predisposed to suspect trouble, but she was loath to raise an alarm lest she disturb Sirona, who had fallen asleep with her head on Raina's shoulder. But when they stopped, Raina spoke to Niall, quietly, urgently.

"Do you see it? Have a care..."

"Stay here," Niall replied. "I'll check it out."

As Niall approached the porch, the figure moved only slightly. When Niall had taken the steps and stood before it, the head rose and the hood fell back to reveal Rowan. Raina could see her mouth move, but could not make out the words. A wave of anger swept over her. Why had Rowan, in all her wisdom, urged them to the Spring? Gently, Raina woke Sirona and helped her from the car. Niall had already brought Rowan inside. *This will be some discussion,* Raina thought.

Rowan spoke first, which was a relief to Raina, as she was struggling to know how to address Rowan, the knot of anger wrestling with her affection for the woman – the woman whose *tree-ness* seemed more evident than ever to Raina, her strangeness more pronounced set against the comfortable familiarity of Sirona's apartment. As Rowan shifted in her seat, the sound was of crisp autumn leaves rustling in a chill breeze; the wrinkles around her eyes like the dark lines around burls.

"I came here shortly after you left this morning, to be here when you returned, eager to see how you'd fared. But as I sat on the porch, I felt your panic. I've been worried sick," Rowan concluded, her sincerity evident. Still...Raina was not entirely mollified.

"We almost lost her..." Raina began, doing her best to keep her voice even, uncritical. And yet, she found she could not continue. She and Sirona had yet to speak of what happened in the Temple. To accuse her friend of trying to take her own life was not a subject to address head on, or at least it didn't seem that way to Raina.

"I wanted to submerge myself," Sirona spoke at last, her voice barely a whisper, "as people often do at the White Spring. But I lost my balance as I stepped into the pool and slipped. Once in the water, I didn't have the strength to get up. Raina got to me just in time..."

"Then you didn't...you weren't..." Niall was nearly beside himself with relief.

"Didn't what?" Sirona asked, then seeing Niall's and Raina's expression said, "Oh my goodness no! How could you think I'd do such a thing?" Sirona's look was accusing.

"Sirona," Raina said, finding her courage, "you've been in dire straits. You'd nearly starved yourself before I got here. You were getting better, but...well, how could we know what might have come over you in that place?"

Rowan heard the edge in Raina's voice. Clearly something else happened there that had yet to be discussed, but Raina and Niall were focused entirely on Sirona who was now crying piteously.

"I'm so sorry! I must have put you all through hell!"

"That you did my love," Niall said, his features, so long creased in worry and fear now smoothing into a slight smile. Weak as she was, he could sense that his Sirona was making her way back from whatever dark place she had been roaming, lost and alone.

"But there's more to the story, is there not?" Rowan said after a time, eyeing Raina.

"There is," Raina said, lifting her arm to smooth back her hair.

"Your arm!" Sirona exclaimed.

Raina raised both arms to reveal the bruises and scrapes she sustained from pulling herself across the stone floor and over the edge of the pool. She'd hardly thought of them herself, so concerned was she about Sirona, but now, as she began to tell her story, they stung and throbbed, punctuating the memory of her body feeling split in two.

When she finished her tale, everyone sat in stunned silence until Rowan spoke.

"I'm sorry for your suffering, but you must know that this was not malevolence on behalf of the Spring or Merlin himself. This was a significant healing for you, a gift even, for which you paid a price."

"And we almost lost Sirona as a result of it," Raina said, this time not trying to hide the resentment in her voice. But Rowan, being Rowan, paid it no mind.

"But you didn't lose her. In fact, you were released just in time," Rowan protested, but she could tell Raina was not convinced.

In his own special wisdom, Niall sensed that what Rowan was about to reveal needed some preparation. And besides, the women were still sitting there in their damp clothes. Nodding to Rowan to indicate that he knew there was more to be said, Niall turned to Sirona and Raina.

"You two are still wet," Niall said, rising. "Why don't you change into dry clothes while I put on some tea and set out biscuits? We'll have a bite and get warm, then we'll let Rowan explain herself." Rowan gave Niall an appreciative nod as he helped Sirona to her feet.

When the women returned to the main room, dressed and combed, they saw that Niall and Rowan had lit candles and arranged the room into something of a circle, the tea and biscuits set in the center, ritually. The effect was one of comfort, safety and abundance. As they took their seats and sipped their tea, Rowan began to sing – or rather rustle. The sound she made was one of trees in a gentle wind, swaying, dancing, catching the wind as a child might reach to catch soap bubbles. Real but elusive, and beautiful in its ethereal nature. As Rowan's singing intensified, each felt their feet grounded, reaching down, drawing strength from the earth, the ancestors, all that has existed since the beginning of time. Raina felt all her negative emotions flow out of her and into the earth where they were transformed, like compost, into a rich, generative humus to nourish the spirit.

Of course, Raina thought, *of course.* She was ready to hear Rowan's words, ready to embrace whatever new and unbelievable thing was now a part of her life. She should be used to it by now....

Rowan ceased her rustling and leaned forward to give weight to what she was about to explain. "From what you describe, Raina, Merlin has come more alive within you. You are correct in assuming that the power of the White Spring called to Merlin's essence in you, the DNA that you share. That it caused you distress is not malevolence, but physiology. The White Spring contains a rich calcite deposit which resonates with your inner ear and the vagus nerve, all of which was excited by the resonance – the awakening, if you will – of aspects of your DNA, causing the dizziness and nausea. For many, the calcite of the White Spring balances the crystals within, hence the clarity and renewal people experience. For you, the effect was a bit overdone, thereby having the opposite effect.

"But," Rowan continued, "what is important here, is the awakening of Merlin's DNA within you. You are increasing in power, which will be unsettling at first. It's a lot to handle, to say the least. But know this, you are a soul-reader, as I am, and as Merlin was. You see the tree nature in me. Merlin held that same nature. That Nimue trapped him in a tree was an exceptionally cruel act. It was a torture to him...and to the tree. It would be like binding you with your own bone and sinew torn from your body..." Rowan was silent for a spell before she could go on.

"Take this gift with whatever grace you can muster. Make your peace with Merlin and the complexity of emotions that have travelled down through your mitochondrial DNA, your *maternal* ancestors. This work will be primarily inner work and highly personal, but I know your character and know this is not alien to you."

Raina found her voice. "And April?"

"The more work you do, the less your daughter will have to face, leaving her free to live into her powers without all the resistance you have struggled with. This has been your gift to her all along, but you are not finished yet."

"And Nimue's curse?" Sirona asked, her eyes darkening at the mere mention of Nimue's name.

"I've thought a great deal about that," Rowan answered. "I begin to think that she sensed the seed of the struggle in Annwyl and merely called it out, intensified it. As such, it is something that can be undone. Perhaps the centuries have weakened it, but they have also obscured its roots. In you, Raina, the whole of it has come together – root, tree and branches. You suffered the mental anguish in your early years, whether that was Nimue's curse at work or the difficulty of having Merlinist power within you, unrecognized. Nevertheless, you found a way to flourish, to participate in the world. Finally, there is April, your daughter, whom you have nourished and now brought to awareness of the heritage to share."

"But to what end?" Raina said, as much to herself as her companions, who, for the moment, all sat silently. No one was any closer to an answer than Raina was herself, until Sirona spoke, a spark of her old self glinting in her eyes at last.

"This time, I don't think we'll find the answer here, as enchanted as this land is. It's time to return to the lake, to Art, and to that spunky daughter of yours, Raina. What say you Raina, dear?"

A laugh burst from Raina like a breath held too long. How much she'd missed this brave and wise woman! "Lead the way, Sirona!"

Chapter 7

A Page Turns

Aries Lake, USA

Leaning awkwardly on a cane, Sirona ran her free hand across the incised pot, outlining vesica-shaped leaves etched in appealing disarray.

"You've been busy, my friend," she said without turning to face Raina who stood shyly behind her, wondering what Sirona would make of her amateurish attempts at ceramics.

"Indeed she has," boomed a voice that startled them both. Art strode into the room, his flannel shirt tucked neatly into his jeans, his carefully trimmed beard glinting silver in the morning light. A quick kiss for Raina, then on to Sirona, his strength and regal bearing emphasizing her diminishment as he stood beside his beloved sister. Raina's throat tightened at the sight. She'd gotten somewhat used to the change in Sirona, focusing on her relief that her friend was at least out of bed and strong enough to make the trip across the pond. Now, seeing the siblings together, the extent of Sirona's frailty was distressing. No doubt Art was struggling to see his sister so, but as was typical of him, he hid his shock and, instead, exuded his usual abundance of enthusiasm and positivity.

"She claims to have no skill," Art went on, putting his hand protectively on his sister's back, "but there's something going on with her decoration. I swear, in just the right light, I see the leaves and vines moving."

"There is a power here," Sirona agreed, so quietly Raina could barely hear her. But what she did hear, loud and clear, was a sigh of defeat. What it must cost Sirona to be using a cane, Raina thought, to lack the vigor and power that had been hers without question, without effort. Surely, Art heard it as well and if Raina knew this man at all, then she suspected he was busy considering how to rescue his sister from wherever she had gone.

"Well then," Art said, shifting course. "I've let you sleep off your jet lag for two days, sister, but now I insist you eat and, when you're well nourished, I must hear of your adventures. Come, I've made us a proper breakfast."

Adventures? Is that what it was, whatever dark night of the soul Sirona had suffered? But so like Art to name it so, Raina thought, purposely lagging behind the two as they made their way to the dining room. For Art, everything was part of the adventure of living. If anyone could bring Sirona's spirit back to her, whether or not her body would be able to follow, it would be Art the Undaunted. Raina felt a tiny smile invade her lips. It was good to be back home.

As the three enjoyed Art's scones and homemade jam, cheesy omelets and perfectly brewed coffee, Raina let her mind wander back to the first meal Art had prepared for her, the night of the Solstice when *she* was the wounded bird, brought into the healing intentions of these magical siblings. Never would she have thought that less than a year later, the magnificent, awe-inspiring Sirona would be the wounded one.

And just as it had been then, now, after the meal, Art brought them into the living room and sat them down before the fire set to chase away the spring chill. Leaning forward in an attentive posture, he went about opening the way for Sirona to tell her tale, which even Raina had not yet heard completely.

Raina watched Sirona carefully, watched as her friend's eyes went distant, her voice pushing through the anguish, telling of her visit to Tuttle, the vision in the cave, the scheming monk, and the young woman whom Morgan le Fay had overlooked...the slight that had such a disastrous conclusion...or so Sirona had surmised.

"And you blame Morgan le Fay for Nimue's actions?" Art asked gently when Sirona paused in her tale. The question was obviously rhetorical, but it called Sirona to acknowledge a fuller picture.

"As always, brother, you challenge me, but appropriately so," Sirona said after a long silence. "I know I was only seeing through Morgan's eyes. There were many players in those events, whose hearts and minds I can never know, but that does not excuse the failure of connection on Morgan's part. And likely she knew it and carried that responsibility forward, so that it lurked in my ancestral memory until the vision brought it to consciousness."

"The warning of which Tuttle spoke," Art mused. "And perhaps that explains the depression that gripped you. But there is another possibility. You have suspected that Nimue's spirit was, or is, entwined in the cave. Is it possible that it had a hand in bring you low?"

"That her spirit cursed me, you mean?" Sirona asked. "As she did Annwyl all those centuries ago? Maybe, but I'm beginning to believe that we must, in some way, be complicit in any curse that affects us. There must be some fertile ground in our unconscious for a curse to take root."

"You seem determined to take responsibility for something that happened over fifteen hundred years ago, dear sister," Art said, not unkindly.

"I see your point," Sirona said, chuckling slightly at her brother's unerring ability to call her out, make her go deeper. "We can't undo the wrongs of our ancestors, but there is a responsibility to acknowledge them and hopefully mend what has been broken if possible. And that's where I'm stuck. How do we do that? I had hoped that releasing Merlin's soul..."

"...would automatically make things better," Art said shifting in his seat. "I think we all hoped that, but likely that was a dream. None of us knows what the reality is or will be. Perhaps the release of his soul is increasing the urgency of the *mending* that needs to be done." A wan smile played across Art's features. "Merlin was never one to make things *easy* for anyone. Like the witches in fairy tales who give out seemingly impossible tasks, perhaps the return of Merlin's soul is calling us to take on more than we ever thought would be asked of us."

No one needed to voice what they were all thinking...if that was so, then what were the tasks? How would they know of them?

Amid a frustrated silence, Raina found her voice. "Besides what I could see for myself, what happened to you at the White Spring? We never really talked about that."

Art's eyebrows rose into his grey locks. "You went to the White Spring?"

"At Rowan's suggestion, yes." Sirona began. "Niall and Raina thought I was trying to drown myself, but I intentionally immersed myself, looking for a message...and I did get one. The voice was sweet and clear...she told me I must battle my way back to functionality. To wallow in my despair was...well...selfish. In that moment, I knew the rightness of it and though it would be difficult, I would do it, could do it. What I didn't realize, however, was how much damage I'd done myself physically. That's another matter."

The day wore on, the fire burned out, making way for the spring sun to play its part. The three talked well into the afternoon until there was a knock on the door. When Art brought the visitor into the living room, there were shouts of glee.

"April!"

Raina sprang from her seat to greet her daughter, hugged her tightly, smoothed her hair from her face, then released her, albeit reluctantly. She could never get enough of April.

"You're home early! Aren't you supposed to be taking exams?" Raina said, joyously playing the role of mother.

"It was all projects and I've finished everything. I'm graduated and done, ready to be home." Then gently breaking from Raina, April went to Sirona where she sat, melting onto the floor at her feet. "Auntie S," she said, grabbing Sirona's withered hands, "you're here! I'm so glad," but she couldn't hold back the tears that sprang to her eyes, and tightened her grip on this treasured woman, as though to send her youthful vigor into her.

"Yes, I'm here dear one," Sirona said, smiling down at the young woman she cherished as though she were her own daughter, "and we have much to discuss, but for now, quit showing off how flexible you are and go find yourself a comfortable seat."

"You're not going to graduation?" Art asked as April reluctantly let go of Sirona's hands and did as she was bid.

"No," April said once seated. "That's a waste of time. We've got work to do here."

"We're not exactly sure what that work is however," Raina said, voicing what she knew to be the consensus, "but I guess we'll figure it out."

"And of that," Sirona added, "we have a better chance now that you're here." And there it was, the flash in Sirona's eyes that had been missing.

Dinner was a festive affair. Art produced a celebratory meal seemingly out of nowhere, as though he had some inside information that allowed him to prepare for April's arrival ahead of time. Not out of the question, Raina thought, that April might have alerted him. She smiled at the thought, delighted at the special relationship Art and April seemed to have developed. Well, she'd let them have their secret. What mattered was that they were all together, smiling, and rejuvenated. A page had turned.

It was decided that Sirona and April would stay at Raina's cottage as Raina had all but moved in with Art, an interesting development that April accepted with no comment, only a small (knowing?) smile. Again, inside information, Raina thought.

"Mom, do you mind if I pull a mattress into the Mother Room? For some reason I feel an urge to sleep there."

But it was Sirona who answered April.

"If it's ok with your mother, the loft is yours. It's only right – your inheritance if you will. Besides, I have no interest in trying to make the stairs."

Raina laughed. "You two do whatever you need to make yourselves comfortable over there. But are you sure you actually want to sleep in the Mother Room honey? I find the mystery of the place best tackled in the daylight."

The Mother Room, or so Raina had named the strange little attic room off the loft with its swirling blues and greens depicting an endless night sky complete with hundreds of string lights to complete the feeling of being lost in the cosmos. Raina had yet to figure out the purpose of the room, evoking in her, as it did, both intrigue and caution. It stood to reason that April would be the next one to have a go at it. Raina knew she had to let April go, to fulfill her destiny according to her own impulses. As Rowan had made clear, Raina's role was to do her own work, to become strong and accepting of her own powers, so that she might stand as a grounding rod for April while she took the next steps in this strange journey.

"I'll be ok," April said. "I'll leave the door open to the rest of the loft. If I get uncomfortable, I'll come out to the other bed. But something tells me there's information in the Mother Room that I haven't been able to connect with so far. When I visited before, I'd sit in there and wait, but nothing happened. I feel like there are words among the swirled paint, but try as I might, I haven't been able to make them out. Everything seems just out of reach. If I sleep there..."

"...perhaps dreams will come," Raina said, fear rising in her despite herself.

"Mom, I know how you feel about dreams, how terrifying they used to be for you, but remember," April said, putting her hand on her mother's, "that has not been my experience and always there has been a guardian, a protective presence in my dreamscapes. I trust in the steadfastness of that presence, as I trust in you and my grandmother before you – who apparently went to great lengths to create that room. There must be a reason. I need to find out what that was – and is – if I can. It seems to be a first step in going forward, in figuring out what we need to do next."

"So there you have it," Sirona spoke up, "the first of our tasks. Baba Yaga declares that you, dear April, must sleep in the dark and mysterious Mother Room for a week and a day, seeking a vision. But beware...the forest of dreams can be a fearful place. To seek your vision, you must face whatever slips from the shadows and do so unflinchingly."

"Not funny, Sirona," Raina said, trying to keep the edge out of her voice.

"And your task, Raina of Merlin's lineage," Sirona continued, "is to let her."

"Sister, I see that you're getting back to your old self," Art said, always the mediator. "But the evening is getting on. Shall we call it a night? Would you two like some help getting settled in the cottage?"

"I think we can..." April began, then, remembering that Sirona was not the powerhouse April had known her to be, changed her mind. "Yes, of course. I'll need help pulling a mattress upstairs at the very least."

Between the four of them, it didn't take long to arrange things comfortably. For her part, Raina was pleased to give the cottage over to Sirona and April. As much as she loved the place she had inherited from her mother – and never really got her fill of – it seemed right and appropriate for her daughter to be there now. Admittedly, she was a little jealous of Sirona having so much time with April – time she had been hungering for most of her life – but she knew in her heart that it was the right configuration of energy for the work ahead. Sirona and April sparked together, and she and Art....well, he was her home now, within whose love she could safely relax, and be happy in her own skin.

Sirona chose to sleep in the Lake Room where the windows on three sides kept her feeling unburied. "I've had enough of caves," she said, eschewing the small bedrooms at the back of the house for anything other than a place to put her things.

April set up the Mother Room with a mattress and a bedside lamp, then propped the door open to the rest of loft with its view through the house and out through the Lake Room windows to the water beyond. With the Mother Room's mural of the night sky, swirling with stars and cosmic mystery, it seemed to April as though she'd gained what every child dreams of – a tree house, open to the night sky, overlooking the world below. In this case, a world which included a lake. Who could ask for more? And how could she not be visited by insight in such a compelling environment?

"How about I fix breakfast for everyone tomorrow?" April offered once it was clear that everything was set for the night. "9:00?"

Art raised an eyebrow. Breakfast was usually his area of expertise. Sirona saw his expression.

"Don't worry, brother," Sirona said. "April makes lovely 'garden omelets' as she calls them. She treated us to them in Glastonbury. Breakfast will be in good hands."

"Then on your word," Art said, making an exaggerated bow, "I relinquish the kitchen."

April dropped a slight curtsey in return. She had taken no offense. Now was a good time for Art to give her the gift he'd brought. Pulling her aside, he produced four red journal books.

"I thought you might like to use these to record your dreams, thoughts, whatever. I've had them for ages and never managed to find a use for them. Funny how we have things that seem to hide themselves until the right time comes for their use. They're yours if you want them."

"Want them!" April exclaimed. "I'll cherish them! They're perfect. Thank you, Art," she said then rose on her tip toes to throw her arms around him and plant a kiss firmly upon his cheek.

As Art and Raina prepared to leave, Sirona disappeared and Art casually waited on the porch, giving Raina and April a chance to be alone.

After a long hug, April gave her mother a penetrating look.

"I'm glad you and Art are together."

"You don't seem too surprised," Raina countered.

"Ok, I admit it. Art and I really connected in those months before I came to you in Glastonbury. He confided in me his affection for you. I've worried that, given your horrible experience with my father, you wouldn't be open to it."

"So wise for your age...the truth is, I was fascinated by Art right from the first when he came to help me move out of my office at the university. And then there was all this," she said, waving her hand to encompass the cottage. "The way he took care of it...and just about everything else. But you're not entirely wrong. It was hard for me to believe in my suitability for a relationship after Malcolm. But when Art is determined he can break through any barrier, that much I've learned. Speaking of...your father...have you had any trouble from him?"

"Haven't heard a word. I think I'm off his radar ever since you and I cleared my stuff out of his house. There's no question he was shocked at our connection...and probably appalled. All those years he worked so hard to keep us apart, and there we were, all his scheming for naught. But what of Auntie S?" April asked, lowering her voice.

"She had a serious bout of depression...I'm sure she'll tell you all about it in time. But she's on the mend, and now that you're here...you are so dear to her."

"I really struggled to finish school," April admitted. "I just wanted to be with all of you. It was a visceral pull; I literally ached to be here. Mom, I can't tell you how much I've thought about everything that happened. I've had some ideas, but mostly I have a ton of questions."

"We all do, sweetie, but I believe that our best chance of answering them is to work on them together," Raina said, giving April a long hug. "But now I need to let you get some rest."

"I can't wait to get all nested in my little bed and fall into the magic of the Mother Room," April said, smiling.

"Well, don't fall too far," Raina warned, knowing all too well the power of dreams to grab the mind and hold it captive.

"No worries, Mom."

And nest she did. Her thought was to leave the fairy lights that lined the room on for a bit, so that she might lie awake and let the feeling of being adrift that the room inspired wash over her. Then as she felt herself getting sleepy, she'd pull the plug and let the night envelop her. But the threshold between wakefulness and dreaming eluded her, leaving her deeply asleep and entering the unknown as the tiny lights shone down on her like stars, or fireflies, or an army of watchful fairies.

She smelled the water before she saw it. Primal freshness, tinged with swimming things and green waving fronds – an aroma she felt she couldn't inhale deeply enough to get her fill. Then the sound of the waves, a gentle lapping, rhythmic beat, again evoking a hunger for more, for immersion. At the shore, she stepped in, clothed or not she couldn't tell, nor did it matter. The lake called to her and she would answer the call. No time to think or prepare. All was the insistent Now of Dreamtime. An osprey flew overhead, a fish jumped, she was no invader but part of it all. A breeze caressed her face, like a lace curtain at an open window. Her heart swelled with joy. Perhaps this was her proper element and she was only human by accident, a momentary glitch in the cosmic order, soon to be rectified if only...if only...

As morning broke, the fairy lights paled to a shy yellow and what was once the glittering cosmos was now nothing more than a wall and ceiling of brush strokes in varying shades of blue and green. April awoke with a burning desire to take a swim.

Tip-toeing through the cottage so as not to wake Sirona, April slid out the door and walked pensively to the shore. Her dreams clung to her like a mist, a slight chill on the skin. The early spring waters felt almost warm in comparison as April plunged into them, grateful and reverent. What a blessing to be held so, the water like arms surrounding her, cradling her, marrying the feeling of the present to the aura of her dreams. Never had she experienced such a connection between the dreaming time and wakefulness. She took long, slow strokes through the still morning waters, mindful of the caress against her skin as she moved. Only when the chill began to invade her core did she give in, abandoning the fantasy of being an aquatic being to return to the shore.

As she grabbed the towel she'd left on the wooden bench, Art suddenly appeared as if from nowhere.

"Welcome home," he said, his eyes glistening in the blue light of early morning.

"Home in so many ways," April said dreamily, doing her best to cling to the experience of the swim. Then, seeing the look in Art's eyes, she dared ask the question.

"Have you felt it?"

"*It?*" he asked, a hint of teasing in his voice.

"The feeling of being held..." April answered, fitting herself to Art's ways of being both mirthful and deadly serious at once.

Art looked out at the lake, then back at April and only after a long pause said,

"Oh yes. Often."

There was nothing more to be said, no words were necessary, even if the right words could be found. The lake had given up her secrets to them and they both instinctively knew they were bonded by them. They sat together on the shore in silence, until it was the right time to move on with the day.

"May I be your sous chef this morning?" Art asked, dying to be a part of the breakfast prep but respecting April's desire to cook. Another way they were the same, he thought, expressing love through food.

"If you can mince vegetables with finesse," she teased.

Chapter 8

Crumbs

Over the next week, April dreamed as Raina, Art and Sirona waited, instinctively feeling that to interrupt April's nocturnal journeys with discussion, analysis, or suggestions too soon, could confound the process. Sirona had pronounced a week and a day for the work, and so it would be. But as the week wore on, April grew more eager to reveal what she was seeing and The Three had all they could do not to open the package early. To pass the time Raina worked obsessively in her studio, churning out pots of all shapes and sizes.

For his part, Art kept busy with the usual springtime repairs typical of living on a lake. Sirona, however, was still acting rather unlike herself, meditating, taking long walks, generally lost in thought, and seemingly avoiding the company of the others. Though she didn't speak it aloud, April suspected that Sirona's behavior was in some way "holding the space" for April's journey and was thankful for Sirona's protection, at the same time that she missed having much interaction with her beloved "Auntie S."

And so the time passed for the companions until the duration was complete. On the eighth day, Art arose early, pleased to see that the chill had retreated from the springtime air, a circumstance that fit perfectly with his plans. By noon he had set up a festive table on the verge of the lake and covered it with all manner of delicious food, meant to signal the breaking of a rather unusual fast, for today was the day that April would, at last, speak of what she had dreamed.

The sun was warm, but not overly so; the sky the kind of baby blue that lightens even the darkest spirit. The trees were budding out, mixing their delicate greens with the welcoming sky and waving gently in the breeze. All in all, the feeling of the day was as far removed from the strange atmosphere of dreamscapes as it could be, which, for reasons he couldn't quite get a handle on, seemed the right kind of atmosphere for what was to come. Maybe it was to protect Raina from her fear of night terrors, or maybe to see if the dream visions held up in the light of day. Whatever it was, Art was following his sense that what was needed was to transcend the perceived duality of dreamtime and reality.

The companions took their places around the table, feeling the warmth of the sun drive away not just the winter chill, but concern and anticipation as well. Once everyone was properly settled, Art lifted a glass of amber iced tea.

"Here's to the first task of our quest completed by our brave April, who has roamed alone in the landscape of dreams while we waited anxiously for her return. If Sirona agrees, let us now hear the result of that journey."

Sirona let a slight smile spread across her creased visage. Seeing it, April was confirmed in her notion that Sirona had somehow stood guard during her vision quest.

"I agree, whole-heartedly," Sirona said. "But it is April who must be the one to say if the time is right."

"Are you kidding me?" April said, clearly bursting with enthusiasm. "The worst part of this experience was keeping things from you until the designated time was completed. But," she added, nodding to Sirona, "it was wise to let me work with everything I'd seen, to process it uninterrupted."

At that, April placed a slender red book on the table, one of the four Art had given her.

"I wrote it all down, every bit that I could remember, and my thoughts about all of it as well. I noticed that my interpretations changed some as the week went on. It was like putting together a puzzle, only in this puzzle the shapes changed as did the overall picture. One day a piece seemed to fit perfectly, then later appeared misplaced. As much as I worked to re-arrange everything into something that made sense, I still don't have it complete, but it's at a point where I'm ready for your input.

"For now, here are the images that have come most clear." April shifted in her seat. Suddenly, the young woman so full of youthful vigor looked...seasoned. Eyeing her daughter with a mixture of pride and concern, Raina saw that April had passed out of a general naivete and into a maturity of purpose...perhaps even a calling? There was more to listen for here than just a vision, or so she suspected.

"First of all, there's more to Grandmother's room than meets the eye. Somehow, there is life in the walls. Many of the understandings I gained came to me as words out of the paint, then followed images, some blurry, some crystal clear. One of the first words that came to me was *circles* – circles of people, bonded by a common need. Then the circles would intertwine, overlapping – strange to explain, but *feeding* each other, drawing others in. The circles grew and collected until they looked like some kind of complex network or... a flower. I tried to draw it, but it defied rendering. I couldn't capture the dimensionality of it."

April paused, as though returning to the struggle of trying to draw her vision. Raina reached across the table to touch her daughter's hand.

"Go on dear..." she said, knowing all too well the power of dreams to linger, seeping into the day, making it difficult to function despite the light.

April looked up and smiled at her mother and as she did so, a strange spark passed between them, a recognition even deeper than they had yet experienced.

"We're all connected, aren't we?" April said, as though the realization was brand new. "You, me, grandmother...and before that and before that."

"I've been known by many names...women all," Sirona whispered, remembering the day she and Raina first visited Rowan and what Raina had spoken in trance during the ritual.

"We all carry Merlin's DNA," Raina acknowledged, wishing, not for the first time, that somehow April had been spared that, though clearly, she had not. But to what extent and in what form, remained to be seen – though there would likely be revelations of it as April's story continued.

Art waited a beat, then encouraged April to continue.

Drawing a deep breath, April offered the next vision.

"I believe that somewhere in Grandmother's cottage, there are loose floorboards that hide a cache of books..."

"Why would she hide books?" Sirona said, incredulous.

"I think because they were...or are...dangerous. Or at least Grandmother thought so. Along with the images of hands pulling up boards and stuffing books into some kind of subflooring, I felt a tightening of my chest. Panic and fear. Urgency. I knew it was Grandmother. In fact, I felt her presence the whole time. Even in waking, I could feel her presence in the room, although more faintly during the day than at night."

"Do you suppose those books are really there?" Art asked.

"I intend to look and enlist your help in doing so," April responded. "But I didn't want to do that during the week...for all the reasons we mentioned. I wanted to be sure about the vision and I didn't want to interrupt the flow."

It was clear from the looks exchanged around the table that all four of them were eager to excavate the cottage in search of the enigmatic books, but they had agreed. April must complete her tale. If the books truly did exist, they had been there for years. They weren't going to disappear in the space of an afternoon.

"There is more about books," April continued. "I saw the Yule Poems, saw a woman writing them..."

"Not your Grandmother?" Raina cut in, urgently.

"Pretty sure not. Her clothes were...older. Her face was similar but not the same. I think it might have been her mother or even grandmother."

"Well one mystery solved...sort of," Sirona added. "But there was mention in them of things that have happened only recently, like the reference to Tolkien."

"Perhaps," April said, her forehead wrinkling as she stitched together more images and impressions, "they were added onto through the years...that would make sense, would explain the confusion of faces..."

"At least we're fairly certain the poems were written by one of our line, which is the important thing," Raina added.

"Books, books, books," April continued. "Hidden, written, all over the place. But there was one that still haunts me. It was a blank book and its pages would ruffle before my eyes, like they were beckoning me, pulling at me. It kept showing up repeatedly. I came to believe that it was encouraging me to take notes and so I did," April said, tapping the volume before her. "I thought once I started doing so that it would stop appearing, but it didn't. It kept showing up at the oddest times, ruffling, always ruffling. It got so repetitious that it started to have a note of nightmare about it..."

At that Raina squirmed in her chair. No. No nightmares. Not for April. Please, no.

"And?" Sirona prodded. "What have you concluded?"

As April began to speak, she heard an annoying whirring sound just on the edge of hearing, but possibly coming closer. Nevertheless, she worked to collect her thoughts enough to give a reasonable answer to Sirona's question.

"Well, the circles make a lot of sense. I keep thinking about the twelve that gathered in Glastonbury and how each of them is committed to following through in some way on bringing Merlin's spirit to bear upon our hope of healing the earth. It seems to me that each..."

"What the hell?" Art said, as he pushed out of his chair and stared into the air above them.

Raina shielded her eyes against the sun and followed his gaze. "Is that one of those drone things?"

"It looks to be so," Art replied, more angry than curious.

Now all four of them were watching the tiny bug-like surveillance device as it buzzed over their heads.

"Probably just some kids from the cottages above playing with a new toy," Raina said, hopefully, though she could read Art's demeanor and knew he was immediately suspicious.

"Well, it's the first time I've seen one of these things around here. It's unsettling," Art said, never taking his eyes off the sky.

"I don't like it," Sirona said at last, staring at it as though she could shoot it out of the sky with just a look. "The sound puts my nerves on edge...and why is it hovering over us?"

It was agreed that there was, if not out-and-out malevolence about the thing, an inappropriate invasion of privacy at the least. As they continued to stare at it, it rose higher and began making wider circles, but not quite leaving. As they tired of craning their necks to watch it, they lowered their eyes and noticed that April was trembling where she sat.

"What is it, sweetheart?" Raina said, alarmed, reaching over to still her daughter's quivering hand.

"It's just that...Grandmother hid her books...and there's something about the Mother Room as well...something hidden..." April seemed unable or unwilling to put a name to it.

"You sense a malevolence," Sirona said, more a statement than a question, "directed at you for what you're uncovering?"

April could only shake her head in the affirmative.

"Damn modern technology..." Art muttered. "A decent enemy would have the courage to show their face. But let's think about this. It just showed up. It can't see any more than the four of us having a delightful *al fresco* lunch. No big deal. Even if it is equipped with audio, which most aren't, it wouldn't be able to record from the distance it's gone to."

"But now he knows I'm here," April said, uncomforted by Art's analysis.

"He?" Raina asked. "You have a sense of something...or someone?"

But April just shook her head *no*, obviously unwilling to say more.

Sirona and Raina exchanged a look while Art stacked plates. "Let's clean this party up and move inside for now."

As they retreated from the lawn, the drone banked hard and flew east, down the lake. Had the four stayed to watch its flight, they would have seen the speck of it make a hard left and head into the woods to the north. They might have surmised that it was circling around behind the lakeside cottages to alight somewhere uncomfortably close, though hidden by the trees. But the group saw none of that, busy as they were collecting the remains of their feast and seeking the protection of interior rooms.

It wasn't until the next morning that anyone dared suggest further discussion or the much-anticipated excavation to unearth the hidden books. After the drone sighting, April had seemed rattled and distant, untouchable even. But the process, whatever it was, had begun. They had some markers now, thanks to April's dreaming. Crumbs, perhaps, but something to get them started at least – a trail to follow. Raina had spent the night in the cottage with April and Sirona, the three staying up late, engaging April in light conversation, trying to dispel her discomfort. It was agreed that henceforth she would sleep not in the Mother Room, but in the loft proper, in the large and well blanketed bed that was open to the comforting spaciousness of the cottage and the lake beyond. Sirona retired to her nest in the lake room and Raina curled up on the couch by the hearth. Despite the lingering warmth of the day, they had set a fire, more for the comforting, woodsy smell of it and the sound of the wood crackling and popping than any need for heat. All slept a dreamless sleep and awoke to the steadfast Art frying bacon and cooking grits and eggs in the cottage's small but serviceable kitchen.

Without being asked, April announced her preparedness to continue the work of the previous day.

"I'm better, my dear ones. I think I was still in the thrall of the intensity of the Mother Room. That place is wonderful and magical, but is meant, I think, to be taken in small doses. Not that I think my vision quest was a bad idea; it was a fruitful task, but not something to make a habit of." April smiled her spunky smile, but it wasn't the pure, unalloyed beam of joy that once was hers. It was like there was a drop-shadow lurking around the edges of it. Perhaps no one but Raina noticed it, but all would agree that April had changed. Now it was up to the four of them to make it worth it – to discern how to move forward in their determination to heal the social fabric and to bring a wholeness back into human consciousness.

"After breakfast," Art offered, "I say we scour the cottage for loose floor boards."

"We'll need some crowbars and the like," Sirona said, scowling. Obviously, crawling around on her knees looking for secret hiding places wasn't much to her liking.

"Already pulled them out. The tools are on the porch."

And so they set to it. Rugs were pulled aside, furniture moved, and the sound of tap, tap, tap filled the house for hours. What made the task even more onerous than crawling around on the floor was the likelihood that what they were looking for didn't even exist. But no one was willing to assume it didn't, and so they tapped and listened until Sirona announced that she'd had enough. Her back was killing her. She'd rest for a bit, but first she'd get some herbs from her bags and make some soothing tea.

As she went to the rooms at the back of the cottage to retrieve her herbs, she heard the tapping from those exploring the loft, a sound like something on the roof, wanting to come in. A chill went down her spine despite herself. She'd never been uncomfortable in the cottage, but now thinking of hidden books and words in paint cast everything in an eerie light. Then again, though she'd made significant strides in her healing, she still wasn't entirely herself. No doubt her dis-ease was just her tired body playing games with her. Her hope was that whichever one of the companions was exploring the loft would be the one to discover the forbidden texts. It was the logical place to hide such things, after all.

Sirona rifled through her bags, tossing things here and there in her exhaustion. As she fumbled around, she accidently knocked a jar off the dresser. It landed with a hollow, resonant sound that caught her attention. Kneeling, careful to avoid the board on which it had landed, she picked up the jar and gently tapped it against the floor. There it was again. A hollow sound. Could it be?

Raina stood at the door, crowbar in hand.

"I came to see if you were ok..."

"Come here and see what you think," Sirona said beckoning Raina into the room. "Does this sound weird or is it just my over-tired imagination?" Sirona tapped the jar against the floor again, as though to illustrate.

"Well, let's see..." Raina said entering the room.

Wedging the crowbar into the largest gap on the plank in question, Raina pried and up came the board, easily, as though by its own volition.

"There's a space," Sirona declared, excited now. "Pull up more."

One more, and another and...

"There they are! They're actually here!" Sirona started to reach for them then stopped. "Let's let April fish them out."

Raina went to spread the news. Once all four were gathered, April bent and gently pulled the books from their hiding place. There were seven books in all. April spread them out across the room and read their titles:

The Christian Heretics; Druid Thought and Practice; A Jungian Primer; Women in the Celtic World; Soul, Spirit and Earth Magic; Healing the Planet; Blood, Bone and Intention: An Alchemical View.

The four sat in silence a long while, each full of questions that could never be answered.

"Where shall we put them?" Raina asked at last.

"Certainly not back in the floor," April said. "I have a lot of reading to do."

"But maybe not out in plain sight either," Sirona suggested, thinking about the intrusive drone sighting the previous day, but choosing not to mention it.

"There's the cupboard up in the loft. That would be a good place," April suggested.

"There's actually a key to that cupboard," Raina said. "I found it when I was arranging stuff up there."

Sirona laughed a tight laugh. "Look at us being all paranoid. Just because these books look to be about heretics and alchemy, this is the modern world, is it not? The Inquisition was hundreds of years ago..."

"You're so right," April said, "but everything tells me we shouldn't broadcast what we've found here."

"If my mother thought them better hidden..." Raina mused,

"...then best we keep them so," Art finished, moving to replace the floorboards. "Good to know we have this little hidey-hole though. Might come in handy."

Chapter 9

The Circle Widens

"Can I tear you away from your books for an afternoon?" Art climbed onto the porch and took a seat next to April where she had spent most of her hours over the past few weeks, her head buried in one or the other of the *forbidden books* as they were now affectionately called.

"It better be good. These books are fascinating," April said, trying not to smile. Truth was, she was glad of Art's company.

"I have a little field trip I'd like to take, some people I'd like you to meet."

The Hedge and Hearth looked darling, dressed as it was in late spring foliage. April couldn't contain her glee and Raina was delighted to be there again and remember not just the camaraderie she had felt there but the memory of that night with Art. So much had changed in that one day.

Lily stood leaning in the open doorway, as though she had been expecting them. Sirona was the first up the porch stairs, grabbing her old friend in a huge hug.

"And this is the famous April I take it," Lily said, extending her hands to April who blushed a delicate pink that matched the bleeding hearts nodding in the breeze. "Come in, come in. I expect you are here for a reason."

The readers looked up at the company, smiling broadly and nodding, then murmuring their approval as they were introduced to April, who took in the strange folk with obvious delight. Raina wondered if she could also see their animal natures, but there would be time later to discuss that. The fairy-girl separated herself from the crowd and, taking April by the hand, brought her to a window seat where the two dove into earnest conversation as though they had known each other for years.

"We've come to talk about circles," Art said, cutting to the chase. Lily nodded, then spoke to a few of the readers who joined them as they retired to an area in the back of the house. It didn't take Art long to catch Lily up on all that had transpired since April's return home.

"April's vision of circles intrigued me, and brought you to mind instantly," he said, leaning toward Lily. "I believe you know something about the power of circles, how to gather them and evoke the best from them."

Lily nodded modestly, while Art continued.

"I was thinking the Summer Solstice might be a good time, if you're willing?"

"Would you like to do it at the lake?" Lily asked, her eyes shining like stars.

"Seems right. Water and all that," Art said rather shyly, knowing his love of the lake was showing.

"That gives me a few weeks until the 21st. That's plenty of time." Lily assented.

Raina wondered at Lily's quick agreement with Art's request, and her apparent understanding of what this "circle" would entail. Something made her hold her tongue though. There was something about Lily that commanded the restraint that comes with deep respect.

Once they had collected April and were on the way back home, however, the spell cast by the Hedge and Hearth, if such it was, thinned and Raina could contain herself no longer.

"Lily didn't seem at all surprised at your request," she said, leaving Art room to dissemble if he so chose – which he did. "No, she didn't, did she?" he responded.

"It's almost as if she knew it was coming," Raina said, unable to stop herself, "just like her standing at the door, like she was expecting our visit." As Raina said it, the oddness of the whole day struck her full force. It was as if *everyone* was expecting them, and yet she didn't remember Art saying he had called, or made arrangements.

Coming to her friend's rescue, Sirona finally chimed in. "I think she's been waiting for us to make this request for some time now. Our quest extends to a much larger circle than we are aware of. If we've been wondering if Merlin's release has had any influence on things, I think this visit to the Hedge and Hearth should give us a clue. For those who can feel it, for those who have desired it, Merlin's release is causing waves."

"Well, certainly Poppie knew all about it," April piped up.

"Poppie?" Raina asked.

"Did you think I was relegated to the kid's table while the grownups took care of business?" April asked. "Not at all. Poppie knew all about it. She explained that the circle is the way to view the world, to raise and share energy, to hold space and invite spirit in. She was thrilled to hear of my dreams, and she gave me a medicine bag full of herbs and stuff to keep me safe while I go deeper."

Raina felt out-numbered. "And what is this event on the Summer Solstice going to look like?"

"You'll see," April said, giving her mother a wink. "By the way, I've been meaning to ask. Do you all mind if I invite Tannen here to be with us? I've been sharing my discoveries with him and I'd like him to be a part of this. He'd like it too," April concluded, a bit shyly.

"I thought you'd never ask," Sirona said laughing. "Of course he should be here with you – with all of us. And Percy too, if he's willing. Seems right to reassemble the company."

"What of Niall?" Raina asked.

"We've talked of it," Sirona admitted, "but we decided he should stay in Glastonbury and work with folks there."

"But don't you miss him?"

"I do, yes," Sirona replied, "but I'm used to spending time here without him each year. He knows I will return soon enough. I can't stay away from Glastonbury too long. As Art draws his energy from the lake, I draw mine from the waters of the Chalice Well. And somehow, together, we connect the two."

"The World River..." April muttered. "I'll gain Tannen, but lose you. It seems there's always a part of me that is far away."

"The only way to avoid that, dear one, is to shrink your circle of care and that is not your fate – not by a long shot. Indeed, quite the contrary. Your circle of care is destined to encompass more than you can imagine."

"It will tear me apart," April protested.

"But it won't," Sirona assured her. "You will learn how to keep things close in spirit. Our hearts defy space and time; they are limitless."

"Well, at least promise me you won't leave right away," April protested.

"I'll stay until after the summer solstice. I must be present for the circle ceremony. You have me until the end of June. By then, I suspect, your path forward will become clear and I can take that back to Glastonbury to great purpose – energize the folks there who are waiting to see what comes next."

"Do we have room for everyone?" April asked, not wanting to tread on anyone's hospitality.

"Room for friends can always be found, but as it happens, I've learned that the cottage next to mine is for rent for the summer at least. I've already made inquiries," Art said.

"More insider information?" Raina asked.

"No," Art laughed. "I just figured sooner or later we'd be collecting folk. I think that's what we *want* to do."

"You'd best get busy fashioning a large, round table then," Sirona teased.

"You jest, sister, but the circle is the way of things, as has already been noted. There was more significance to King Arthur's round table than many realize. Most focus on the democratizing effect of there being no head to the table, but there is so much more. Roundness is the way of nature and the cycle of life, death, and rebirth. Sitting in a circle mirrors that. It literally puts us in physical harmony with the way of life, so that perhaps the mental harmony has more chance to follow. So much of what humans create does just the opposite. All our straight lines convince us that things are linear, that we exist in isolated points of time as discrete beings…"

"While, in fact," April said, "we are connected in many ways most of us never come to understand. I'm starting to get a strong sense of what it means to be connected to my female ancestors. It's more than just knowing I carry their DNA, which, in itself, is mind-blowing, but there's also a strong sense growing in me of how what I am and what I can do is a product of what *they* did."

"And there are lots of ways that is true," Art continued, "*including* the DNA stuff. There's more and more research on how people's behavior can affect their DNA and then those changes can get passed down. So, say you write a book, as your Grandmother Quinn did with the Yule Poems. Yes, those poems, in your hands, are an influence and inspiration, but there is also what happened to your grandmother *as a result of the process of writing the book*, and that can be passed down as well as the book itself."

"A good argument for living a full life," Sirona said.

"Imagine what the world would be like if everyone was convinced that everything they did in their life would have an effect on the future," April said.

"It might be inspiration for more confidence in expressing themselves creatively, more awareness of purpose," Sirona agreed.

"There would still be those who would use such knowledge for destructive ends, for power..." Raina said.

"There's always evil in the world," Art said, sympathetically. "That, too, gives us purpose. We cannot let it deflate or defeat us."

"Except when it does," Sirona said quietly, gazing out of the car window, speaking more to the beautiful spring day as it flashed past than to her companions.

"Except when it does," Raina echoed, knowing all too well how one's spirit can be trapped in despair.

"That's what the circle is for," April said, her heart going out to her two beautiful mothers. "The circle binds us and keeps us upright when we struggle to stand alone."

Something had changed in April. Over the next week, while she awaited the arrival of Percy and Tannen, she continued to read, but spent a good deal of her time writing as well, taking abundant notes in her journals. Whenever possible she would work outside, on the porch or down by the lake. As her companions watched her, they marveled at her intensity and the way she seemed to draw insight not just from her reading but from the very air as she lifted her head, facing into the wind that flowed across the lake daily. At times, it would seem that she was in a trance, her eyes closed, her hair flowing around her head, the breeze lifting her auburn locks as though to reveal openings for its mystical whisperings.

Poppie would often come to visit, sitting head-to - head with her new friend, in earnest conversation, while the elders kept their distance. Whatever was happening between them had the air of new inspiration, fresh thought coming from young minds, unburdened by the weight of long life.

Until the day of the return of the drone. Poppie and April were sitting by the lake, in their usual posture of intense discussion, April frequently writing in her notebook. Engrossed in their work, they were oblivious to the whir of the surveillance device, even as it hovered above them, but Art saw it from where he had been splitting wood, and rushed toward the lake, grabbing a stone as he went. When he was sure he could aim at the drone without hitting the women, he let fly. The rock nicked the side of the craft, not enough to disable it, but clearly enough to dissuade it from its mission. Again, it headed east down the lake and banked into the woods to the north.

"What on earth was that?" Poppie asked, her eyes wide.

"This is the second time that thing has come around," April said, her gaze fixed where the drone had disappeared. "I can't imagine what it's after, but clearly it's taking an interest in us."

"I'll be better prepared next time," Art said.

"You think there'll be a next time?" April asked.

"I suspect so. This second fly-over doesn't seem coincidental and the surveillance seems focused on our lakefront. What I really want to know is who is behind the damn thing."

"Do you think it's been here more than the two times we've seen it?" April said, panic rising in her despite her efforts to stay calm. But Art just gave her a look.

"Like I said, I'll be better prepared next time," he said over his shoulder as he returned to his cottage.

Percy and Tannen arrived the day of the Solstice gathering so there was little time for an elaborate welcome. Art had indeed secured the neighboring cottage and managed to give them the keys and show them around before he was called off for other chores. Lily was due later that afternoon with some of her people, so chairs had to be gathered, the fire arranged, food prepared, and tables set. Before the other members of the company found the time to wander over to the cottage to welcome them, Tannen and his father were already among them, their sleeves rolled up and ready to be of use.

With Lily and her people came drums and rattles, flutes and brightly colored garments. As Raina moved among them, welcoming each and every one, she saw their animal souls shine brightly, so much so that she experienced a slight vertigo. Human, animal, which? Tannen and Percy showed no hesitancy with the newcomers, taking it for granted that friends of Art and Sirona's were friends of theirs. Food and drink were present in abundance as people milled around, making new friends, greeting old ones, spinning in and out of knots of communion, as though weaving threads of connection between all those gathered, smoothing the ground before the much-awaited ceremony.

As the day waned, the pace slowed as folks made their way to the shore. All day, the wind had been from the East, not fierce, but significant, blowing hair this way and that, ruffling the coverings on the tables, carrying a variety of scents that made it intriguing to be outside and part of the ebb and flow of the elements. But as the sun lowered, the wind receded, as though bowing out of a great hall, leaving the king of the sky the center of attention. Clouds that had been pure white and sailing the blue sea of sky during the day, now paused and radiated delicate shades of orange and pink. A hush fell over everything – animal, human, and elemental – as each person found their place in the circle. Raina sat to Art's right, while Lily sat on his left, the two of them assuming their roles as guides for the ritual. Tannen, April and Poppie sat together, while Percy sat with Sirona, though his eyes were often on Lily, as hers drifted toward him from time to time as well.

At sunset, Lily rose to speak an invocation, thanking all beings, both earthly and cosmic, and speaking other words Raina could make no sense of, but the sound of them was soothing, relaxing. A member of Lily's company rose to light the fire, motioning to Percy to assist him in the honor. Art had set the fire well, and it took quickly. As the sky dimmed, the firelight brought light to all the faces around the circle. Quietly, the drumming began, then the rattles and a flute joined in as the darkness defined the gathering and the flames made each visage dance. The music intensified and singing soon followed.

The drums beat in sync with her heart, and though Raina knew her body was still, she felt her spirit soar, weaving in and out among those assembled, spirit-dancing with each in turn. Now the fox and bear, eagle and dove shone clear in the amber light. And to her surprise, each seemed to come to her to pay homage in their own way, offering gifts of recognition, gratitude and blessing. Hesitant at first, despite herself, Raina felt Merlin's spirit rise in her, at one with her own. Slowly, slowly, but inexorably, she came to accept her agency as one revered, one who *knew* – and one who carried the hopes of many in her hands. Then she was carried higher, into the night sky, a nightscape not unlike that of the Mother Room and there she floated, stars on her fingertips, her body infinite and immortal, alone in the void. Or was she. For there, drifting toward her was April, as though a mirror image of her own infinite being. And there it was, a feeling like giving birth, a transfer of being, a cosmic umbilical cord between herself and her daughter, through which flowed spirit, wisdom, power, a multi-strand helix of untold generations, the mystery of life.

Raina awoke to the pre-dawn light, the chill of dew on her face. As she slowly came to, she saw that everyone had fallen asleep where they had sat. The shortest night of the year, spent asleep on the grass, and yet she felt surprisingly alert and alive, albeit a bit embarrassed to have fallen asleep on the ground without even knowing it. In the soft, predawn light, people stirred, stretched, and wiping the dew from their faces, pulled themselves up to properly reform the circle. As the sun slivered above the eastern shore, Lily rose once again and praised the morning, giving thanks for the safe passing of the night and the wisdom bestowed.

"Each soul in this circle is now connected in a sacred bond. Let this coming together be a source of support, insight, and inspiration for our task of healing the earth and the minds of the humans who have been blessed to live within its web. Let us embrace our role as stewards, and each find our individual roles in the work that lies ahead."

Murmurs of assent rose from the assembly, smiles passed from person to person in recognition of what they had shared. As Art pronounced the circle open, people found their feet with varying degrees of agility. Then, with nods and hugs, began making their way away from the shore and back into the every day.

Amid the leave-taking, Lily pulled Art aside.

"Give us a week to process what we've experienced here and then let us come together in council, agreed?"

"Agreed," Art replied, "and thank you, Lily. Shall we meet here or at the Hedge and Hearth?"

"I've heard you've had a robotic visitor..."

"Ah, yes," Art admitted.

"We needed to have the Solstice here on the lake, but I think it wise to vary our venue, so I suggest the Hedge and Hearth," Lily said, her voice belying a concern that Art hadn't heard until this moment.

"Wise," Art answered his friend. "I'm not sure what that drone was after, but I sense malicious intent."

"As does Poppie. She told me she felt her spine turn cold. Such a response is not to be ignored," Lily said.

"So, a week from today at the Hedge and Hearth," Art said as Sirona approached.

"Oh," Lily said, as she turned to leave, "and do be sure to bring the Owl with you."

"The what...?" Art stammered, but Sirona was at his side, laughing heartily.

"I doubt we could keep him away," Sirona said to Lily, then to Art, "I'll explain later."

At that moment, a shriek was heard coming from Raina's cottage. The three sprinted up the hill with Raina and Percy catching up from where they were saying good-bye to Lily's people. Bursting through the door, they found Tannen and Poppie trying to calm April who was in quite a state.

"What...?" Art began.

"My notebook! It's missing!"

"Are you sure?" Raina asked. "You could have left it any number of places."

"I know I left it right here on the coffee table. I was writing in it yesterday morning while all of you were busy getting ready for the ceremony. And it's not on the floor, or anywhere around here..." April concluded.

"Let's look everywhere, just to be certain," Percy said, hoping to instill some calm. He hated to see April so nearly hysterical. "Someone could have moved it thinking to keep it safe before everyone came."

While the rest began the search, Art walked Lily to the door.

"Best you get your folks home," he said.

"Do you suspect foul play?" Lily asked, well out of earshot of the others.

"I certainly hope not, but there's the matter of the drone which seems damn suspicious. I'll keep you in the loop. We'll see you and your crew in a week in any case."

"I'll let you return to the search," Lily said. "But I will say, as well as the ceremony went, I do feel something is off. The balance is not without some ripples here and there. I didn't think much of it until now. Take care, my friend," Lily said, leaving only after giving Art a respectful nod.

Art watched her return to her people, his protective disposition on high alert. He had known, the minute he met Raina, that something was going to shift, that the life defining search for purpose that had been Sirona's and his to bear for so long, was finally coming to an end, their purpose revealed. Getting to know Raina, experiencing the revelations, had been exhilarating – the promise of gathering folks to their cause heartening, prophetic even. But in all that excitement, he had forgotten that what they sought – a return to ancient ways of knowing the earth as sacred – had been repressed, demonized, branded heretical by the powers that had developed a strangle hold on the minds and lives of the masses for centuries. Wars had been fought; people tormented, tortured, murdered; entire cultures brought to ruin. Lily's people and other indigenous groups brought to the edge of extinction. The investment in the Catholic doctrine of *ex nihilo* – denying the sacred nature of matter – was huge. Without it, empires could not survive nor could humans use and abuse the earth with impunity.

Of course they were being spied upon. Perhaps that was the least of it. Suddenly, painfully, Art was fully aware that all the people who mattered most to him were now in harm's way. His heart told him to pull back, to deny his destiny, to draw a tight circle of protection around those he loved – to pull them out of the battle. But the part of him that knew what ancient kingship meant spoke with a different voice. The land must be protected above all else, and it was his sworn duty to see to it. Humans come and go, but the land must persist. It is the font of all being, and at this point in history, its health was challenged as never before. Art's chest constricted and for a moment he felt his knees threaten to buckle and his breath cease. For so long he had waited to step into his destiny and now that he could see clearly what that meant, he would flee from it if he could.

Then what kind of King would he be to run from the battle? Besides, a true battle cannot be avoided, only postponed, or in the running, one's dreams and loved ones are slaughtered from behind. Now was the time. He must find his best self, call upon all his soul had experienced in its journey from ancient England to the present day. Loosening his grip from the porch railing, he turned and made his way into the cottage.

Everyone but April had reconvened in the living room, having failed to find the notebook. As Art entered, he felt the anxiety among the group, the sense that something was amiss, and knew that part of his job now was to keep everyone away from the despair he had wrestled with on the porch, but at the same time dealing realistically with the situation.

A loud bang echoed from the loft, followed by April running down the stairs.

"The others are safe," she said breathlessly.

"What others?" Raina asked, going to her daughter's side.

"I keep my dreams in a separate journal," April explained, "and the one I was working on that's missing is the second book of my notes, the other one being full. I decided to keep them upstairs, locked in the cupboard with the books. They're all there."

"That's a relief," Sirona said.

"Yes, but it's more about the fact that it's missing than what's been lost..." April said, the fear alive in her face.

"Let's talk somewhere else," Art suggested, then led the group to his cottage, saying nothing until they were inside.

"Clearly, you suspect foul play," Sirona questioned Art once they were all seated in his living room.

"That's not where my mind would naturally go," he admitted, "but that drone has me spooked."

"And I keep thinking about Grandma being so careful to hide her books," April added. "Obviously, she must have sensed some danger, that someone would have a problem with her studies. Still, I find it hard to believe that my notes would be of interest to anyone..."

"You underestimate what you're about, dear one," Sirona said. "You've been studying those very books that your grandmother hid, bringing those ideas to life once again. Ancient wisdom and heresies...these ideas run counter to corporate, religious, and governmental interests..."

So, Art thought, sister Sirona wasn't oblivious to his concerns. Of course not.

"But I'm just...me," April protested. "Who gives a leap what I'm studying?"

"You are truly your mother's daughter," Art said, striving for a lighthearted tone. "Neither of you quite get the magnitude of what you carry. Being heir to Merlin's DNA, your potential to be leaders and prophets in our time is limited only by your reluctance to own it..."

"...and any notion of what to do with it..." April protested.

"I think we'll get to that, or it will come to us," Art said, "but for now it seems that someone might be aware of who you are and what we're up to and is concerned...enough so that they're spying on you...on us. By the way, was the cottage locked last night?"

"No," April admitted. "There was so much coming and going and I never imagined..."

"I didn't think of it either," Sirona added. "But we were outside all night long, singing, drumming. Easy enough for someone to slip in and take the book, especially as it was right in plain sight."

"This is giving me the willies..." Tannen said.

"So we need to take precautions," Art advised. "I'll go out tomorrow and visit some of the neighbors, see if anyone has seen a stranger hanging about. Not to sound too paranoid, but the drone makes me wonder if whoever took the book might have put a bug somewhere in the cottage. I think you should be careful of what you say there. Assume someone may be listening, and in the meantime check around for a bug."

"Maybe we should just move out..." April said.

"It might make more sense to just keep on as though nothing has happened," Raina said, speaking for the first time. "Don't let on that we're concerned or even that we think someone stole the book. Whoever it is, they will be more likely to get sloppy and reveal themselves if they don't know we're on to them. Or maybe the person we're dealing with is just trying to intimidate us, rattle us."

"And you know such a person," Sirona said, following Raina's train of thought.

"Do I ever..." Raina admitted.

"You think this could be dad?" April said, aghast.

"It makes sense," Raina said. "He's devoted his life to destroying mine. It must eat him alive to know that you and I are reunited and living together. And he knows about the cottage. Whether he gives a damn about what we're doing or not, it is in his nature to enjoy messing with our heads, playing games with us, to throw us off ours. If he can rattle us, he's won."

"Be like fairies twinkling in the dark," Poppie declared, drawing everyone's attention. "Well, that's how we do it! We just keep doing our thing, not oblivious to the danger that lurks – careful about that and taking precautions – but just keep shining on. The life-suckers don't like the brightness. Sooner or later, they will retreat, while we've continued to move forward, not wasting precious time."

"*You* are brilliant," April said, hugging her friend. "We'll just keep on as you say...but, I will keep *all* my notes locked in the cupboard from now on, all the same."

"Which brings up another point." It was Percy's turn to speak. "What of your notes, April? You've lost all that work. How much will that set you back?"

"Not sure yet," April admitted. "My thoughts have been pretty tangled. I needed to sort things out anyway. I'll get on my computer and recreate as much as I can remember. All my dream notes are safe, as are the earlier notes I took. And all the books are still there...I can go back and review, maybe even see more on second look."

"I must learn more of these books you speak of," Percy said.

"I'd love for you to look them over. I'm at the point where I could benefit from some discussion of the ideas in them," April said.

"We're ready, dear one," Sirona assured her, shining brightly herself. "Nightly *salons?* After dinner discussions? We have a pretty good group evolving here. I can't think of a better way to spend our evenings than to delve into heretical thought and make our plans for how to give it life!

Our circle is now seven. A good number. Poppie, you are a part of us now, if that suits you."

Poppie dropped a subtle curtsey in assent.

"I think we have a plan then," Art said.

"I look forward to those discussions," Tannen ventured. "Seven minds working together...it has potential!"

"You're all making me tired just talking about it," Raina said. "I don't know about the rest of you, but a night of sleeping in the grass has left me a bit disoriented. I'm going to take a nap."

As the group dispersed, Art held Sirona back.

"So, what did Lily mean by her comment to *bring the owl?*"

Sirona laughed her signature laugh.

"Well, that's Percy, of course."

"*What?* Please explain dear sister."

"Did I not tell you before?" Sirona teased. Then seriously, "Oh I'm sorry if I left that out! So much was happening, so fast. I thought I told you. Percy carries the spirit of Merlin's owl, and it's strong in him."

"You're kidding," Art said, delighted. "How wonderful!"

"Well, not all that much, for him," Sirona said. "Apparently Nimue rather gruesomely magicked the owl away when she ensorcelled Merlin, and Percy holds the memory of it. It was what helped him to find the cave for us, but it was painful for him to revisit the memory as vividly as he did on our behalf."

"Admirable. Then I'm especially glad he's here. He's quiet," Art observed.

"Yes and no. He's reserved and careful. His powers of observation are strong, but he waits before he speaks."

"Lily was rather adamant that Percy be included in any discussions," Art said.

"Did you not notice that she and Percy barely took their eyes off each other last night?" Sirona chided.

"Honestly, I didn't...but if he has strong owl spirit, that's the kind of thing Lily would notice right away," Art said, everything adding up now.

"Owl spirit and presence," Sirona said. "He's a force and he's devoted to Tannen. There's an uncanny similarity between his relationship with his son and Raina's with April. It's rather like a mirror. And April and Tannen have deep chemistry. It will be interesting to see what happens there, both between them personally, and what they bring to our circle as a pair. Quite honestly, brother, I suspect we are close. The players are on the board."

"As are those of the opposition it would seem," Art mused. "Raina might be right about Malcolm, but I suspect there is more here than meets the eye. You know as well as I that as our goal is to inspire a major cultural shift, we will have enemies a-plenty."

"It's the way of the world, is it not?" Sirona countered. "Life requires resistance, otherwise we have no form, no volition. A cultural shift requires something to shift *from.* I, for one, am ready for the game."

Chapter 10

The Red Notebook

On the verge of the woods, Malcolm kept himself hidden until he was sure the ceremony was well under way. As he neared the cottage, the sound of the drums slowed his steps and invaded his mind, distracting him from his intentions. He could feel his heart beating to the same rhythm as the drums. And the singing – it was like everything he had ever hoped for, dreamed of. It beckoned to him, tried to pull him toward it. With one foot on the porch he hesitated, but he thought he saw someone looking his way and the spell was broken.

Unwise to tarry. His mission must be accomplished and quickly. The drone had shown him images of April with a red notebook she carried everywhere, writing in it feverishly. How fortunate for him that his daughter preferred to be outside, making it all that much easier to spy on her – and spy he did. Once or twice the drone was spotted but there were all those other times when either her concentration or the wind or whatever kept her from noticing the surveillance.

He knew what he was after. If he could find that notebook, he was certain that Ignatius Vas would be pleased. Not that Vas's approval was his primary concern. What he sought was something that would bring Raina down. Much to his delight, the Society for the Preservation of Heaven emerged as the perfect proxy for his vengeance –

a desire that, should someone ask him, he could not quite explain. All he knew was that it burned in him like fire.

At first, he had mistaken that fire for passion, a desire to have her, the beautiful Raina. But once they were married, and had a child, the fire turned to a heat of irritation with everything about her. There was something not quite right about her. Something that went against the grain. If he would let himself acknowledge it, he would have to admit that it was a kind of power. But that would be giving Raina more than he was willing to give. Instead, he read what irritated him in her as unnaturalness, especially for a woman.

When she began having persistent nightmares that rattled not just her sleep, but her waking hours as well, his feelings were validated. Clearly, she was frail, unfit, and of no use to him. In her distressed state she was easy prey for his incendiary temper. To convince her she was mad and a danger to their daughter was easy pickings for him – and, he had to admit, pleasurable in the sense that it proved he was the righteous one and a hero for saving his daughter by cutting her mother from their life.

But now she had seemingly gotten control of herself and, moreover, had pulled his daughter into her orbit. For that alone he could hate her to the end of his days and wish any manner of ill fortune to befall her – ill fortune that he had found a way to orchestrate by revealing her to the SPH. That it now seemed unavoidable that April would be drawn into the ill wind of his revenge bothered him some, but he'd convinced himself that, given her alliance with Raina, the two were now one. He would make no distinction. And anyway, as it happened, it was April who was producing hard evidence that he could bring to Vas.

The door was unlocked, but the sun was near to setting; he would soon lose the light. But if he'd been concerned that his search would be extensive, he needn't have worried, for there on the coffee table sat the red notebook. Reading the cover, he felt a wave of anger. Under the word "Notes" was scrawled the name "April Quinn." So, she'd even denied him and taken her mother's last name. Such hubris! If he'd had any niggling doubt about exposing April to the venial Ignatius Vas, they were dashed at the site of the name *Quinn.* As Raina had kept her mother's last name, now April was doing the same. Well, let them have it, this lineage of odd and annoying women. He would out their schemes to the High Priest of the Society for the Preservation of Heaven and then see how they'd fare.

Malcolm slipped the notebook into his shirt, but rather than leave immediately, he couldn't resist using the last of the day's light to sniff around the cottage. It reeked of women. The kitchen sink was spotless and a vase of flowers adorned the table. In the room facing the lake, he saw that someone had set up a bed. Odd place to sleep, he thought, but then what did he expect? Even now, they were down at the lakeshore drumming and singing like barbarians. They probably howled at the moon as well. He shivered at the thought, then made his way toward the back bedrooms. Women's clothes and accessories were scattered about, along with books piled here and there.

But he'd saved the best for last – the loft. When he'd been there previously, though Raina wouldn't let him past the door, he'd caught a glimpse of that upper room and what looked like an open door in the far wall. There was something there, something evil. He could feel it. He was half way up the stairs when darkness fell rather abruptly. Despite his burning desire to continue his snooping, it would soon be fully dark and he couldn't risk a light. Disappointed, he made his way down the stairs, but as he headed toward the door, he made himself a promise he would return and discover what strange thing lurked in the loft that made the back of his neck tingle. Then he slid through the darkness and back into the woods, his trophy tight against his chest.

Would he read it? He wondered. Of course he was curious. Then again, could he risk being infected by whatever it was that April had been so diligently writing? Admittedly, he wasn't much of a reader anyway. If the thought came to him that reading his daughter's notes might soften his heart toward her, or, worse, stir up feelings of regret at having lost her to Raina, it never made it to his consciousness.

Anyway, there was no time. He was anxious to get his trophy to Vas, to enjoy his praise but more importantly to put the wheels in motion for whatever retribution Vas would conjure against the plans of these women. It wasn't entirely clear to him what was at stake here. He had heard Whitestone's story of Raina and others thinking they had released Merlin's spirit into the world – a ridiculous notion to his mind, but clearly of some considerable concern to the SPH brotherhood. All that mattered to Malcolm was that Raina was connected to this odd series of events and that, the more he thought about it, the more fitting it was. Of course crazy Raina would do something like think she'd freed the spirit of a mythical wizard. And from what he could tell from his spying, April was right in the middle of whatever they were planning next. Malcolm pressed his hand to his chest, feeling the leather of the notebook against his skin, reassuring himself that in those pages would be sufficient evidence to make trouble for Raina – hopefully to expose her unnaturalness to the light of day and squash it.

Stepping into the woods for cover, he nevertheless kept close to the verge. The deep woods frightened him in the same way Raina did. When he watched the video footage from the drone, he'd experienced waves of vertigo as it banked over the woods on its return flight. The blanket of various greens, punctuated by silver flashes where the sun hit water – too otherworldly, chaotic, uncontrollable. Too much *not* the world of mankind, with its defined corners, crisp asphalt, and rules. And most of all, where a man's word was law, indisputable. Where he knew his place and felt safe. As those thoughts revisited his mind, suddenly the leather-bound book against his skin felt slimy, oddly alive. In a panic, he pulled it out from beneath his shirt, and held it with the tips of his fingers. Vas could have it and the sooner it was out of his possession and into that of the High Priest, the better.

Somerset, England

The book felt like skin in his hands. How long he had been sitting there, rubbing his fingertips across the soft red leather he could not say, but for Ignatius Vas, the feel of it was intoxicating. So much about it was proof of his power. The slim volume was not meant for his eyes, and yet here it was, procured surreptitiously from its author by one who seemed more than willing to do his bidding. Obsequious even. American. And devoted to the cause of the Society – *his* society. The notebook and, he assumed, its contents would, now more than ever, reinforce his place as High Priest, as the one who could guide the brothers of the Society for the Preservation of Heaven through these troubled times. Ignatius Vas allowed himself a wheezing chuckle. *Troubled times indeed.* Merlin's spirit on the loose, poised to bring down the Order. What foolishness. He believed none of it. Dead is dead and Merlin, if he'd ever even existed, has been dead for centuries. And yet the mythic narrative of the powerful wizard was strong in the imaginations of the people and he knew how to play it to overwhelm reason with the fear of loss...end times, even. After all these years of living in the light of God's promised kingdom, the threat of pagan ignorance and Devil worship has returned to cast all into darkness. Vas chuckled again. Oh, yes. He knew exactly how to play this. And now...now...he had concrete evidence.

He breathed in the scent of opulence that pervaded his rooms. Gold fixtures, sacred relics from around the world, paintings that depicted the subjugation of unbelievers, all safe behind heavy drapes drawn to keep out the harsh light of the secular world. This was his haven, but soon the whole world would be his domain. He was sure of it. How fortunate for him, this amateurish attempt to reinvigorate the earth-bound beliefs of an ancient age. He couldn't have set a better trap himself. Rome will be proud, perhaps...

He rubbed his fingers over the leather volume again, enjoying the surge of blood in his loins as he imagined the skin of the woman whose thoughts were laid bare inside.

Private thoughts, heretical thoughts, the simple word *Notes* scrawled across the cover. Perhaps even better than spying on a woman in her bedchamber, he was about to pull back the curtain on a woman's secret mind. A woman who believed she had released a fabled magician from ensorcellment. Oh, too rich.

At last, Ignatius Vas opened the cover and cast his eyes upon April Quinn's hand-written notes. An image flashed in Vas's mind – a witch imprisoned in a cage, pleasingly available to an inquisitor for his interrogation. An enviable situation, but perhaps what he had was even better. A mind exposed, free of resistance from the owner. He would savor the excursion and when he was finished, he would use it to frame the narrative that served him.

So, I'm in possession of the same DNA as Merlin, ancient Druid, source of untold tales of intrigue, magic, and manipulation.

Vas sat bolt upright. So, there was more to this than he had imagined! Not just that this group of crazies had ventured into the forests of France thinking they had found the location of Merlin's supposed enchantment and released his soul. Fantasy, all of it. But this! This was different. This was real. The tales say nothing of Merlin having offspring. It was always Vas's sense that Merlin was, how to say it, *above* such things. To imagine that he had had offspring and that this woman was aware of her ancestral connection to this monster – this was more than just a handy narrative – it was downright dangerous. He read on...

What does that mean really? What do I do about this? It nearly drove my mother mad, and my grandmother...I wish I had paid closer attention to her in what little time she and I shared. But what matters now is that here I am, all hopes resting on me. I could walk away from this I suppose, but to deny what's within me, madness that way lies as my mother knows all too well. So, I'll accept it, but what do I do with it? Even Auntie Sirona isn't sure.

Ah, Vas thought, Sirona. The enchantress Abernathy Whitestone spoke so despairingly of. *Auntie* Sirona is it? How quaint. Vas skipped over a few pages, anxious to dispense with a young woman's angst and get to the meat of the thing.

Grandmother's books have been a blessing. I've been reading almost non-stop. I find that I am in love with a fourth century Welsh monk named Pelagius. Perhaps I can travel back there in my dreams and have a chat with him. He was known to value women, even to teach them to read – just one of his many heresies. To know such a man!

Pelagius! Of all people! The vilest of heretics. Vas scanned the next pages of the notebook which outlined in detail all of the man's despicable heresies, beginning with his rejection of the *ex nihilo* doctrine, so central to the foundational principles of the Church. Imagine! Arguing that the earth itself and all living beings are sacred. Where would civilization be if that thought had been allowed to persist? And then there's the idea of the *Anam Cara*, the "soul friend." Leave it to the Celtic pagans to believe that simple human beings could provide spiritual sustenance for one another without the intervention of priests and the sacred confessional.

Vas felt his temperature rise. What he thought would be a delightfully voyeuristic adventure was turning out to be an infuriating reminder of the essential threat to the preservation of an entire worldview and the triumph of the religion of empire. Pelagius and his teachings had been banned repeatedly, over centuries, and yet here he was, cropping up again, and in the heart of a young woman who dared to imagine she might have the power of the druids running through her veins. Had no one told her that the Romans, God bless them, had driven all the remaining druids to the edge of the earth and slaughtered them as was their due, relieving the world of their pernicious notions of the sanctity of the earth?

Against his inclination, Vas began leafing through more pages only to find that the text soon ended. Most of the notebook was blank.

"That fool!" he bellowed into his chambers. "He stole the book too soon!" Vas should have known better than to trust an American to be a canny spy. With some difficulty, Ignatius Vas rose from his chair and paced the room as he beat the little red notebook against his forehead. He had wanted more information, more insight into what this woman and her cohorts were planning, but...then he stopped suddenly. That was it. There was no plan! She said so herself. *What do I do about this?* His path forward was easier than he had imagined. All he needed to do was to eliminate this April Quinn, and all her Merlinist DNA and passion for heresies with her. That's what the Society was for after all. He could arouse the fears of the Brotherhood and keep his own hands clean. The hard part would be getting her to England where he could bring her before the Society and egg her on until her own words doomed her. Then the Brothers, already thoroughly women-hating and prone to violence, would do the rest.

Perhaps there was a use for Brother Malcolm after all. Might he find a way to lure this April Quinn across the pond? If he could manage to steal her notebook, perhaps he could steal the young woman as well. Vas would look into it.

For now, he thought it best to dispose of the leather volume. He considered one last caress of the leather cover, one last fantasy of the touch of a woman's skin, but now he knew by her own admission that she was a witch and so not to be suffered to live. Besides, even he, High Priest of the Society for the Preservation of Heaven could be seduced, enchanted away from his God. After all, was it not Satan who had created women for no other purpose than to tempt and destroy men?

With resolute steps, he strode to the hearth and with a flick of his wrist sent the book into the heart of the fire. As it curled and writhed in the flames, he was visited by a welcome vision of a woman burning at the stake. Oh, to have lived during the time when such sights were plentiful and very real. Still. His God had seen fit to bless him with his own witch to dispose of. With a brief prayer of gratitude, he turned away from the fire and rang for his servant.

It was time for lunch.

Chapter 11

The Way Forward

Aries Lake, USA

The lake drew him. A frequent visitor to the Chalice Well in Glastonbury, Percy was no stranger to the mystical power of water, but there was something about Aries Lake that had a different quality to it. Perhaps he was influenced by April's apparent connection to it. As he ventured out that morning, coffee in hand, to sit in front of the little cottage Art had rented for him and Tannen, in the near distance he could see April taking her daily, early morning swim. The way she moved through the water intrigued him, more like she was caressing it than propelling herself through the liquid element.

His own feeling about the lake was similar. As he sat there in the blue light of morning, gazing across the water, he saw the lake as though it were a being, a body, waking from its dark slumber in the well of its earthen depression. *The lake bed, a body of water* – perhaps there was deeper meaning to those expressions than most people realized. It was a common notion in his home of Glastonbury that the Goddess was part and parcel of the Chalice Well. Artistic renderings and personal stories evidenced as much. But here, it was more like the lake itself was the body of the Mother Goddess, all flowing hair and welcoming arms, lake life living within her, the bounty of sacred water available to anyone brave enough to immerse themselves in it.

A gust of wind loosened a wisp of Percy's snow-white hair from its pony tail. Usually scrupulous about his looks, today he actually enjoyed the play of wind in his hair. Life seemed easier here. To think that he had initially resisted the trip, not able to imagine himself separated from the gardens, the Chalice Well, the Tor. But Tannen was determined to come, to be with April. If Percy was forced to choose between his comfortable environs and being with his son, there was no contest. Leave it to Tannen to bring him to this new place, this new perspective. Sitting on the verge of all this openness, he felt his own being open up, as though his soul could take a full breath at last. Instead of being the weight it had always been, his soul now felt like the wings that were his birthright.

"Mind some company?" It was Art, carrying his own cup of morning joe.

"Not at all," Percy said, shifting in his seat. He did prize these quiet mornings, but now that Tannen seemed to have moved into Raina's cottage with April, there was a tinge of loneliness to them. And anyway, he looked forward to getting to know Art better.

"I don't think I've ever felt this relaxed in my life," Percy admitted, before he could think to be cautious. The feeling was too close to the surface to hide.

"Be careful," Art warned playfully, "it's pretty addicting. It's part of the reason why Sirona's trip to Glastonbury every year is taken without me. I can't seem to leave this place."

"In turn," Percy countered, "Sirona seems to be wedded to Glastonbury, as I have been, though she seems able to comfortably keep a foot in both worlds."

"You and Sirona have been friends a long time, then?" Art ventured, wondering to himself why she had never mentioned such an interesting person before.

"Actually not," Percy answered, feeling the leisure to give thought to what had brought him into Sirona's orbit. "We lived in the same town, but never connected. Actually, I think it was Raina who drew me. Don't get me wrong. It's a wonder I never connected with Sirona. She's much beloved by all who know her." Percy drifted into his habitual reticence, but Art wasn't going to let him stay there.

"It was Raina who drew you? How was that?"

"A strange story. Perhaps you'd rather just enjoy the morning..." Percy hedged.

"Actually, I'd very much like to hear the story, if you're willing to share it," Art admitted.

Percy took a deep breath. "Very few people know my story. Sirona only knows it because she intuited it. But," drawing another deep breath, "it seems that the time has come to reveal things that have long been kept protected."

Art nodded his agreement, his over-sized capacity for empathy on full alert.

"I saw Raina at an Imbolc gathering – surprised I even went to it, but I had a rare urge to go, and there she was. She was amazing. Dressed in a beautiful cloak, emanating ancient magic, totally unaware and looking even more out of place than I felt. For my part, I felt I knew her, but couldn't figure out how. I couldn't take my eyes off her, until she spotted me staring and got spooked. I left quickly, hoping I had seen the last of her and she of me. But that night, I had a soul dream. I trust you know of what I speak..."

"I do," Art said. "More like a memory than a dream. Our souls carry us back..."

"...whether for good or ill," Percy agreed. "As is often the case when I soul dream, I was carried back to the most horrific day of my soul's journey. Perhaps Sirona has told you. I carry the soul of Merlin's owl..." Percy said, shivering as he spoke the truth aloud.

"Actually, she has spoken of it," Art admitted.

Another deep sigh, then Percy pushed on. "Merlin had been trapped by Nimue but, at Merlin's behest, the owl flew from Brittany to Cornwall, on the wings and winds of magic, to where Merlin's daughter, Annwyl, had been ensconced in his cave beneath Tintagel. The owl drew Annwyl and one of the Duke of Cornwall's knights, Tanan..."

"Your son's name," Art interrupted.

"Yes. A loyal and selfless knight. The owl drew them back to Brittany, to the cave where Nimue had trapped Merlin. Annwyl was determined to save her father, though she had no idea how. Valiantly, she entered the cave while Tanan and the owl kept guard, but Nimue was ready for us...them. She worked a spell to eliminate Tanan and the owl, but Tanan put up enough of a fight to give Annwyl time to flee. In the end, Tanan and the owl were dissolved in an excruciating spell of dissolution," Percy resisted being overcome by the memory, but he had not yet made the connection Art was waiting to hear. After a pause, he added, "In my dream, I saw Annwyl's face and Raina's as one."

"So you knew that Annwyl was Raina's ancestor, that Annwyl had survived Nimue's wrath, and that Raina was of Merlin's lineage," Art said, "but you said nothing."

"Would you have?" Percy countered. "Glastonbury is full of magic and people who believe such things, true enough, but I didn't know either Raina or Sirona. To come to them out of the blue with such a story would have been madness. Instead, I chose to watch and wait. Little by little I gathered clues that perhaps these two women *were* seeking something, and perhaps Glastonbury itself would draw them closer to it. Imagine someone of Merlin's lineage coming to that sacred ground for the first time. Unless the line had grown too thin over the centuries, if there was any of it left, the Tor, the Well, would certainly draw it out."

Percy drew a breath, as though to calm himself. Shifting in his chair and leaning forward, he made a conscious decision to bring his tale to closure. He had gotten this far; the rest should be easy.

"Over the next few weeks I dreamed of Annwyl/Raina incessantly. It nearly drove me mad. And always I would wake feeling the anguish of Nimue's spell, tearing at my body and for that matter, my soul as well. She came close to dissolving the soul as well as the owl body it had inhabited. Close, but the soul prevailed. Gradually, I came to realize that the anguish I was feeling was also that of Merlin in his ensorcellment, Annwyl in her failure to save her father, and Raina in some way as well, the details of which I did not know at the time. Eventually, I came to the realization that I needed to tell her – even if she tore me apart for doing so. Which," Percy let out a rare chuckle, "she nearly did. It was your sister who came to my rescue. She recognized the owl soul in me immediately."

"I'm not surprised," Art said. "Her connection with her soul life as Morgan le Fay is strong, along with it her affinity for Merlin."

"There was instant recognition..." Percy admitted, then, visibly relieved, he concluded with, "the rest you know."

"Except the part about Raina being angry with you for telling her what you knew..." Art said, clearly not satisfied until he'd wrung every bit of the story out of Percy.

"She was angry because I hadn't told her *sooner*..."

"Raina has her own struggles..." Art said, protectively.

"I know some of it. Some from her, but most of it from my own dreams." Clearly, there was more to be said there, but Percy was shutting down.

The two men stared out across the lake. The breeze had come up, gently rippling the waters, making the pebble-strewn shoreline sing its gentle stone-song. April had long since left the arms of the Mother to return to her books.

"And what of you?" Percy asked, feeling it was Art's turn.

"What of me?" Art laughed.

"What is your story?"

"My story..." Art began, serious now. Tit for tat. If he was going to forge a friendship with this fascinating person, he needed to uphold his end of the bargain. "It's been one of waiting and wondering. Sirona and I spent our childhood gradually coming to the realization, or at least the belief, that we were the incarnated souls of King Arthur and Morgan le Fay. I say belief because how does one know such things for certain? Is it true or does one just want it to be true? And to whom does one go to ask, or even share one's notions?"

"For some of us, it's inescapable...undeniable," Percy said, gently.

"I realize that now, but either way, it separates one from the herd, so to speak."

"Indeed," Percy agreed. "It makes one cautious, reclusive, at the very least."

"I was lucky to have Sirona to share it with..."

"Enviable..." Percy said.

"True. Thick as thieves we've always been, united in our belief that we had some important destiny to fulfill. But the years went on with little inkling of what that destiny consisted of. Except for one thing. We longed for Merlin – the completion of the Three."

Percy felt his throat tighten. He knew what it meant to have a deep longing for the wizard and everything he represented. So hard to live in a world where people cherished their cell phones and ignored the trees.

"Until...?" Percy prodded.

"Until Raina. Sweet, oblivious Raina. Talk about fate, her mother had lived in that cottage for years and I never had the slightest idea. I wonder about that. Why didn't I sense in Morgan Quinn what I immediately sensed in Raina the first time I met her?"

Percy shrugged. "The Turning of the Wheel, planetary conjunctions? So many things we can never know."

"Until we do," Art agreed. "Sirona and I suspected Raina might be Merlin incarnated, but we sought more surety. The rest, you know better than I. Then came April..."

Now Percy was beaming. "I'm not sure who loves that girl more, my son or me. She is absolutely brilliant."

"She is the center of whatever this is..." Art said, his demeanor belying his concern.

"And as the center, potentially in danger?" Percy asked, the answer suddenly obvious.

"Visionaries, world-changers, don't tend to live into old age, or if they do, they do so discredited, incarcerated, exiled," Art said. "I'm not sure I can protect her, but I will willingly die trying."

"We're not sure yet what's at play here," Percy said, "but as for protecting April, or anyone of our group, the burden does not fall on you alone. We're in this together. My soul gave its all trying to protect Merlin and failed. Now, it's been given another chance. I couldn't back away from this if I tried."

"Your words are a comfort, Percy," Art said and meant it sincerely. "We'll have a better sense of things when we meet with Lily's people in a few days."

"Tell me of this woman, Lily..." Percy ventured.

Art exploded in laughter. "Oh my friend, you thought Sirona had your number! Lily will spy you out like you're made of glass, if she hasn't already. But I say too much. Best you see for yourself." Then, slapping his knees, he rose from the chair. "We should all gather later for lunch and an ample portion of stout. I'd best get to it."

The minute he laid eyes on the Hedge and Hearth Percy was enchanted. For him, it was a little piece of English countryside plopped down in this sprawling country of America. It wasn't a stone cottage, but the way the gardens cozied up to it, as though they were kin, had a feel Percy recognized, like the house had grown out of the garden rather than the reverse. To Percy's mind, it was auspicious that this should be where they would meet Lily. Percy had thought of little else since his lake-side chat with Art. What was it that Lily would see in him? What was the link that Art hinted at? He knew she was of indigenous lineage – of the old ways as he was, but of a different place and culture. There was much to learn here.

She stood on the porch, ready to greet them, her long ebony hair gleaming in the sun. In her he saw a depth of character, an openness, a person relaxed in her own skin. It was not like Percy to be so taken by a woman. Watch and wait, was his modus operandi. But on this day, he had to fight not to quicken his step to be the first on the porch.

As the company entered the Hedge and Heath, they were joined by Lily's people, six in all to match the six of the "lake tribe" as Poppie had come to call Raina, Sirona, Art and April and now Percy and Tannen. It was not lost on them that they numbered twelve, Poppie, for the purposes of representation, being counted on Lily's "team" though she had come to spend most of her time with April at the cottage. By now, Raina had grown used to the dual nature of Lily's folks and April, practically living with Poppie, thought nothing of it. But Percy, though he had met these people at the ceremony, was struck anew by their visible manifestation of non-human soul-lives. For the first time in his life, he didn't feel like a freak. Here were others whose animal soul-history was a conscious part of their identity, and they seemed to thrive in it, if the way it shone through them was a valid indication. Never before had Percy experienced such excitement. Undoubtedly, something momentous was afoot.

As they formed themselves into a circle, alternating between the two groups, Lily took the lead.

"We've talked at length about what we felt and saw during the Solstice ceremony, and it appears that three things have emerged, those being circles, a book and blood. Circles makes sense to us. It is in harmony with our way of seeing the world. It is what we did on Solstice, what we are doing now. The book, that is a different story. As Indigenous people, we come from an oral tradition, so a book isn't the first thing we think of. But a single book loomed large in many people's visions. The last, blood, is not entirely clear, but of course, blood is life, blood is how we talk about the connections through generations. Without too much interpretation, we offer these visions to you for your consideration. Together, we may find some threads that make sense..."

April leaned forward, a bit nervous about speaking first, but knowing that it was she who needed to speak. "Two of the three of your visions correlate with what came to me from a week of intense dreaming in the pursuit of insight. Those two are circles and a book."

There were murmurs among those gathered.

"Circles are the best way to share information, generate new ideas and make decisions," said Ben, a handsome man with wolf eyes.

"The early Christian 'churches' were gatherings at people's homes. Circles," Art added.

Raina moved to the edge of her seat. "I think of the Vesica Piscis figure -- two interlocking circles. Two circles join and share what they know."

"In the same vein," Sirona began, "there is the flower of life, popularized by DaVinci. Multiple interlocking circles, interdependent, infinite...and beautiful."

"Based on the golden mean," this from Gladys, a woman with black eyes, snow white hair, and a graceful bearing – swan-like. "A spatial relationship that universally elicits pleasure and balance, perfection."

"One could see the flower of life as a visual representation of harmonious and interlocking relationship between beings, cultures, ideas," Lily offered.

"So we start a bunch of circles, and then those circles interact and start other circles. We create a living flower of life," Tannen said, full of youthful enthusiasm and, clearly, a vision of a path to action.

"Sound idea, from both a Western and Indigenous perspective," said Darla, a woman so wrinkled with age her skin looked like bark, but with green eyes that shone like emeralds. "But now I want to know exactly what it is we will be discussing in those circles. What will they share with others? What is the thread that will connect them all? We've come up with a workable *how*, but we have not discussed the *what.*"

The silence that followed attested to their arrival at the heart of the matter. What indeed?

Percy wrestled with his desire to watch and wait, but the phrase was playing through his head like the shard of a song, maddening, impossible to ignore. He literally clenched his teeth to keep from giving it voice, hoping that someone else would speak. But no one did, and the mood of the room was changing. The positive energy they had called up was beginning to dissipate.

"A new myth. What we need is a new myth," he said at last.

Lily smiled at him from across the circle. "Of course," she said. "Taking the best of what we've learned through the ages, bringing together the wisdom of many cultures and times..."

"But also breaking free of the old patterns of thought," Poppie added. "Being free to imagine something entirely new. Taking mental flight!"

"And of course, a book is the way to articulate and share this new myth..." Art said.

Sirona frowned. "I suppose that makes sense, but I'm suspicious of a single book articulating the way forward. We see where that's gotten us. Books can lead to dogmatic thinking, be misinterpreted intentionally or not so, even weaponized."

There were murmurs of assent from Lily's people.

Gladys spoke up. "I see your point entirely. But maybe it takes a new book to dethrone an old one. Besides, what other way do we have of articulating what I assume will be rather complex ideas?"

A question hung in the air that no one seemed willing to ask, until John, a burly man with rough features and huge hands, spoke in an authoritative baritone. "That young one there. April. She's the one to write the book. I saw it the night of the Solstice."

April opened her mouth to protest, but suddenly the room was abuzz, as though some kind of restraint had been loosened.

"Of course you have all of us as resources, and all of this place to help you," said Darla, waving her hand at all the books stacked around them.

"You've already been reading your grandmother's books," Percy added.

"I'll be your beta reader," Tannen said, smiling at April like the cat who got the bird.

"It will take forever..." April stammered.

"It's already over-due by hundreds of years. A few more won't matter," Lily smiled warmly.

Poppie was beside herself, clapping her hands in glee. "We're going to write *a book!!!*" she squealed.

Beaming at her daughter, Raina rose from her seat and crossed the circle to kneel before her. "John is absolutely correct," she said. "You are the obvious one to do this for so many reasons. In fact, I think you've already begun."

"Perhaps, but some of it is missing," April said.

"Maybe so," Raina said, soothingly, "but it's all here," tapping April's head, "and here," she added, touching her heart. "And in your genes as well, and your dreams, and perhaps in those words you think are hidden in the paint in the Mother Room."

April nodded and squeezed her mother's hands.

"What of the third vision," Art asked, "the blood?"

Lily turned to April. "The first two visions correlated between our understandings and your own visions. Was there a third vision for you?"

"There was," April replied, "but it doesn't seem to correlate with *blood*."

"Still..." Lily prodded.

"I saw a vision of loose floorboards in my grandmother's cottage. We checked it out and found a cache of books under the floorboards in one of the bedrooms."

"Books again," Gladys commented. "Of what sort?"

"The kinds of things my grandmother thought it best to keep hidden," April replied. "Books on Christian heretics, alchemy, earth-based spirituality."

Looks passed among the company.

"Perhaps your grandmother had already come to the same conclusion we reached today," John boomed.

Chet, a small man whose hair ran in rich brown and black streaks into a long braid, ventured a thought. "Perhaps there is a connection to blood here. You could see it that your grandmother had done some ground work for you – that the task of a new myth runs in your blood."

April felt tears sting her eyes as she thought about her mysterious and beloved grandmother hiding away books she hoped, or somehow knew, April would find. The power of connection with her maternal ancestors hit her full force. If this was her fate, to write this new myth, she was hardly doing it alone. She had a world of support at her back, both from the past and the present and now, she saw, this was her task to complete and send into the future.

"And you all promise to help?" she asked, though she was fairly sure of the answer.

Wordlessly, spontaneously, eleven people stood up and clasped hands. At April's side, Lily grabbed April's hand

and brought her in to complete the circle of twelve. One by one, each made a pledge.

"...we are family by intent..."

"...let our minds become as one..."

"...April is the beginning..."

"...and each of us a piece of the whole..."

"...pledged to forge a new myth..."

"...a new way of mind..."

"...all souls touching each..."

"...animal, bird, human, tree, elementals and elements..."

"...together calling on the cosmic soul..."

"...where the answer must lie if it lies anywhere..."

"...with pure mind and heart we seek..."

And now the circle had come around to April herself. Without hesitation, she spoke what came to her lips unbidden.

"...and pledge to share it with the world."

No one knew quite what to make of what had just happened, where the words had come from or what gave each of them the impulse to speak. Hands clasped, gripped tightly around the circle, the twelve stood in silence. Tears for some, heat rising from hearts in others, each keenly aware that henceforth, they were all inextricably linked, an indissoluble unit, yet a small part of something immense...and true.

The sound of tiny bells broke the silence. Poppie, not one to sit still for too long, had shifted her feet, causing the string of bells she wore around her ankle to sing. Smiling, Lily dropped the hands of her neighbors and brought her own into a gesture of thanks, then waited a beat for the rest to come back to the every day.

"We have prepared a picnic for our friends from the lake," she announced, "if you'd do us the honor of staying for a bit." Lily gestured to a door at the back of the Hedge and Hearth that led out to a yard bounded by blossoming shrubs and all manner of flowers and herbs. The air was sweet and dreamy while a stream in the near distance burbled its melody just on the edge of hearing. On the table, sweet bread and iced strawberry tea shone in the sunlight, with plenty of edible greens providing accenting colors. The twelve chatted like a murder of crows, weaving in and out of each other, as though wanting to all talk at once, to be as at one in body as they were in spirit. Joy sat upon the gathering like a blessing.

After a time, Lily drew Percy out of the crowd and walked him to the stream, where they found a convenient log along its edge.

"Forgive me for pulling you away from everyone, but I sense we need to speak with one another," Lily began. Refreshingly direct, Percy thought.

"I believe we do," Percy admitted, "but I'm not sure where to begin."

"Shall I begin by saying I see the avian nature in you and suspect there is a story there?" Lily offered.

Percy chuckled. "Art warned me about you. Said you'd see through me like glass..."

"A bit over-stated I think," Lily returned. "If that were true, I wouldn't need to be so bold as to ask you about it. And normally I wouldn't, but these are strange and urgent times and I suspect you hold an important piece of the puzzle we're trying to assemble."

Percy found Lily almost too beautiful to look at, and yet he was drawn to take the measure of her. He sensed this present boldness was somewhat out of character for her, that it was hard for her to be so direct. He could respect that, and acknowledge that she was driven by purpose. Well, then. So be it.

"I seem to be acutely aware of my soul life as an owl," he said, pausing for her reaction.

"Yes, I see that. It speaks loudly," Lily said. "But not just any owl I gather."

Percy took a deep breath. "No, not just any owl. I...belonged...to Merlin."

To her credit, Lily barely blinked. Softly she said, "You've been given a rare gift to have that particular soul awareness."

If it had been anyone else other than this radiant woman beside him, Percy would have laughed derisively at such a statement, but coming from Lily it aroused in him a different turn of mind.

"I have never seen it as such," he admitted. "It's always been more of a torment than anything else, an unbearable longing."

"I see that in your face," Lily said, holding Percy's eyes with hers, "but I also see the power, the potential."

"For what?" he asked.

Lily stood up, paced along the edge of the stream for a bit then turned to face Percy, her arms casually folded across her chest.

"All the wisdom we need to live in right relation with all that is, is here, in the very stones and roots and water...and still, faintly, in some humans, especially those who can access soul memory of being other than human, as you see in the gentle folk feasting on the lawn. Your crew believes it has released Merlin's spirit, a belief for which there is neither concrete evidence nor any way to know what that means or will mean. On the one hand, we are elated by the event, on the other we are as much in the dark as we ever were about how we might bring earth-wisdom to the fore."

"Exactly," Percy said, struggling to keep his voice even. "Because humanity has so thoroughly turned against it, what I know, what I feel, is a torment."

"And how do you imagine we indigenous peoples manage it?" Lily said, sympathetically. "For centuries, we have watched people defile what we know to be sacred and essential, not just to a life well lived, but to any life at all."

Percy nodded, getting a glimpse of what drew him to Lily so inexorably. "So how does an owl spirit from 500 AD make a difference?"

"You not only have the knowledge of an avian creature, but you shared spirit and wisdom with Merlin. Whatever shreds of that we could recover would be valuable in our quest. And..." Lily seemed almost reluctant to continue, "perhaps you could sense if Merlin's spirit is abroad, and if it is, where."

Now Percy did laugh, but gently. "I hate to disappoint you Lily, but I'm afraid I'm not capable of any of that. When I reach into my spirit past, all I feel is pain, and not just the pain of living in this misguided modern world. There's more."

Lily returned to the log and, sitting close to Percy, took his hands in hers.

"I'm listening," she said.

And so Percy told Lily the story of his dissolution at the hands of Nimue. He tried to keep it short, upbeat even, but he trembled at the memory nonetheless. Upon conclusion, he admitted, "I can't get past it. I don't know how."

"I might," Lily whispered.

Out of the corner of her eye, Lily saw Tannen and April ambling down the slope to where she and Percy sat. With a final squeeze, she surreptitiously let go of Percy's hands.

"Can you come sometime next week, alone?" she asked. "I have something to show you and I think we have more to discuss."

Percy nodded, then turned to welcome his son and April to their log.

Chapter 12

Of Bees and Trees

Hypnotic, thought Percy, as he stood just outside the studio door, watching Raina at her wheel. The whirring hum was hypnotic, and oddly organic for a machine. From time to time, there'd be a clicking sound, the whirring would stop and Raina would reach to re-wet her hands or pick up a sponge, then the whirring would begin again. How long he had stood there watching, he had no idea, nor, obviously, did Raina, who was indistinguishable from the rhythm of the wheel. *Whir...click...reach...whir...click...reach.* Percy felt a pinch of envy. To be so lost in one's work, woven seamlessly into the dance of creation. He'd never experienced that, never felt at home enough in his own skin to let himself dissolve so.

But now the whirring had stopped and as Raina rose to take the finished pot off the wheel, she caught sight of him.

"Dear Percy!" she said, clearly delighted to see him, "what a pleasant surprise. If you're not afraid of a little mud, come on in." Rinsing her hands in a bucket of muddy water, she used her chin to point to a chair in the corner. "That's probably mostly clean."

"You're getting good at this," Percy observed as he dragged the chair toward her, but only as far as what he hoped was a safe distance from the clay-splattered work area. "You don't mind the mess?"

Raina laughed off the question with a lightheartedness that he'd never heard from her when they were in Glastonbury.

"What do they say about omelets and eggs?" she replied. "It is somewhat of a tedious clean up, but always worth it. But what brings you here?"

"We haven't had much opportunity to talk, just the two of us," he answered, but where to go from there, he wasn't quite sure.

Raina took off her clay-covered apron, but there were still smudges of mud on her arms, her jeans, even on her face. With a relatively clean edge of her arm, she attempted to push back an errant lock of hair, but to no avail. "It must be rather urgent for you to brave the mud," she said.

"Not really, just thought it would be a likely place to find you alone," he admitted. "Plus, I've been wanting to see what you've been up to in here. I am impressed."

"Oh, I wouldn't be," she laughed. "I'm very much a novice. My goal is to someday make a cauldron like the one we used in the ritual, although I despair of ever being able to do it."

"A shame such a beautiful artifact was lost to the world, despite my agreement that it was no doubt necessary," Percy said. "Actually, I barely remember what it looked like."

"About that," she said, walking over to a shelf full of various pieces, some hers, some not, some not even entire pieces. From among them she pulled out a shard and handed it to Percy.

"Is this..." he asked.

"Yes, a surviving shard from the cauldron. Sirona literally stumbled on it when she returned to the cave."

"It's...." Percy stammered.

"Vibrating, yes," Raina assured him. "I can't figure it. Sometimes, when it's really quiet in here, I almost feel like I can hear it...singing."

"You've kept this pretty well under wraps," Percy observed, though not accusingly.

"There's so much going on...I thought I'd wait to see if I can learn more about it before I get the others involved. I will say this, it's a comfort to have it here. It almost feels like it guides me in my work. At the very least it resonates with it, quite literally...but," she said, returning the shard to the shelf, "you had a reason for coming here."

"I have a personal question to ask you, but you don't have to answer if you don't wish to," Percy said.

"I think we've established that we have a deep connection, Percy. If I can offer something that will help you, I will."

Percy shared one of his rare smiles. Indeed, he and Raina did have a unique relationship.

"Ok, so, do you still have those horrible dreams?" he asked, diving straight into the deep end.

Now it was Raina's turn to smile.

"No, thankfully. Ever since our experience at the cave, there have been no more of the horrifying nightmares. And since April has started intentionally dreaming, my own dreams are full of a sense of...how do I explain it...holding a space. For her, I think. It's like I'm holding open a door for her to walk through but not going through myself. Like you and Niall at the cave, I'm fulfilling the role of the guardian at the gate."

Raina paused, waiting for Percy to go further, or not. In the silence that followed Raina had almost concluded that Percy would keep his need to himself, when at last he opened up.

"Lily thinks I may have a special ability to sense what's going on with Merlin's spirit, if indeed we did release it."

Raina leaned forward in her chair. "Of course. Your spirit once belonged to his owl. There might be a resonance..."

"Except for a few glimpses of Annwyl, my memories, my dreams, are stuck in the horror of Nimue's dissolution of the owl." Percy drew a long breath. "But Lily thinks she can get me past that."

"And you're terrified," Raina said kindly, knowing all too well the shape of his fear.

"I am, yes."

"Do you trust her?"

"I barely know her, but...I'm drawn to her...fiercely I have to say, though I will only admit that to you. But is that the same as trust? And can I trust myself to make a wise decision where emotions are so intense?"

"It's complicated, isn't it?" Raina said. "But I will say this, and maybe this is what you came to me to hear. Art and Sirona have known Lily for ages and trust her completely. She's a healer of a strange sort -- a soul healer, most particularly for people like you. All the folks you've met at the Hedge and Hearth, they are her people because she has helped them live with the non-human soul-lives they carry. And you see how Art reveres her."

"I guess I should take one for the team..." Percy sighed.

Raina moved her chair closer and took his hands in hers, clay be damned.

"Every piece of the puzzle we can acquire is a help, but our choices should always be made in the context of assessing the potential danger to ourselves. You and I know the psychological risk that lurks here. None of us could bear to see you lost to us, Percy. You are...how can I say it...the embodiment of a deep and contemplative wisdom. A constant that we look to and depend on."

Bowing his head so that Raina could not see his expression, Percy whispered,
"No one knows what it takes for me to even come close to that."

"I might have a sense of it," Raina whispered in turn.

They met at the Hedge and Hearth. Lily had already packed a cloth bag and insisted on explaining the process as they walked. *Best to speak of it in the company of the trees,* she had said. Percy's heartbeat throbbed in his throat. Always so careful, he now felt like he was standing on a ledge, his toes chilled by the cool air that raced to the infinite gulf below. Had it been anyone but Lily, he wouldn't even have considered this, but there was something about her way that soothed him. Oddly, he felt like she was straight out of the Tor, a goddess of Avalon, but how could that be? She was of the lineage of the indigenous peoples of North

America, a world away from Glastonbury. And yet, who could say?

"We're headed to a lodge deep in this woods," Lily began as they ambled across the lawn behind the Hedge and Hearth, but heading north, away from the curve of the stream they had sat beside not so long ago. "Once there, we will smoke the *dream leaf.* I will join you so that I can travel with you, be your guide and your tether. Know that I have done this many times. You will never be alone, nor will you be in any danger of not returning. You can do so at any time, and yet I caution you, to return too soon will fail to accomplish what we've set out to do. You must face the terror, face it and see through it – walk through it in your mind."

"But..." Percy began to protest, but Lily put her hand on his arm.

"No *buts,"* she insisted. "You can. I am taking you to a place of sacred energy. The earth wants you to succeed. The *dream leaf* is the messenger it has sent to help you. I'm assuming you believe the earth has consciousness, connected through all its complex being...and beings. Or have I misread you?"

Percy watched his feet as they pushed through the understory, drew in a deep breath of the early summer emergence, thought of the Chalice Well and all the times he'd felt the presence of the Goddess there. Something deep within him stirred and for a flashing moment he saw the woods from above, through the eyes of a bird in flight.

"Of course I believe that," he answered at last, a catch in his voice.

Lily pulled them to a stop and turned to Percy, wordlessly searching his face, for what he could not tell, then released him from her stare and continued on. Not long after, in the near distance, he saw a rude hut made of stacked stone and woven branches, a more perfect version of the kind of shelters children build, or dream of building. Inside were mats of woven reeds and herbs that gave off a calming scent as they sat upon them. Lily busied herself with unpacking her bundle while Percy let himself relax into the soothing aura of the place, the *rightness* of it.

Lighting the pipe stuffed with dream leaf, she took a deep inhale, then passed it to Percy. As he reached for it, he realized his previous trepidation was now replaced with a calm excitement. How could he want to do anything else but this? He drew deeply and let the aromatic smoke escape his nostrils like the tendrils of morning glory vines, curling through the air, tethering his soul to the root of creation.

"One last instruction," he heard Lily saying as if from some distance. "When you touch the terror, let it fill you, drink in the energy of it, and then know that you have the power to convert that energy into a force that will move you beyond the event and into the world beyond it. You have owl spirit. Use your wings to propel you through the darkness and into life again."

She urged him to take another draw then gently took the pipe from him and guided his head into her lap as he fell into a dream, the sound of wings loud in his ears.

He was exhausted. He'd been flying all morning, frustrated that the humans behind him couldn't move through the woods more quickly. His avian ears were full of the sounds of the forest, tiny creatures ripe for the picking, scurrying to and fro. When was the last time he'd eaten? He was half dead, suffering the excruciating pain of separation from Merlin. But nothing held his attention above the sound of his master's heartbeat, steadily growing louder as they approached the cave. When at last he perched on the rock ledge, he watched with anticipation as the young woman, Annwyl, entered the cave, while the knight, Tanan, stood guard, all tense and determined, sword drawn and ready. So intent was he on the sense of Merlin struggling within, that he did not hear the enchantress enter the glade and disarm Tanan with a flick of her wrist. Then all was chaos. Manic laughter, Tanan's screams, his own strangled screech...

Percy's body writhed where it lay. Placing one hand on his heart and the other on his forehead, with her dreaming mind, Lily stepped into the chaos. *Ride the energy,* she thought into Percy's mind. *Make it yours. Owl of the great wizard, fly the winds of power back in time, back to your master...*

Wind like knives, cold and sharp, whipped through feather and bone, straight into the essence of the owl, tearing his body apart while Nimue's shrieking laughter threatened to shred his soul. Then, just when he thought he could bear no more, like the thinnest ray of light finding an opening in the storm, appeared the visage of a man, hair as white as his own beautiful plumage, eyes as clear as his master's. Wordlessly, the man's presence spoke to him, a promise of more to come, a role yet to play, a kind of life over which Nimue's evil intent could have no dominion.

And then he was a young and eager owl, perched on Merlin's shoulder as his master rode through the countryside on some righteous errand. Through his talons, tightened just enough to keep him attached, he felt the energy emanating from the mage, matching perfectly with the energy in the wind that gently ruffled his feathers, the sunlight that warmed his head, the smell of the trees as they swayed slightly in homage to the respected presence of the wizard and his owl as they passed beneath them. The owl could not claim that all was right with the world, elsewise why were they abroad? Something needed mending, rebalancing. That was the way of things. But there was balance to be had, his life with Merlin had proved that time and again. Never in his experience had the scales tipped too far in one direction, making the rebalancing impossible to attain. The Earth itself was on their side and Merlin, human though he was, had achieved the ability to resonate in harmony with all that was not human. And there was hope, the cherished dream, that in time all of humanity would find their way to such resonance. Those who had achieved it – the Druids, the Fey – did all they could to help others do the same. The songs, the stones, the stories. Of all the Earth's creatures, humans were the newest arrivals and therefore the least connected, and yet their promise was immense, and the power to achieve it near at hand and ubiquitous.

Awash in tears, Percy's eyes opened onto the waking world. Sitting up, he bowed his head and wept piteously, aware of Lily's presence, but unable to hold back the tide. His heart ached, for Merlin, for the owl, for all of humanity...and the planet. A deep vein of existential sadness washed over him, while Lily sat quietly, knowing full well what he was experiencing.

"Must we leave soon?" he asked when he'd regained some control.

"Not at all," Lily reassured him. "Perhaps you'd like to rest for a bit?

"There's much to speak of, but..." Percy stammered.

"We're fine here. Sleep. You have travelled far, your heart and mind opened to the winds of truth. I will rest as well, and welcome it."

For a brief moment, Percy thought to wonder what the ceremony had been like for Lily, but the need to rest was overwhelming. There would be plenty of time to speak of things...in that he trusted. And then he was asleep.

When he awoke, he saw that Lily had laid out food -- bread and cheese, fruit and nuts, and a sparkling golden liquid brought to life by tiny rays of sunshine finding their way through the gaps in the walls. Never had anything tasted so good, nor had he ever been so aware of the power, the energy in the bounty of the earth. He ate gratefully, reverently, wondering if the grace he was experiencing would last. As though reading his thoughts, Lily spoke.

"It will never leave you, the connection, the resonance. It has always been yours, but it needed to be...activated."

"It's both a joy and a sorrow at once..." Percy said, struggling to find words to share his experience.

"You feel your connection with the all that is, and yet you must continue to live in a world where most do not," Lily said, almost shyly. Percy caught her tone.

"You..."

"Yes," she replied, "and all the good people at the Hedge and Hearth as well. It can be painful, but knowing it, would you give it up?"

"Not for anything," Percy said, then he laughed slightly. "*I was lost, but now I'm found.* Amazing Grace indeed."

"It's the great existential longing," Lily said. "I doubt anyone has escaped the longing but despite the songs, the words, the huge cathedrals and the myriad religions, too many are ignorant of what it actually is they're looking for or where to find it."

After a comfortable silence while they ate, picking at a sprig of sage poking out from the mat beneath him, Percy spoke.

"So while we slept just now, I dreamed again. Was I still under the influence of the leaf?"

"I doubt it," Lily replied. "It's efficacy usually ends after you wake. If you dreamed again so soon, it was from your own being, of your own volition. What was the nature of it?"

"Calming, welcome, albeit a bit confusing," Percy admitted.

"Can you recount it?"

"As the owl, I was sitting on Merlin's shoulder, enjoying my connection with him in a quiet moment, when suddenly, his black robes became a stunning white, his nest of tangled grey hair became a sleek fall of blue-black hair with a feather woven in, and instead of his gnarled hand holding his oak staff, a graceful hand held a pipe adorned in feathers and leather strips, and," here Percy paused and lowering his head, "he, I should say now she, looked like...you."

Lily let out a gasp, then a small laugh.

"Goodness. Actually that sounds like White Buffalo Calf Woman."

"Who?" Percy asked.

"A cultural prophet of the Lakota peoples."

"Her shape and Merlin's kept blending in and out of one another..."

"The two as one," Lily offered.

"Signifying..." Percy began.

"The connections, the similarities between the ancient druidic culture and indigenous peoples," Lily finished. "What a wonderful vision. And I'm not surprised. Art and I have often talked of the similarities between the two cultures. The ancient Celts, pre-Roman, were, after all, the indigenous peoples of western Europe."

"An important intersection to consider," Percy said, his voice rising in excitement.

"And a significant potential alliance going forward," Lily said.

They fell into deep conversation, comparing the indigenous cultures of western Europe and the Americas, wondering at the closed hearts of those who placed empire above the balm of connection to the earth, and speculating about how the release of Merlin's spirit into the world might break open the cage of desolation into which so much of humanity had fallen. It was not lost on them that they were representatives of the two separate but similar cultures, drawn to each other with more than a physical pull.

As they spoke, the woods darkened. The night was warm, the trees whispered around them and the hut provided adequate shelter. No point in trying to find the way home before morning. Exactly when their hands touched, neither could say, but they fell asleep with their fingers entwined and their hearts in harmony.

They could smell it before the house came into view. Honey. Sweet, alluring, sticky Tannen was skeptical about this visit to the *Bee Witch*, but April was more animated than Tannen had seen her in a while. She all but ran up the steps to the modest house painted in a variety of amber shades, as

though it had been smeared with honey rather than paint. Some houses have four-legged doorbells – dogs that bark wildly at the approach of strangers, alerting the occupants within. In the case of the home of the Bee Witch, it was the bees themselves who raised the alarm, a general atmospheric hum rising to something akin to the scream of a chainsaw as Tannen raised his hand to the knocker and barely pulled it back in time to avoid hitting
the face of the woman who had opened the door before his knock was complete. Framed by the doorway, she appeared as a living portrait, her skin the color of wildflower honey, her beauty vibrant, energetic.

"You muzzt be Tannen and Aprilll," the woman buzzed at her guests. "I've been ezzpecting you. I'm Eudora, but zzome people call me..."

"The Bee Witch," April exploded, eagerly extending her hand, unable to hold back her enthusiasm.

Eudora grabbed April's hand with matching good will. "ZZZZZ, yezz, zzo they like to zzay. The nickname ticklezz me. Nothing witchy about me, but let them have zzeir fun. No harm in it, not in thizz century at leazzt. But how rude I am! Bring yourzzelvezz inzzide."

Oh such wonders! As Tannen and April stepped into the house, they were immediately surrounded by an arresting sight. Every wall was covered in paintings, each of them brilliantly, stunningly alive. Eudora let her visitors gawk and exclaim all they liked without interruption. April and Tannen spun around, exclaiming at each window into another world, each more thrilling than the last. It was some time before they could find their manners and act like proper guests.

"You like my paintingzz then?" Eudora asked, smiling a knowing smile.

"Is it my imagination or are they singing?" April asked her host.

"Oh, I think it'zz vvery much your imagination that allowzz you to hear it," Eudora said, eyeing Tannen, who just shrugged. No, he didn't hear it.

"I'll ezzplain evverything, but firzzt letzz have zzome tea," Eudora suggested.

"With honey, of course!" April replied, very much in tune with the atmosphere of the Bee Witch's magical home. In fact, she almost seemed to be buzzing herself, her whole body subtly vibrating.

Eudora sat them in the living room while she disappeared to make tea.

"Are you ok?" Tannen asked, the concern evident in his voice.

"I'm great! This is wonderful! I feel like I'm at a bee concert!" April said as she fairly bounced where she sat.

"What are you talking about?" Tannen asked.

"All the buzzing coming from the paintings. It's like bee music – no, not *like* it, IS it! Seriously, you don't hear it?"

"No...I mean this whole place smells like I've been dipped in a bucket of honey, but from what I can see, the only thing buzzing is you," Tannen said, trying hard to not sound petulant, but April's extreme animation was making him uneasy.

"I wish we'd brought Poppie. She would LOVE this!" April said, her nose in the air to better take in the aroma, her eyes closed to better appreciate the "concert."

"Good God," Tannen couldn't help saying as he imagined Poppie, who barely touched the earth as it was, even more energized than usual.

"Here we are," Eudora sang as she set the tea tray down in front of her young guests.
"Zzo, how much did Lily tell you?"

"Well, she didn't prepare us for this," April said, smiling broadly as she waved her arm at the apparently *living* room. "She just said that you were someone we should meet...and that you'd be pleased to meet us."

"Which I am, indeed!" Eudora said, leaning forward in her chair. "But I almozzt wonder if thizz izz a tezzt."

"A test?" Tannen asked, irritation rising in his voice despite himself.

"Wrong word, perhapzz," Eudora said, sensing Tannen's discomfort. "Letzz zzay more of a 'letzz zzzee'. Better?"

"Let's see *what*?" Tannen persisted.

"Letzz conzzider what we have zzeen, yezz? That being April'zz senzzitivity to the beezz."

"Then she's passed with flying colors I'd say," Tannen concluded.

"Dear Tannen," Eudora said, laying a golden hand on his arm, "you love zzith woman for her zzpecialnezz, do you not? Hazz no one prepared you for how zztrange, how challenging zzat will be from time to time? You muzzt learn to be zzhe zzaucer to her teacup, yezz? She izz zzo full of wonderouzz abilitiezz which you are only now finding out. Your job izz to zzupport her, create a zzave zzpace around her." As an illustration, Eudora traced a finger around the edge of the saucer in front of Tannen. "A humble role perhapzz, but honorable and ezzential. And the ezzprezzzion of the deepezzt love."

As Eudora withdrew her hand from Tannen's arm, she turned her attention to April who seemed completely enchanted by the "bee music."

"How izz the tea my dear?" Eudora asked, gently pulling April away from the sounds that had her so spellbound.

"Oh!" April said, reddening at the realization that she hadn't touched her tea at all. Taking a sip, she could then honestly reply that it was lovely. As her cup clattered back into the saucer, Tannen gave a small start. *The saucer to her teacup.* Despite himself, he felt the image take root in his consciousness. There was an expansive steadiness in it that appealed to him.

April had edged up on her seat and leaned forward toward their hostess. "Will you tell us about all this, please? The buzzing, the paintings? Why do you think Lily sent us to you?"

Eudora waved her hand above her head and swept it across the room with odd movements, as though she was sweeping something away. As she did so, the bee singing receded to a slight background hum and when she spoke, the buzzing of her voice had likewise mellowed to a more human timbre. But the paintings continued to shine as though lit from within.

"These paintings you see are done with the encaustic method..."

"I've heard of that!" Tannen said. "It's done with beeswax. Of course! Don't know why I didn't realize that from the beginning."

"It's not something you see every day," Eudora said, smiling broadly at Tannen. "Beeswax, colored pigment and a tree resin called *damar.* It's a rather complicated process, but as you can see, quite worth it."

"Beeswax and tree resin. No wonder they feel so alive! They actually are!" April said, the faraway look threatening to return to her features.

"I've been doing this for years. It's part of the *contract* I have with the bees. Through me their experience of the world is made visible to others. Layer upon layer I work, entering a kind of trance state. I hardly know what I'm doing until somehow I know it's done and then there it is, a glowing image of flowers, trees, ponds, critters, sometimes with hints of humans and houses, but always as a small part of the larger landscape."

"And how do others get to see these?" Tannen asked. "Do you sell them?"

"Mostly I give them away, but if someone offers me money for one, I take it. It all goes to maintenance, but mostly I make an income with my honey. But now, dear ones, we must get to the real reason you are here." Eudora sat quietly for a moment, although April could sense a buzzing coming from her, not quite like a snore, but more like the sound of thinking – if thinking were to make a sound.

"April," Eudora began, almost apologetically, "tell me about what you were hearing earlier."

"You mean the bee singing?" April asked. "Don't you hear it?"

"I hear a slight buzzing – it's in my head all the time. It *invades* me, as you probably could tell from the way I spoke when you first came here." Eudora let out a little buzzing chuckle. "When I'm here alone, with no one to talk to, I just kind of buzz all the time, like breathing. When I need to speak, the buzzing is still there, until I'm in human company for a time, then I can reclaim a more typical way of speaking...mostly. But from the way you talked, I think you actually hear more than I do, so please tell me about it."

April squirmed where she sat. How could she hear more than this woman who looked like she was *made* of honey? "It was like singing...like...the harmonic sound one gets when hitting a string instrument just right. It's hard to describe. It's so pleasant. It sounds like sunshine would sound if it made a noise. It's like lying in a bed of flowers on a perfect day, watching the wind making the trees dance. It's like...I could go on and on, but why is it that I'm the only one who experienced this?"

Eudora looked like she didn't want to say what she had to say next. "Do you still hear it?"

"Somewhat," April admitted, "but you turned it down...and it seems to know that we need to talk, that I needed to bring myself back to...I can't say *reality*. It's all reality, but *this* reality, us talking, here."

Eudora took a deep breath, like she was about to jump from a great height into deep, deep waters.

"Lily sent you here to see what would happen when you were in the presence of the bees – bees that, because of their relationship with me are prepared to connect with the human world under certain conditions."

"What conditions?" Tannen asked, bracing himself for the answer.

Eudora looked down at her hands, putting them fingertip to fingertip. The buzzing got a bit louder for a bit, then subsided again.

"You know you are of Merlin's lineage, yes?" she asked at last.

"Yes."

"What does that mean for you?" Eudora prodded.

"I'm not sure, honestly. Somehow, I knew the way to the cave in the Forest of Broceliande and I can enter the dream world like I'm opening a door to a room, but other than that..." April shrugged.

"You see the animal spirits in Lily's people I presume?"

April thought of Poppie, the friend who was so delightfully otherworldly. "Yes, I do see that, but I thought that was because my mom told me about it. Predisposed me to it."

"I don't know what it's been like for people in your lineage before you, but in you, Merlin's abilities are awakened. Your experience here today is evidence of that." Now Eudora sat back in her chair and folded her hands in her lap. Any hint of buzzing was gone. It was as though she was speaking from another place and time.

"There are still people who can connect with the natural world, who readily experience their kinship with all the beings of this planet, but they are few and growing fewer all the time. Time was, when all people had at least some sense of the connection and many just lived with it naturally, knowing it was the way of things. Then there were the special ones, like Merlin, who were the epitome of that connection, who were human, but not human at the same time, if being completely connected to the natural world defines non-human, which alas, seems to be the case."

"What makes the difference?" April asked, a sadness growing in her. "I see it that some people care deeply about the planet while others can't wait to cut down the trees, pave over the ground, or leave the planet altogether to live under a dome on some distant world. What makes the difference?"

"I've been trying to figure that out my whole life," Eudora said, the sadness in her voice heartrending to hear. "When I'm in my encaustic trances, I get the feeling that it's in all of us, the connection to the planet. It has to be. We are part of it, made of the same elements. The bees whisper that to me...I find the place in me that is like them and they do the same with me and...we connect. Naturally, inevitably. But then, as you say, why cannot others do the same? I believe the potential is there, indelibly locked in the genetic code, but has been turned off in some way."

"Epigenetics," Tannen interjected. "We're learning that genes can be turned off or on, due to any number of factors. As civilizations have progressed – if you want to call it that – our genetic expressions have changed. I would be tempted to say that those changes were meant to be adaptive, more suited to survival..."

"...but now they actually threaten our survival..." April said. "Maybe they were misguided from the get-go."

Tannen disagreed. "I'm not sure that makes sense or correlates with current research. Our genes want us to survive. Maybe becoming more independent from nature was adaptive at a certain point, but we've gone too far in that direction and now we need to reclaim the knowledge of the old ways."

"But," Eudora said, "the indigenous peoples of this land have kept to the old ways for eons and would no doubt still be living that way if Europeans had never come to this continent."

"So what does this mean for April?" Tannen asked, warming to his role as protector.

Eudora shone the beauty of her gaze directly into April's heart. "You must be brave and trusting. You are likely to encounter challenges, perhaps even some frightening obstacles, but rest in the knowledge that you are an integral part of the natural world and it wants you to survive and explore what your Merlinist DNA has in store for you. As I am a voice for the bees, you are the voice of Merlin, reborn in this crucial time. It is, perhaps, the last chance we have to bring humanity back into its proper place in the scheme of things."

"No pressure," April said.

"Not if you don't let there be," Eudora said gently. "You have heard the song of the bees. They have sung for you and you alone. There will be more such messages to come. Follow them, do your best, put yourself in the hands of the Way of Things. All you need do is not resist. What will happen, will happen." With that, Eudora rose. "And now," she said, "I would be honored if you'd choose a painting to take with you."

It should have taken some time; there were so many to choose from. But one painting in particular had caught and held April's eye all afternoon. It was a field of delicate pink and purple poppies adored by a myriad of tiny but perfectly rendered bees and butterflies, all bathed in a golden light that filled April's heart with confidence and optimism. As she approached the painting, she was pleased to notice that if she listened carefully, she could hear the bee song that had so enraptured her earlier. It was as though it was coming from the tiny bees in the painting, and maybe it was. To take all this with her, to have access to it whenever she needed it was a gift for which no thanks would be enough, and so April said as much to Eudora.

"Your thanks will be in what you do going forward," Eudora said as she handed the painting to April. "I have no doubt that you will earn this gift one hundred-fold."

Tannen and April were nearly at their car when Eudora called out, "Keep the painting cool, lezzt it melt!"

The two turned to wave and as they did so, a line from Yeats came into Tannen's mind..."and live alone in the bee loud glade." *Yes,* he thought, *just so.*

Chapter 13

Return to Glastonbury

It was a simple dream, direct, nothing complicated or symbolic that needed interpretation, at least not in April's sense of it. *She stood at the edge of the Chalice Well, surrounded by the smell of summer and the sound of sweet birdsong, unable to imagine anything more delightful, when arose from the Well a vision of the Goddess, her head reaching toward the heavens, her feet just below the surface of the sacred waters, her eyes staring straight at April. With one graceful hand emerging from the gossamer threads that whirled around her, she reached toward April. "Come" was the unmistakable message of the beckoning fingers.*

"You can't leave me!" Poppie pleaded. "We have so much work to do together!"

As was their wont, the three were having a late breakfast in the cottage, ignoring the concern about the house being bugged as they milled around the kitchen, grazing and stealing food from each other's plates.

"And going back to Glastonbury right now is, we think, part of that work," Tannen explained, as gently as he could. "April has had a vision. We're pretty confident it's the next step."

"It isn't just that Sirona is leaving and you will miss her?" Poppie asked, reaching for a thread she hoped she could follow back to a convincing argument for them to stay.

"I don't think so," April said, not wanting to flat out contradict her friend's logical explanation. And anyway, maybe there was a tiny bit of that, but the dream was unambiguous. The sacred waters were calling her back. "You of all people know that I should not ignore my dreams and this one was clear as crystal. At the very least, we need to connect with our people there, especially now that we have some direction. That Sirona is returning now as well is a happy circumstance."

"Come with us Poppie," Tannen said, suddenly delighted at the thought of their fairy-like friend in Glastonbury. "You would absolutely love Glastonbury. You'd fit right in!"

At this, Poppie was uncharacteristically silent, dropping her eyes and turning away from her friends.

"What is it, Poppie? We'd love to have you come with us!"

Poppie only shook her head and refused to speak.

"Is it something I said?" Tannen asked, distraught at the possibility that he had somehow insulted their friend.

"Please, Poppie," April said, putting her hand on her friend's shoulder. "Don't shut us out. Whatever it is, you can tell us. We'll take no offense. Nothing you can say would..."

"I'm afraid!" Poppie blurted.

"It's a long trip, yes, but we'll be together and Sirona will be with us as well..." Tannen said.

"It's not that at all," Poppie replied, raising her tear-damp eyes to meet theirs. "I'm afraid to leave here. Please try to understand. This is my ancestral ground, my soul's home place. If I leave it, my connection could diminish. Do you ever wonder why so few people are conscious of their soul's journey? Moving away from their ancestral home is not the only reason, but it's a significant one. The soul must be nourished, *seen* as it were. When it's safe in its ancestral place, that's not hard to do, but if it is uprooted, then the carrier of that soul must take extra pains to keep the soul's connection strong. I cannot risk losing my connection. It is precious to me."

"As it is to us!" April said. "Oh, Poppie, not for a moment would we want you to lose any of what makes you so uniquely, wonderfully, you! But as you must stay, so must we go. We'll not stay long. As you said, most of our work is here as are the people we love, but we dare not turn our backs on a vision. We'll write, and Facetime, and return as soon as possible. In the meantime, you can take care of Raina, Art and Percy for us. I believe they've grown to depend on your perky spirit to keep them optimistic."

"Perhaps none of that is necessary." It was Sirona, coming in from the lake room. "Pardon me for overhearing, but I may have a solution -- and I think it might actually be well to have Poppie with us in Glastonbury. Come, let me tell you a bit of a story."

Sirona led them all to seats by the hearth and placed herself between Poppie and April so she could hold their hands as she spoke.

"As you know," Sirona began, "I always spend part of my year in Glastonbury. Most likely, you thought it was just because I love the place -- which I do. But I love this place as well – Art, and the Lake. So there is a deeper reason why I must periodically return to the legendary Isle of Avalon, and it is because that is the place of *my* soul's ancestry. Poppie, you are absolutely correct to believe that our connection to our ancient soul is strongest in our ancestral home, and that all the movement humans have undergone over the long ages has contributed significantly to the severance of that soul awareness from our consciousness.

"Perhaps the three of you are not aware," Sirona continued, "that both Art and I were born here in the States. Not far from here as it turns out."

"Then how did you know your ancestral home was in Somerset?" April asked.

"It took many years and many twists and turns. Art and I were lucky, if that's what you want to call it. Or perhaps we were chosen in some way. At any rate, as we grew up, many interesting and unusual things happened to us which encouraged us to investigate, ask questions, and give our imaginations free rein. It helped immeasurably that we had each other – another trusted person with whom to compare notes, commiserate, and, as we grew older, to cover our backs as we took certain risks. A child alone would likely give in to accepting a definition of "strange" or "mad"..."

"...like my mother," April interjected.

"Exactly so," Sirona said, giving April's hand a squeeze before continuing her story. "As our felt connection to the Arthurian tales got stronger, I decided I needed to go to England, to the sites connected to the tales."

"Did Art not go with you?" Tannen asked, his accepted role of protector on high alert.

"Not this time. I was headstrong at that point. I insisted that I needed to test things on my own, without the potential for Art's influence. I did travel with a friend, however. One who knew very clearly that her ancestral line was firmly rooted on this continent."

"And?" April asked, thirsty for a story of confirmation, if not her own (which she so fervently wished for), at least that of someone else.

"That was a very long time ago and so much has happened since then...events, visions, feelings...they've become somewhat of a blur. But I do remember some of it clearly. I started at Stonehenge as so many seekers do. I had a strange interaction with a crow, but I didn't think much of it, although I remember it sending chills down my spine and being the stuff of my dreams for many nights thereafter. From there we travelled to Tintagel and Merlin's Cave beneath it. Climbing to the top of the cliff, I lost my breath and couldn't continue. That made no sense. I was young, in good shape. But there was no question that I could not complete the climb. When at last I felt strong enough, I made my way back down and then down a bit more to Merlin's Cave, poised on the edge of the tide. It was little more than a hole in the rock, but it spoke to me, pulled at me. I didn't want to leave. In fact, I stayed much too long and had to wade through the incoming tide to get back up to the road.

"Things were strange – clearly more was going on with me than what would comprise the typical experience of an interested tourist or even a researcher of antiquarian sites. But it wasn't until we came to Glastonbury, to the Chalice Well, the White Spring, the Tor, that I experienced an overwhelming feeling of transformation, though many specifics of that time are lost to me. I do remember that my heart would ache as though it was being pulled from my chest, or my vision would blur and it would seem I was looking at things as they were hundreds of years ago, yet, strange as that was, all of it felt as familiar and comfortable as my own skin. There was no denying that this was indeed my ancestral soul home. I visited many times after that, growing stronger and stronger each time."

"Did Art ever go with you?" Poppie asked.

"Once. Only once. Something happened to him on that trip that he's never talked about, his only comment being, 'my destiny lies in the States, on the lake.' "

"So he's not as connected or as concerned about his ancestral soul as you are then" April asked.

"That's for him to say, but it's not a topic he addresses." Sirona answered.

Poppie leaned forward in her chair, signaling the importance of her next question.

"You said that each time you grew stronger. What do you mean by that, exactly?"

"Ah, that's not an experience you would have had, is it Poppie?" Sirona said, smiling benevolently at the young woman. "You have always been connected to your ancestral soul and so you would not have experienced any transition. Let me put it this way. Most of us, despite any accomplishments, have a nagging feeling that we are not yet complete – that there's something more out there, perhaps just around the corner, that will complete us. As my awareness of my full soul grew, that feeling of incompleteness diminished, leaving me in what I can only say is a state of grace."

"But if I go with you, am I not putting all that at risk?" Poppie said.

"I honestly don't think so," Sirona replied. "You are well-rooted, your connection habituated. I wouldn't recommend staying away for months, but, aside from perhaps a vague sense of dislocation, you should be fine for a short visit. If you decide to come, I will take you to my friend Rowan who will be delighted to meet you and, I suspect, will have some teas that you will find useful. It is in great measure thanks to her that I can travel back and forth from here to there as much as I do."

"Rowan!" April sighed. "I can't wait to see her again."

Poppie sat quietly, still not ready to make up her mind.

"Talk to Lily," Sirona suggested. "See what she says. We leave in a few days."

That night, everyone met at Art's for a last "gathering of minds" before they went in separate directions. As usual, Art was the perfect host, his living room by now oozing with the atmosphere of a sacred space – safe for honest and penetrating conversation.

"What, still no Round Table?" Sirona chided as she entered.

"No room. Besides, it exists in our imaginations, does it not dear sister?" Art countered with raised eyebrow, as if to say *surely, Sirona, you of all people should not need an actual TABLE....*

As before, Lily's people wove themselves into the lake group, using their bodies to signal the unity of the various perspectives. John found his seat next to April, beaming at her with genuine affection, placing his over-sized, paw-like hand gently on her wrist, offering a comfort April did not shrink from. Lily eyed Percy with what could only be described as hunger, but took her seat next to Art, while Gladys floated to Percy's side, settling into her chair as though onto a nest. Sirona sought out Darla, so like Rowan, while Ben asked Raina if she minded his company. Poppie gravitated to Percy, quietly inserting herself at his other side, while Tannen, never leaving April's side, installed himself protectively next to her. It was a tight fit, the twelve of them in a circle in Art's living room, but once settled, they fit together like beads on a prayer bracelet. The energy that flowed around the circle was palpable, each person so unique, and yet, increasingly interconnected with the others. Most likely, the knights who populated the legendary Round Table, while united in their fealty to Arthur, never achieved the unity of mind shared by these twelve.

Art opened the meeting. "Welcome all. We meet tonight to share our experiences to date and to offer what we can of direction to Sirona, April and Tannen as they leave us to reconnect with our counterparts in Glastonbury. While I hate to see them leave, I'm convinced that this is the next step toward quickening the pattern we're attempting to weave. The energy we're generating here is strong – strong enough, I believe, to carry across the ocean to that other place of power." As Art spoke, he felt arise in him the sense of connection he felt between Aries Lake and the waters of the Tor that seeped into the everyday world at the Chalice Well and the White Spring. He rarely spoke of it, this connection, mostly because he had no words to logically explain it, but it wouldn't surprise him in the least if the legendary Lady of the Lake were to someday rise from the center of the water he looked upon daily. This land was only a "New World" to the invaders from Europe. The land itself was as ancient as any other, and carrying as much power, certainly, even if of a different nature.

Art took his seat, signaling an opening of the floor for sharing. With a nod from Lily,
Percy told of his experience with the dreaming leaf, though carefully skirting around the more intimate details.

"And since then?" Ben asked, no doubt asking the question on everyone's mind. "Have you had any insights?"

"Actually, I have," Percy admitted, realizing he'd shared none of this with anyone until now. "I'd like to wait until others have shared before I bring it up, as I suspect a discussion might ensue."

"Fair enough," Ben agreed, sitting back in his seat.

Next to speak was Tannen, he and April having agreed that he would be the one to begin the tale of their encounter with the Bee Witch, since April's experience had been so overwhelming, and perhaps rather unbelievable to others. As he spoke, April drifted into a reverie of the day, the bee song still accessible to her senses. Fortunately, Tannen's account was so riveting few noticed that April had fallen into a kind of trance – few except John, who had his own special kind of relationship with bees. His hand still on hers, he felt the vibration and, as though from miles away, heard the faintest echo of the song. His smile was camouflaged by his beard, but his eyes twinkled merrily. Whatever Tannen was relating, while important to be sure, it was nothing compared to what John knew April could now add to her understanding of the *way things are.* The bees had shared with her their story of interconnection and flower alchemy, of invisible highways built of song. Eudora had done her part. He must pay her a visit.

When Tannen's story ended and everyone had had a chance to ask their questions and mull over what he had shared, Gladys leaned forward slightly in her seat, while her head swung gracefully, side to side, taking in each member of the circle in turn.

"Grace," she said, speaking the word as though it was a jewel she was laying out for all to marvel at. "Grace is both received and bestowed, the province of both Spirit and the individual mind. Grace is all around us, it is the *effect* of touching spirit." Gladys arched her neck and turned her head to meet Percy's eyes. "I believe you are now quite clear on that point."

Percy nodded in assent, losing himself for a flashing moment in the dark pools of Gladys' gaze.

She continued. "As we grow in our experience of grace, as we take the gift into ourselves, we can move beyond gratitude into the understanding that grace is a tool to be employed in even the smallest of every day events. As we learn to make grace our way of being in the world, we are making our mark, our contribution. As we grow our souls, how our behavior is informed by grace is our legacy."

"Just as the tree, in doing what it is designed to do for itself, is contributing to the wellbeing of all, so the soul work we do for ourselves *exhales* grace into the world," Darla said, clearly thrilled by the insight.

"Exactly so!" Gladys beamed.

Quiet ensued as the twelve processed all that they had heard. After a spell, Art spoke into the silence.

"If there are no more reports, let us open up to general discuss...."

"Wait," Poppie said, the westering sun having finally found a window from which it lit up Poppie's presence as would a spotlight. "I have something to share."

Art gestured regally for her to continue.

"I'm going to Glastonbury with my friends!" It was just in that moment that Poppie made the decision, so not even April and Tannen knew of it. Hearing all the stories and insights from the collective quickened her desire for adventure. As comfortable as she was in her familiar environs, what more could she learn or experience here? Accompanied by her friends, she could swallow her fear and open her wings to something new.

"Yes!" April exploded, as a murmur of approval went around the room.

"Excellent," Art announced. "It was my hope that someone from Lily's group would go. It will help to make the connection between the groups. Who better than Poppie to literally be a seed that travels across the waters?"

But while Art's words spoke approval of the development, the look he shot to Sirona said something much different. *I fear for her. So pure and protected here. I sense a potential for danger for her in the Old World.*

I've got this, brother, Sirona shot back. *I share your concerns, but I will stay vigilant and enlist Rowan's help. That she has made this decision is evidence, to me anyway, that she would suffer more from being away from Tannen and April than she will in the swirl of energies that is Glastonbury.*

Just saying it that way gives me chills, Art thought. So much for Sirona's assurances.

When the excitement around Poppie's announcement faded, Ben reiterated his question to Percy. "So, you have learned something about Merlin's soul then?"

"I have," Percy stammered. How he disliked being the center of attention. But, he sadly concluded, this was a significant part of his contribution. He thought of April having to bear the burden of leadership at so young an age. If she was willing to step so far out of her comfort zone, then he must find a similar kind of courage.

"Perhaps this is not exactly what we had hoped for, but it is a beginning. Consider the nature of Nimue's ensorcellment of Merlin. What has come down to us through the tales, and it is logical that it should be so, is the lament of the loss of Merlin's imminence – the body through which he is known. We suffer at the thought of his human body being entwined with a tree."

At this, Sirona squirmed where she sat. Her heartbeat quickened and it was only with an effort that she kept herself present and relatively calm, to appearances at least.

"But it was not just his body that Nimue captured. It was his soul. And that...that is the cosmic crime. As we are all aware, it is the natural state of the soul to be released when the human body expires – released to quicken in another physical host and continue the journey through time and experience. To trap a soul, particularly one such as Merlin's, is an egregious act, a cessation of the flow of sacred energy."

"Almost like tearing a hole in the universe..." Poppie said, feeling the power and presence of her own soul.

"So if we indeed have freed that soul..." Raina began, unable to finish her thought as questions crowded her mind.

"I fear none of us is wise enough to even hazard a guess," Ben said. "But what I do know is that whoever becomes, or has become, the host for that soul..."

"Has their work cut out for them..." Lily said, completing Ben's thought. "I pity that person. Whether that individual develops soul awareness or not, where there should be nearly fifty generations of evolution there will be only..."

"Nothingness..." Darla said, her voice laden with loss.

"Worse," Sirona said, her voice cracking. "Not just nothing, but torture, entrapment."

"Then perhaps we've made a huge mistake!" Raina cried, voicing a fear that had nagged at her from the beginning.

Sirona remembered the dense fog she awoke to the morning after their ritual in the cave. It had unnerved her then, but she had had no idea what to make of it. Now she wondered if it was a foreshadowing of the spiritual "fog" the next host of Merlin's soul was likely to experience. Or perhaps it was a manifestation of the agony and confusion of the soul itself, spilled out upon the earth. Despite the warmth of the evening, Sirona shivered.

"I don't think it was a mistake," Art said. "If it was a horror to trap a soul, to leave it trapped would be a continuation of that horror. Coming back to life, re-entering the eternal stream that flows beneath the life and death of the material world won't be easy, but I think you were on the right side of the natural order of things in doing what you did. And now I have another thought." Art paused, stroked his chin. What he was about to share was only half formed in his own mind. He would have preferred to be more confident in his thinking before expressing it, but there were times when one had to trust to the community of mind, and this was one such time. He could not hoard the insight, but must share it, even in its infancy, and thereby let the whole group nurture it.

"I would not for a moment diminish the importance of freeing Merlin's soul. But it occurs to me that perhaps the act itself, that is to say, the effect on each of you of taking that action is profoundly significant." Art paused, to see if anyone had caught the thread and would carry it forward, but he was met only with curious looks. There was nothing for it but to continue what he had begun.

"Everything that went into the preparation for and execution of the ritual, everything you experienced in the cave, all the feelings and thoughts you have had since, everything that has happened here within this group and between its members...absolutely all of it has gotten us where we are today."

It was like plunging into the lake in early April, well before the waters had warmed to a comfortable temperature, but unable to wait any longer to be immersed, to feel the embrace of the elemental. So Art literally plunged on.

"I am no philosopher of the soul. I really don't know how soul works. I am a man of the material world, devoted to right action and the protection of others. But what of this? What if your ritual successfully undid Nimue's spell and when the soul was released, somehow *pieces* of it," (he knew that was the wrong word, but he was struggling), "entered each of you, quickening in you a determination to move forward at whatever cost, guiding your hands and your minds to surge forward in your understanding, your actions. I have witnessed many of you, all of you really, moving out of your comfort zones, taking risks, finding in yourselves new facets of your being. Look at us," he implored, gesturing around the circle. "Crossing cultures with our trust, our visions, our ancestral knowledge. Percy, Tannen, Raina, Sirona...and of course April, each of you engaging things you're unsure about, but doing it anyway, despite the fact that there are no maps of the territory you're entering. Lily, you and your people engaging with us, risking giving up those things which you have so wisely kept secret for so long..." Here he paused, worn out, even a bit terrified by his own insight.

"All this from a simple trip to Paimpont Forest?" Sirona teased.

"You know nothing was simple about that. You know what went into it, what it cost all of you to undertake it. Our actions, if done with intentionality and mindfulness, are the link between the imminent and transcendent. They exist at the center of the Vesica Piscis, the manifestation of the coming together of the sacred and the mundane. Yes, we change the world by our actions, but we must also attend to the way in which our actions change us."

"I've not been the same since that day," Raina admitted.

"Nor I," Percy added. "It... opened me up to things I'd kept buried for years." His owl nature, yes, and his connection to Merlin, but more than that, he realized, glancing at Lily, his heart. But that change, he knew, would never be voiced, only lived into.

"It almost killed me," Sirona said, but so quietly only those closest to her properly heard it.

Lily reached over to where Art's hand gripped the arm of his chair, white knuckled. At her touch, his hand relaxed. The respect between them was profound and rarely needed words. Lily could easily have had much to say about what Art had shared, but she chose to keep her counsel. What needed to be said, had been said. Now she needed to hold the space for others to find their way into the story, on their own time, in their own way.

But for now, the council had come to an end. Folks said their good-byes amid many hugs and well-wishes. They would meet again if need be, but likely not until April, Tannen, Sirona and Poppie returned from England. As everyone left, Lily lagged behind with Art. Together, the two walked out onto the porch and sat on the steps, free to bathe in the radiance of the night sky.

"It's not easy walking between two world views, is it old friend?" Lily offered.

"Well, something's not easy, but I'm not sure I've been much compelled by the Western worldview for a long time. Thanks to you, I've walked through the door in the sky and seen clearly that most of the world has no idea the extent to which they're living in a constructed reality. It's more the struggle between the imminent and transcendent that gives me a headache. If the whole thing needs to be sorted, I'm not the one to do it."

"Why do you think religions are so important to people? They reduce all those struggles to simple, dogmatic answers and vacant rituals that convince people that everything will be ok as long as they don't question anything."

"But so not ok..." Art mused. Then not exactly changing the subject, but shifting it, "I see you are now schooling Percy in the Indigenous worldview..."

Lily laughed. "No schooling needed. His owl nature already knows it intuitively. He just needed confirmation that it was ok to trust his deep knowing."

"So what is the deal with all this soul stuff? How does it work?" Art asked.

"You're asking me?" Lily said. "I've been gifted with the ability to sense previous lives in people and help them accept that influence if it is strong in them, but beyond that...it is as much a mystery to me as anyone and likely will remain so."

"But what determines which past life creeps into our present one? There must be myriad soul iterations floating around in us. Why, for instance, did Sirona and I get snagged by Arthur and Morgan le Fay?"

"Mystery, my friend, mystery," Lily said, pointing at the stars. "The important question is, if we're lucky enough to be aware of any aspect of our soul's history, what is it that we will do with it?"

Taking off his headset, Malcolm congratulated himself with an ambitious swig of whiskey. Double points for his craftiness. Putting a bug in Art's cottage rather than Raina's – what a stroke of genius. And now he had the joyful news that April was going to Glastonbury of her own accord. How perfect, and how easy for him. Relieved of the challenge Vas had set for him – to get April to England – Malcolm let his mind take a break. Another swig of whiskey as his mind replayed the events leading up the present moment.

He'd been delightfully successful in obtaining April's journal, but after the vigilance the theft had evoked in April and her friends, his original plan to bug the Quinn place seemed less than ideal. Malcolm's spying had revealed that any gatherings subsequently seemed mostly to happen in Art's place. So from his perch at the edge of the woods and the information he gathered from the drone, Malcolm watched and waited until the day came when it seemed most everyone had gone off somewhere, leaving Art's cottage unattended. He had not seen Sirona leave the Quinn cottage since morning and Art and Raina had taken off for what looked to be a rather long swim. Judging by their distance from the cottages, he figured he had a good twenty minutes or so to put the bug in place. If he was lucky, the door would be unlocked. If not, he would find a window near the main room of the cottage and wedge the device there.

Careful to stay out of eyesight of Raina's place, Malcolm made his way to a door at the back of Art's house. Trying it, he found it unlocked and was surprised to see that it let into a pottery studio. So, who was the potter? Having little time to wonder, he walked through and into the rest of the house. Despite himself, he was impressed. So, this was Art. Solid, secure, perfectly arranged and nothing out of place. Malcolm fought the urge to take a seat and wait for his host to return. He'd only had one encounter with Art, and that an uncomfortable one, but being in this house, Malcolm couldn't avoid the feeling of wanting to chat with the man whose home spoke so clearly of an orderly calm.

But as an image of Ignatius Vas intruded on Malcolm's daydreaming, he was brought back to his goal. He saw that chairs and sofas were arranged in a circle which included the hearth in its design. Clearly, this is where the conversations took place. He searched until he found the perfect spot – a convenient depression between the wooden mantle and the stone of the fireplace. The bug plopped into the hole as though it was made for it and sunk down just enough to be out of sight, but with its receiving end facing outward. So perfectly did it fit that Malcolm couldn't have retrieved it if he'd wanted to.

Curiosity pulled him toward to rest of the house, but distant laughter halted his step. Back already? Had he misjudged the distance, or had he stood mesmerized longer than he thought? His heart beating painfully, he made his way to the back door, remembering now his first encounter with Art and the power he exerted with his manner alone. No, Malcolm did not want to be found by this man a second time, especially as a trespasser in his home. Palms sweating, he turned the knob on the studio door and hastened to the road and the woods beyond.

That was yesterday. Now his reverie was halted by the reality of an empty glass. Reaching for the bottle, he returned to the practicality of considering how to proceed going forward. He would return to Glastonbury, make an appointment to see Vas, as much as he disliked being alone with the man, and, hopefully, let Vas and the Brotherhood take it from there. He had made it clear to Vas that he would not be the instrument of April's capture, though Vas would never be privy to his reasons – not if he could help it.

One thing was certain. He'd be glad to be done with this espionage. When Vas first tasked him with spying on Raina, April and crew, he saw it as a welcome opportunity to exact some revenge against Raina for stealing April from him, and the surveillance technology they'd provided for him was top notch – a thrill to use. But the room he'd rented near the lake was a musty, insulting hovel, and prowling around in the woods was not at all his thing. Worse, what he hadn't counted on was watching his former wife obviously happily involved with another man, and his daughter wrapped comfortably in the surety of a host of new friends. It had taken a chunk out of his ego in more ways than one, but though he wasn't entirely certain what Vas had in mind, he was confident that it would inject some chaos into the smug little world of the women who'd rejected him, and so, he told himself it was worth it.

Malcolm gulped the last inch of his whiskey then turned the empty glass upside down over the top of the bottle. *Done and dusted, as they said in England,* he thought. Then, rather than retire to his lumpy excuse of a bed, he fell asleep where he sat.

Chapter 14

Bargains Fulfilled

Glastonbury, Somerset, England

No worries that in Glastonbury Eudora's painting would get too hot, even arranged on the wall in Percy's great room in such a way that the morning sun would hit it directly, a clarion call to rise early and face the day prepared to work diligently and enthusiastically. It did liven up the room, but as of yet, had not brought Poppic out of her funk. She had suffered piteously on the plane, barely able to breathe the recycled air. Had it not been for Sirona's tea which helped her sleep, April feared she would have begged to be let off mid-Atlantic.

Only slightly reassured by a promised trip to the Chalice Gardens, Poppie sat curled in a motionless ball while Tannen and April unpacked and assessed their needs for the coming days. Niall had already stocked the kitchen with basics and breakfast fixings and insisted they come to Sirona's for dinner. That Percy's place was so close to Sirona's was an immense convenience. There was much to do, so it was assumed there would be much coming and going between the two places. April wondered, not for the first time, how it was that two such mystical beings had lived so near for so long and not discovered one another earlier.

"Dad's a loner," Tannen explained. "Has always done his own thing."

"Until Lily," April teased.

"Oh," Tannen objected, "I think it started with your mom, and then there's Sirona. Once a person knows her, well, there's no getting over that! But I agree, Lily has inspired another level of engagement altogether."

The two laughed softly, but then fell into mutual silence. Poppie wasn't the only one missing the folks in the States. For April's part, she had to continually remind herself why she was here. And while Tannen appreciated being back home, without his father things felt...incomplete.

"We need to get to the Chalice Well," April pronounced. "The sooner the better."

"Agreed," Tannen said, his head deep in the refrigerator. "Hey, looks like Niall made us some bag lunches. Let's take them and get out of here."

Flanked by her friends, Poppie stumbled out of the door and did her best to hold her own, but the closer they got to the Gardens, the stronger she felt. At the entrance, she halted, tears streaming down her face.

"What is this place?" she asked as though she expected the flowers themselves to satisfy her query.

"Come on," April said, gently pulling her friend up the slope that led to the Well. It being early summer, the garden was in full bloom, more abundant and alive than even April had seen it. Amazingly, they encountered no one on the path, and when they rounded the tree and walked onto the patio to stand, circling the Well, they were in a world all their own. Poppie's eyes glistened and her face glowed with the light of recognition as she threw her head back, spread her arms wide and began to sing a strange, high-pitched chant.

April and Tannen stood transfixed. There was nothing they could do but marvel at the transformation in their friend. Poppie's singing, if one could rightly call it that, continued, wordlessly, in notes that defied replication. As it intensified, the still waters of the Well began to ripple, as water does in a sudden breeze. Still Poppie sang and still her friends stood mesmerized, until from the waters a mist arose and encircled them, each of the three surrounded by a spiral of shimmering cloud. Without falling, it seemed to both April and Tannen that they lost consciousness for a brief time, until at last, Poppie ceased her chant and the mist evaporated as though it had never been. But at Poppie's feet lay a single blossom – a delicate peach-colored poppy whose petals gave way to perfect purple fingerprints that highlighted a yellow seed-head. Poppie stooped to retrieve the flower then looked at her friends, and, putting her finger to her lips, turned to descend from the Well, following the stream to where it pooled in the flats.

Finally coming to the very bench where April first met Percy, the three sat, waiting for the story to be told. Twirling the flower between her fingers, Poppie could only manage, "It recognized me! The Well recognized me!"

That the story could not yet be told, all three intuitively understood.

"Let's find a place to open our lunches," Tannen advised.

When the three arrived at Sirona's for dinner, they saw that a surprise guest would be joining them.

"Rowan!" April exclaimed, rushing to the older woman and surrounding her with a gentle but determined hug. "So good to see you!"

"And you, dear April," Rowan replied, brushing April's hair back from where it had caught in her own. As she did so, she felt the vibrations of all the young woman had experienced since their last visit. *What a long night this promises to be,* Rowan thought. *So many stories to tell.* Then she eyed Poppie over April's shoulder. *So many stories indeed!*

Niall's dinner was scrumptious, demanding their full attention. Rowan limited herself to the greens and sautéed mushrooms, but the rest tore into the roast Cornish hens as though they hadn't eaten in days, which, of course, they hadn't – not like this! But once bellies were full and dishes cleared, the air was heavy with untold tales.

"I understand you had a rough crossing, Poppie," Rowan began, as innocently as she could manage. Her surreptitious observation of Poppie at dinner had revealed a being the likes of which she had never seen before. The only word that came to mind to describe it was *clean* – a connection between a present body and an ancient and magical soul uncontaminated by the usual detritus of the centuries. Even in someone as tactful as Rowan, it was only with studied effort that she could control her curiosity.

"Much better now, thank you," Poppie admitted shyly. A look passed between the young people, April and Tannen anxious to tell of their experience at the well, but respecting Poppie's ownership of the tale.

"And I expect you'll feel even better when we get you to the Chalice Well," Sirona said, brushing at some unseen particle on her pants. Niall knew the gesture. Sirona was being cagey. She knew they'd already been to the Well and that something was afoot.

Tannen could hold back no longer. "We went this afternoon," he said.

"And?" Sirona queried, imperiously.

Glances exchanged again. Poppie gave the slightest of nods to April.

"We had an...experience," April began. "More to the point, Poppie did."

"The Well spoke to you?" Sirona posed it as a question, but it was more of a statement. She already knew the answer.

"More like she spoke to it, or...sang to it," Tannen blurted out, then bit his lip. He hadn't meant to hijack Poppie's story, but why was she being so reticent? Niall raised an eyebrow, while Sirona hid a smile behind three delicate fingers and Rowan sat forward, bursting with curiosity.

Poppie blushed, then in a whisper said, "It pulled it out of me...a song."

"It was beautiful," April said, relieved to have the story begun at last. "Poppie, I didn't know you could do that."

"Neither did I," Poppie admitted. "It just came out of me. But it wasn't *of* me. It was like the well was playing me like an instrument, using me to...make its own voice audible to humans...or maybe just to me. I'm not sure."

"How did you feel while you were singing?" Rowan asked.

Poppie blushed again. "Like nothing I've ever felt before. It was like I was fully alive and yet outside my body at the same time, and also like I was vibrating at the same frequency as all the growing things around me – the flowers, trees, everything."

"Do you think you could do it again?" Rowan continued with her questions.

"I'm not sure. I think so, but I also feel like I shouldn't do it casually. Does that make sense?" Poppie pulled her knees to her chest. Clearly, Rowan was following a thread, now it was her turn to share what she was thinking.

"All the sense in the world," she replied. "I need to think about this more, but I can safely say this much. Clearly the Well resonated with you, found something in you it recognized and at the same time awakened a power within you. I expect your singing, should you find the right place and time to do it, carries great power."

Poppie fidgeted. "I'm not sure I'm comfortable with that."

"It will take time, and some instruction," Rowan said in her uncannily calming voice. "We'll talk more. For now, what about the rest of you? What was your experience during all this?"

April deferred to Tannen, curious to see if his experience was the same as hers. It was becoming achingly clear to her that "reality," such as it is, is often perceived differently by different people.

"A mist rose out of the Well," Tannen began, "then curled around each of the three of us, like that Celtic design..."

"The Triskele," Sirona said, obviously enthralled.

"It held us," April added, "but not in a frightening way. It was like an embrace, bringing the three of us together as one."

"But then it seemed that I lost consciousness," Tannen continued. "until Poppie's singing stopped."

Sirona and Rowan exchanged a look. Niall ran his hand through his hair, not entirely sure whether he was jealous or relieved that so far in his life, the world had offered no such mystical moments.

"When it was all over," April offered, "and we all came to, so to speak, there was a single poppy blossom at Poppie's feet. Poppie picked it up and signaled us to remain silent – not that any of us could speak. I know I certainly couldn't. Then Poppie led us down the far path to the pool where we sat until reality returned."

"You haven't been here a full twenty-four hours and already the magic is swirling around you like a swarm of bees," Niall said, totally unaware of the appropriateness of his metaphor. All anyone could do was laugh and so they did until their bellies ached and their eyes were awash in tears.

Finally, Sirona calmed herself enough to speak. "I thought we might consider next steps tonight, plan out the days ahead, but we all have much to consider and I think a good night's sleep is in order. Shall we meet tomorrow for lunch and dive into more mundane topics?"

It was agreed. The three held hands as they walked back to Percy's house in the evening half-light, strengthened in their mutual bond and the wisdom of Rowan and Sirona. If truly they had been called here by the Well Goddess, She had already made herself known and fulfilled her side of the bargain. Whether there would be more to come or not, April considered Eudora's words in a new light...*do not resist.* She was here and surrounded by her people, safe enough to surrender to whatever was meant to be revealed.

The next morning, April rose before the others, full of nervous energy. Something was in the air, but she couldn't put her finger on it. Good or ill, she couldn't tell. A walk, she thought, would do her good. She'd get some fresh pastries for breakfast and surprise her friends with a delightful meal. She grabbed a basket hanging in the kitchen (Percy, it seemed, was a master of melding the practical with the beautiful) and left the house, closing the door without a sound. It was a lovely morning. Not sunny, but warm enough with a hint of the sea in the air. As she walked, she hummed quietly, a kind of buzzing hum without melody, but soothing. The coffee shop was just opening its doors and as she entered, the smell of warm dough, sugar and cinnamon mixed with fresh brewed coffee filled the air. It reminded her of college, when she and her friends would end a night of study with carbs and caffeine.

Having secured her bounty of cinnamon buns, she strolled around the side streets, finding one particular alley that begged to be explored. The shops were not open yet, but their windows offered a delightful array of goods, all, it seemed, offered to her alone as she was the only thing (besides a foraging crow) moving on the charming street. That is, until a black sedan pulled up beside her. From an open window, a man in hat and sunglasses drew her attention by asking directions, but before he finished his sentence, she felt rough hands grab her from behind and a bag put over her head and cinched around her neck, plunging her into darkness and fear.

Inside the car, she was wedged between two large bodies that emitted an odor of wet wool and sweat. Her fear choked her, but her mind was clear enough that she knew there was no point in calling out. There was no one to hear. No one. How could such a common morning become so unreal? Perhaps this was one of her dreams, more vivid than any she had had before. But the press of bodies and the movement of the vehicle told her otherwise.

She must have passed out because the next thing she knew she was being pulled from the car and dragged into a building. When at last she was forced into a seat and her hood removed, she found herself in a cavernous room, lit, oddly, with torches rather than electric lights. Her seat faced a raised dais upon which sat a man elaborately dressed, holding a staff of some sort and wearing an odd crown-like hat. To either side of her in multiple rows, people in black cloaks with hoods pulled low over their faces, sat in an arc. Judging by the crawling feeling along her back, she guessed that those rows extended behind her as well. Fear threatened to overwhelm her, but something she couldn't name seemed to whisper, *breathe...I am here.*

"Thank you, Miss Quinn, for joining us," spoke the man on the dais. "You are Miss Quinn, April Quinn I trust?"

April sat in stony silence. No point in confirming what this man already obviously knew and besides, she doubted she could trust her voice.

"I apologize for the cloak and dagger stuff," Vas said, his voice oily with no apology at all, "but you see, or will see, our need for secrecy. Please don't think ill of us. All we want is to hear from your lips the account of your attempt to, what was it, to bring Merlin back to life?"

Who the hell are these people? What is it they think they know, and why me? April's thoughts were a jumble. Silence was her only gambit at this point, at least until she had some sense of what was going on.

"Come now, Miss Quinn," Vas persisted, impatience creeping into his voice. "I'm sure you'd like to return to your friends. Let's get this over with, shall we?"

"I'm not clear on what you want from me," April managed at last, "or who I'm speaking to."

Vas made a short, barking sound – a poor excuse for a laugh. "Let's just say we're a group of concerned citizens. Grave robbing is a serious offense, not, please be assured, that we are accusing you of such."

"I'd like to see some proof of your authority..." April began, only to be interrupted by a now much more animated Vas.

"Our authority, young lady, is that we have you here, alone, with no sense of where you are nor any way to escape. It is up to you entirely to satisfy our curiosity sufficiently that we might choose to release you." Vas sat back in his chair and steepled his hands before him. Something changed in his demeanor that made April tremble. If she had seen silence as her weapon, she now saw it crumble in her hands. In its place, she saw nothing she could use to protect herself.

"Very well then," Vas oozed, "perhaps you are tired and in need of refreshment." Vas nodded to two hooded figures who had been standing to the side of the proceedings.

"Bring Miss Quinn to my quarters if you will. Perhaps a private conversation would be more to her liking."

The hood came back over April's head as she was pulled from her chair and marched out of the room, through musty corridors and into what she assumed was Vas's quarters. Everything in her wanted to fight, but she knew it was useless. There was no world, dream or reality, in which she could escape the bruising grip of the men who held her.

"Please bring her inside. I've prepared a space for her," Vas told the men.

A few more steps, then she was thrown against a wall. Before she could regain her balance, she heard a steel door slam and the click of a lock.

"Oh, do remove the hood, my dear," Vas said, his voice now just inches from where she stood. As April slowly, shakily removed the cloth from her head, she saw that she was in a cage of sorts, apparently in an alcove in what appeared to be a well-appointed room. Vas stood on the only side of the enclosure that was not walled, with only the bars to separate them. His proximity was terrifying. There was something about the man that made April's skin crawl, a vacancy in him like the fetid air of a tomb.

"I promised you refreshment, did I not?" he spoke, his voice mild and unconcerned, as though April were a guest, comfortably seated and willingly present. "I'll get my man to prepare something," he continued. "For now I think it best if you rest." With that, Vas pulled heavy curtains over the bars, submerging April into impenetrable darkness. Fumbling for her bearings she found a wooden bench upon which she sank in despair. Lying uncomfortably on her side, she curled into a ball and let oblivion take her.

Chapter 15

The Space Between

"Sirona, come here. You must see this," Niall called from the kitchen where he had just finished clearing breakfast. Perfectly framed in the window above the sink sat a crow, a rather large one. When Sirona entered the kitchen, it turned its ebony head and stared directly at her.

"My, my, friend. What brings you here?" she asked as she strode slowly to the window. For a long moment, the woman and the crow held one another locked in an unflinching gaze, and would have stood so longer, no doubt, had there not been a knock on the door. Sirona turned to address the visitation, but saw, from the corner of her eye, that the crow had not moved, had not been disturbed by the arrival of humans. Odd.

It was Tannen and Poppie.

"Rather early for lunch my dears..." Sirona began, then saw the look on their faces. "What is it? And where's April?"

"She's gone!" Poppie wailed.

"Poppie and I got up late," Tannen explained, "and April was nowhere about. Her phone was on the table, but she was nowhere to be found."

"Let's go back to the house and look for clues," Sirona said. "Niall, best you stay here in case she comes here, yes?"

"Of course. She may have just gone out for a walk..." Niall said hopefully.

Back at Percy's, the three looked around the house and called out for their friend. Sirona checked April's phone to see if there had been a missed call that might have explained her absence.

"It's been hours now," Poppie said, distraught. "It's not like her to leave without a note or something..."

"Wait," Tannen called from the kitchen. "My dad's shopping basket is missing. That suggests she may have gone out to the store."

As Sirona joined Tannen in the kitchen, she saw that a crow was now in Percy's kitchen window, staring directly at Sirona as it had done earlier.

"So, you have something for us then?" Sirona addressed the crow which, in response, tapped on the window and lifted a wing.

"Come, my dears," Sirona instructed Tannen and Poppie. "We've been summoned."

The crow kept them in sight, but they had to maintain a good pace to keep up with it as it flew from tree to tree, leading them toward the center of town. Before long, they turned into a narrow street of shops, busy with people going to and fro, the shops having long since opened their doors. When they caught up with the crow, they found it pecking at a paper bag, from which had spilled a cinnamon bun.

"Dad's basket!" Tannen cried. "And April's wallet. She's been here."

"But is no longer," Sirona said, vainly searching the street for some sign of the young woman.

As the crow took flight, a fragment of bun in its beak, it flew close to Sirona's face, brushing her forehead with its tail feathers, then was gone.

Opening her eyes made no difference. Her cage was as dark as the room behind her eyes. The experience gave her vertigo, only her body on the bench suggesting any sense of what was up and what down. It was better to keep her eyes closed, but unless she was asleep, that was against her nature. Surely, sooner or later her eyes would adjust and she would see *something.* Her heart was beating too fast, nausea rising in her in waves, her throat too dry to swallow. Then, from somewhere behind the fear, a memory flowed into her consciousness – a vision from the dreaming she had done in the Mother Room. In the dream there was something fearful lurking, but she was not afraid. Somehow, she knew how to flow above the fear. Now, painfully, she rolled onto her back and locked her hands over her stomach, mimicking her posture in the dream. Then she copied the pattern – one deep breath, then another. Panic would solve nothing. Deep breath. Push the fear down, down, into your spine and out your back, into the wood beneath you. Deep breath. Now find the space inside you, between waking and sleep, the place of connection and knowing. Deep breath. Count...*1...2...3...*

Daughter, I am here.

Count...*4...5...6*

He will come. He wants something from you.

7...8...9

Feed him, but slowly.

10...1...2

Make him captive to what you know.
3...4...5
I am here. I am you...

Whether she slept, she could not tell. What time had passed she had no way of judging. The darkness cradled her until at last, the curtains were pulled aside to reveal Ignatius Vas seated just out of reach beyond the bars. *Out of physical reach, yes, but not that of words, winged things that they are. Choose wisely*, the voice inside her admonished.

"Feeling better I trust?" Vas said, signaling to his servant who strode forward and opening a small door near the floor of the cage, slid in a tray of bread, cheese and a beverage. April eyed it suspiciously. It could wait.

"Could you tell me where I am?" April asked, doing her best to keep her voice even and unconfrontational. *Feed him, but slowly.*

"No, I think not. Ask me another question."

So this was to be a game.

"Who are you?" April ventured.

"Warmer, but not on the mark."

"How is it that you know me?" April asked, with a genuine wish to know.

"Well, by your notebook, of course. I've seen into your mind young lady. I would prove it to you, but your book met with...an accident."

The notebook! So, whoever purloined it was working in the service of this unsavory individual. April would have preferred to take some time to process this startling information, but the game was afoot and she sensed that to wait too long before she made her next move might inspire her captor to fold the board.

"What do you want from me?" April knew this was the right question, but asking it made it harder for her to remain calm. It evoked a host of unsavory answers. *I am here. Breathe.*

"Now we're getting somewhere!" Vas enthused, shifting in his chair. "I want to know what your plans are."

"My plans? I'm nobody. What can any plans I have matter to you?" Another question she sincerely wanted to know the answer to.

"Oh, but you are indeed somebody. You are a young lady who loves a dead monk who spouted heretical ideas. Moreover, according to you, you are of the lineage of Merlin. Not that I believe that, mind you. Merlin is a myth. But the beliefs that swirl around that myth are very real...and very dangerous. And... though you cannot be the descendant of a myth, just believing you are – and convincing others of the same – is potentially, profoundly dangerous." Vas stopped suddenly, as if to catch his breath.

He is afraid.

Arguments gathered in April's mind like so many angry demons, but she resisted them. *Feed him.*

"What are these dangerous ideas you speak of?" April felt a shift. The game was beginning to make sense and... she was beginning to enjoy it.

"Well, I believe you know full well, quoter of Pelagius," Vas sneered, "but to clarify, the idea that anything other than God is sacred. That the earth itself is sacred. That it exists for any other reason than to be used by men in the service of God."

In the service of Empire, more likely played in April's mind, but she did not give it voice. Instead, she offered a gentle challenge.

"Did not your God make the earth and all its creatures?" April held her breath.

"God made all, of course," Vas said, an eyebrow raised, quick to sense an ambush but unable to refuse to answer.

"Then isn't that which God has made sacred by definition?" Perhaps too much too soon, April lamented. But the play had been made.

"Don't play theologian with me, little girl," Vas said, anger rising in him like vomit, but he quelled it quickly. "Enough of your singing for today, little bird. Nighty night." And with that Vas rose and pulled the curtains shut.

He'll be back. But for now there was the darkness again. April fell to her knees and felt around for the tray of food, but finding it held back. What would he gain by poisoning it? But another thought stuck her. If she ate, she would eventually have to...but where? The thought appalled her. Why hadn't she taken a look around her cell when she had the chance? Now she was blind again. Perhaps...she took the food off the tray and moving toward the bars, turned the tray sideways and ran it back and forth between them until she found the separation in the curtains, then rotated the tray as far as the bars would allow, revealing a sliver of light. It wasn't much, but it was something. She paced out her cell, found a bucket in the far corner, and gauged the distance between her "bed" and the bars. Then she carefully removed the tray and replaced the food, which she still did not eat, but rather returned to her bed and resumed counting her breaths in the dark until she returned to the in-between place.

It took Malcolm no small amount of effort to find the whereabouts of Abernathy Whitestone. The Brothers' natural paranoia, enhanced by Malcolm's newness to the order and, worse, that he was an outsider, an American, kept many of the Brothers claiming ignorance. With diligence and cunning, however, he found a crack. Apparently, there were those who knew that Vas had special dealings with the new Brother, so playing on that, Malcolm was able to gather information that he cautioned the Brothers "not to bother Vas with." Vas was secretive and mercurial enough that few would dare risk tattling on Malcolm lest they incur Vas's wrath, of that Malcolm was fairly certain.

But now that he stood at the door to Whitestone's rooms, uncertainty filled him. Trusting Whitestone was another matter altogether. He had nothing to hold over him. Malcolm lowered his hand. Perhaps his plan was ill-advised, after all he had gone through to bring April to Vas in the first place. But he'd seen the cage, seen his daughter tossed into it and the cell locked tight. He'd also seen the wolf-like look on Vas's face and didn't like it. Vas had assured him that he just wanted to meet the girl, to intimidate her a bit, to warn her against any grandiose notions that would counter the interests of the Society for the Preservation of Heaven. And Malcolm bought it, but now he asked himself *why*. What had he to gain from their bargain? Revenge on Raina? The camaraderie of the Brotherhood and validation of his mistrust of women? The

Brotherhood was turning out to be a bunch of fanatics and he didn't see himself in that light. And seeing his daughter caged had aroused what few paternal feelings remained in his heart.

He had to take the chance. Besides, Whitestone had nothing to gain by outing him, and he remembered the day he watched Whitestone testify before the Brotherhood. The man was no devotee of the SPH. Malcolm knocked. Waited. Knocked again. When the door opened, he was overcome with the stench of moldy books and unwashed clothes, because of which he would have been content to say his piece from the doorway, but the nature of his business precluded anything other than utmost caution. Introducing himself as one of the Brothers of the SPH was a gamble in itself, he feared, but the effect on Whitestone was useful. Clearly, the old professor would have gladly shut the door in Malcolm's face, but his fear of the SPH trumped his reclusive nature and so, reluctantly, he invited Malcolm into the malodorous apartment.

Breathing as shallowly as he could, Malcolm was determined to keep his story short and to the point.

"You might recall," he began, "that your visit to the Society caused quite a stir, that story about a handful of women releasing Merlin's soul."

"I meant no harm," Whitestone stammered. "It just seemed that they should know..."

"Well, the upshot of it is that they have captured the young girl." Malcolm eyed Whitestone as if to make it quite clear to him that Malcolm held him responsible for any evil doings that transpired as a result of the professor's story, a look that made Whitestone squirm. "Vas," Malcolm continued, "initially put it out that he just wanted to question her, as he did you. To get more of the story. But it has come to my attention that he has gone beyond that and has caged the girl in his quarters."

"Caged? Good heavens? Whatever for? And how on earth did they manage that?"

Malcolm felt the slash of his own guilt in the matter, but was determined to hold to the narrative of Whitestone's culpability.

"Never mind all that," Malcolm said, hoping the man's feebleness would overcome his curiosity. "The important thing is that we have to free her."

"Oh, no, no, no," Whitestone said, jumping to his feet and turning his back on his visitor, waving his hand dismissively, "I'm not your man for that. I study wizards, I'm not one myself."

"Nor I," Malcolm said, a strange feeling of inadequacy flowing over him. "I think we must leave the rescue to others. But I believe you know the people who are associated with her and would know how to get in touch with them."

Whitestone groaned. "You mean that woman, Sirona. Please. Spare me." Then, as though a light came on in his antique brain, he asked, "Why don't you do it yourself?"

"I have good reason not to," Malcolm parried, suddenly coming to the happy realization that he'd cleanly escape having to reveal himself as April's father. "Besides, I don't know her or her people. I doubt they'd trust me or believe my story. You at least have had some dealings with them."

"Much to my displeasure, I assure you." Whitestone replied, moving around the room as though he was looking for something.

"May I remind you, sir, that it is you who set all this in motion? And now there is a young girl in Vas's clutches. In my opinion," Malcolm was struggling here. How to discuss this without revealing his special concern for the young lady in question. "Vas has gone a bit...overboard. Look, I'm not asking any more of you than to deliver a message to this Sirona and let her do the rest." Malcolm held his breath, hoping his arrow had hit the mark. Then another thought came to him. "If you dislike this Sirona as much as you imply, you can put her in a difficult position at the same time that you assuage your guilt about the young girl by delivering a plan for her rescue."

Whitestone paced the room, fingering books, pulling his jacket tight against his chest.

"A young girl, caged you say? Never liked that Vas guy. Something off about him, about that place." Whitestone seemed to be struggling with something, a memory perhaps. "Deliver a note you say? No more than that?"

Malcolm pulled out a folded paper on which he had written a plan, directions to the SPH and a rough map of the interior and outside doors.

"Just this, sir, nothing more," he said.

When Vas returned, he had abandoned his formal vestments in favor of his dressing gown. As he cast aside the curtains, his gown parted briefly revealing that he wore nothing under it. April's pulse quickened and she could feel heat rise on her neck. Vas eyed the uneaten food, but said nothing. Instead he launched into a lecture. As he spoke, he paced back and forth, close to the bars, as though *he* was the caged beast, occasionally pausing to stare hungrily into the recess where his pray shivered, just out of his reach.

He lectured on the value of the Church as a bastion against mankind's inherently evil nature. Asked if April was aware of the Age of Inquisition when brave and learned men sought out and eliminated women who were possessed of the Devil. Warned against the licentious urges one can fall prey to in the woods, the wild places. Lamented that women were necessary for the continuation of the species, when they were such dangerous instruments of temptation, that without them mankind could and would rise to the perfection God intended. All the while, his dressing gown would flow with his movements. April did her best to avert her eyes, choosing to fix on a crucifix hanging just behind and above Vas's head. Was this indeed what the tortured prophet had in mind when he surrendered to his enemies? Is this what he died for?

"I will bring you to the Church," Vas was shouting now, clinging white-knuckled to the bars of April's cage. "I, Ignatius Vas, High Priest of the Society for the Preservation of Heaven, am God's Sword and so help me, I will bring you to the Church. God's light will sear into you and burn this fascination with wizardry from your mind and heart." Then, as though remembering himself, he backed away and in a calmer voice said, "Enough of the darkness. I will leave the curtains open that you might see, that your eyes might fall upon the truth." With that, he turned and walked to the door, but before leaving, he turned back and, having recovered himself, spoke in his oiliest tones, "But mind you, I will be watching."

April sank onto the bench, her head in her hands. *Where are you?* She pleaded. *I am lost. There is no reason here, no reality. I don't know how to fight this...and I'm scared, so scared.*

Her bladder burned. There was no holding back. The pail in the corner was all too visible now. There was nothing for it. She made her way to it, humiliated, telling herself no one in their right mind would waste their time spying on a girl in a cage. Then again, there was nothing right about the mind of the man who held her captive.

At the last minute, Malcolm was overcome with the fear that Whitestone, though having agreed to deliver his letter, would either forget, change his mind, or wait too long. He'd have to be sure it got delivered.

"I have a car, I'll drive," he insisted to the old man.

"Now, just now? I'm not ready, it's late."

"How ready do you have to be?" Malcolm said, stifling an unkind remark about the state of Whitestone's lifestyle. No amount of time would find him a clean shirt. "Might as well get it over with."

Malcolm all but pushed the man out the door. Amid Whitestone's protestation, Malcolm managed to get directions to Sirona's place and park some distance from it but in clear view.

"Just deliver it. That's all you have to do." Malcolm leaned across Whitestone and opened his door.

It was Niall who answered the door. "Can I help you?"

"Is this the home of Sirona?" Whitestone asked.

"Who's asking?" Niall countered.

"Abernathy Whitestone. She knows me," then he broke down. "Oh my God, they have the poor girl hostage!"

Niall grabbed Whitestone by his jacket and pulled him into the house. The moment Sirona saw him she went to him. Poppie and Tannen edged toward the door, but kept their distance.

"Abernathy, what is it? Do you bring us news of April?"

"I'm afraid I do...oh please, do not think I had anything to do with this! A man came to me, explaining that a young girl had been kidnapped by the Society for the Preservation of Heaven and gave me this to give to you." Whitestone held out the paper with a shaking hand.

Sirona took it and moved to the light, her own hand shaking as she read it aloud.

To Whom It May Concern,

I am aware that April Quinn has been kidnapped by Ignatius Vas, High Priest of the very secret Society for the Preservation of Heaven. Below you will find the location of their quarters and a map of the interior of the place. In three days' time, there will be meeting of the Brotherhood in the great hall over which Vas will preside, and so will not be in his quarters which is where he holds the girl. It is common knowledge that his man servant is wont to take himself off to the pub when the Brotherhood meets. You will have only a brief window. The meetings begin at 7:00 and generally last about an hour. There is an X on the map marking a rear door which will be propped open. Everything else you need to know is marked on the map.

Sincerely,

A Friend

Poppie cried out, prompting Tannen to pull her to him, muffling her sobs in his shirt.

"Who gave you this?" Sirona demanded.

"Please, I really don't know him," Whitestone whined. "He said he was a member of the Brotherhood, but obviously, not a particularly loyal one. He was upset about what he thought might be happening to the girl."

"And exactly what is that?" Niall asked, fury rising in his voice.

"He didn't know for sure, only that she was...*caged* in Ignatius Vas's quarters," Whitestone said, watching with dismay Sirona's horrified reaction and feeling his gorge rise despite himself. "Really, I must go. Godspeed in your attempt at rescue." Whitestone backed out of the room, fumbled for the doorknob and left, stumbling down the porch steps.

Had they thought of it, they might have watched where he went, but they were so shaken by what they now knew they could barely think straight.

"*Caged...*" Sirona cried.

"And three days before we can attempt a rescue," Niall said, his hands in a fist.

"We can't wait that long..." Tannen said, breaking off before his voice broke.

"Couldn't we call the police?" Poppie said, her face a veritable flood of tears.

"Not sure it would do much good," Niall said, obviously weighing their options. "This organization might be fairly powerful and all we have to go on is an anonymous note. I suspect the police would be reluctant to charge into a religious establishment on such flimsy evidence. Besides, once we get the police involved, that will limit what *we* can do. We'd be at the mercy of their processes...our hands would be tied. A civilian rescue would then be out of the question."

"What if we tried to break in earlier?" Tannen offered. "We have the map..."

"But not a propped open door or the assurance that Vas will be away from where he's..." Sirona's voice cracked, "keeping April."

"Why would they do this?" Tannen cried.

"Perhaps our actions have caused some consternation among certain kinds of people," Sirona mused.

"But how would they have any clue what you were about?" Niall asked, genuinely perplexed.

"The drone..." Tannen said.

"And the stolen notebook..." Poppie added.

The gravity of the picture that was shaping up as they put the pieces together was terrifying. To think that this organization had been spying on them and was aware enough of their activities to actually kidnap April was beyond even their most paranoid thoughts.

"But how did they know about this in the first place?" Niall queried.

Sirona searched her mind. Certainly none of the original twelve who helped plan the ritual of release would have given anything away, at least not intentionally. Her mind went to Whitestone...he knew of their plans and was hardly reliable. But what would his connection be to this society, and what about the spying in the States? Only one other name came to mind – Malcolm. But a connection between him and the Society for the Preservation of Heaven? She wished Raina were here to help her puzzle this out, but she wasn't, nor was Sirona ready to tell her friend that her daughter had been kidnapped. Not at this point anyway. To burden her with such incomplete information over the long distance that separated them would be like a knife to Raina's heart.

"That's a good question," Sirona replied to Niall's query at last, "but right now we have to focus on getting our girl back. We can hope to unravel the riddles later."

Chapter 16

The Wizard Awakes

It had been a while since Vas had come, but surely, he would make his appearance soon enough. April trembled at the thought, rocking back and forth, her knees pulled to her chest, getting more desperate by the moment. How long could she do this? What were Vas' plans for her? She was faint with hunger and exhausted by loneliness and fear. Should he attempt to abuse her, she feared she hadn't an ounce of strength with which to resist him. And if it was her fear he was feeding on, she was full of it. He could gorge himself, and in the process create more. He might as well draw the curtains and cast her into the inky well of despair for all she could see a way forward.

If this was the result of her carrying the DNA of an ancient druid, she wanted no part of it. She would have cried aloud, but if Vas was watching, she wouldn't give him that satisfaction. Time wore on; her anxiety eventually exhausting her. She fell into a half-sleep, imagining the smell of the coffee shop, the satisfaction of cinnamon buns stowed in her basket...

Daughter, I am here.

What of it? Something in her mind shot back.

Calm yourself, focus. There is a power in you, it is your birthright. Words have power, sounds have power, you have the power to wield them as a weapon.

Dispair welled in April. She had no power. The only thing her "birthright" had gotten her was to be kidnapped and caged. Then a memory stole into her mind. Her mother, confident, secure, standing before her father with April at her side, and in a powerful voice telling him April would be leaving with her, that she was free to get her belongings and leave Malcolm's house. Malcolm standing like a rock, pinned by Raina's gaze, his face slack, his shoulders slumped in submissiveness. April had never seen her father so disarmed, doubted it would last. In a rush, she had grabbed what she wanted and stuffed it into a sack, then she and Raina left the house without incident.

That power is yours. Reach deep into your ancestral knowing. Be clear in your intention. The words will come. I am here.

April was deep in a memory of that fateful day in Paimpont forest, finding the words to complete the ritual as her mother faltered, when she heard Vas at the door. This time, he was dressed more appropriately, his demeanor significantly changed. Loose trousers and a sort of tunic shirt that flowed slightly as he swaggered into the room did nothing to set April's mind at ease. Rather his apparent self-control was even more frightening than the mania he had exhibited earlier. The hairs on April's neck prickled. What had he in store for her today?

Daughter I am here. Trust me. Trust yourself.

As she watched Vas toss himself into the chair just outside her cage, with a false air of innocent friendship, she saw the world as she had once seen it during a partial solar eclipse – things as they always were but with a sliver of another dimension, a cosmic drop-shadow. She took a deep breath and with all the control she could muster, addressed her captor.

"What is it you have for me today, High Priest?" her voice asked, but something else was present in her tone as well.

Was that a raised eyebrow? Did he sense the change in her?

"What would you like, little bird?" he answered with false amiability, showing no sign of sensing anything amiss. "I see you've barely touched the food we've provided. Perhaps you'd like some company..."

As a small part of her panicked, from her deep consciousness she heard *Urge him on. He'll have to open the door...*

"As you like, or not," she said, an ever-so-slight hint of flirtation in her voice.

Confidently, Vas strode to a wooden chest and drew an oversized key from a drawer. Returning to the cell, he opened the door, leaving the key in the lock, and dragged the chair just inside, across from April, but between her and the now open door. He took his seat regally and steepled his fingers in his habitual pose of superiority. April pushed herself back on her bench as far as she could, her shoulders touching the wall. Surreptitiously, she eyed the open door. A pressure, a presence in her egged her on.

"You've told me of your world view," she heard herself say. "Would you like now to hear mine?"

Vas gave a sneer. Back to the game. Why not let his prey imagine some kind of escape? It would make the final pounce that much more rewarding.

"Of course. It's only fair," Vas said inauthentically.

"Then you will hear me out as I have done for you," April said, the voice that was both her and not her full of power, her weakness dissolving in an inner strength that flowered in her as she spoke. Watching Vas' face carefully, she noticed a slight drift in his confidence.

Where the words came from, she wasn't entirely sure, but she recognized them from her studies, from her grandmother's books, from Sirona and Rowan's teachings, and from her own deep knowing. So, this was what all that was about.

"You imagine yourself the voice of your God," she began, gaining strength as she spoke, "secure in your self-righteousness, but I tell you that, for all those who prop you up with similar beliefs, you are disastrously incorrect. You believe that this earth exists for your pleasure and gain. I tell you that it is the earth that owns you and all you need to survive."

Vas' face grew pale, his hands dropped to the arms of his chair. April pressed on.

"You imagine that women are yours to toy with and disparage. I tell you that women are the seat of life, yours included."

April pictured her mother, Sirona, Poppie, Lily, all the women who had loved and supported her. A trickle of anger nagged at her mind, but she held firm, focused.

"You imagine that your salvation exists in some off-planet realm. I tell you that if you are not rooted in this earth, you are lost."

Rowan joined forces with her, as Vas' forehead wrinkled in a disbelief that kept him paralyzed.

"You torture your prophet and ignore his words, but I tell you that his teachings of compassion and interconnection echo the truth you despise."

And now the "heretic" Pelagius was there and it was clear that she had hit a nerve.

"You long for your silent God to speak to you, when in truth spirit surrounds you with its joyful song of interconnectedness for all to hear if they but listen."

And now the image of a cloaked figure carrying an oaken staff stared out of his hood and spoke through April with the pent-up anger of the ages.

"You cling to what you call civilization at your peril. Though the earth-denying might of the Roman way has dominated for two millennia, it is not in harmony with the reality of earth, life, and all that is truly sacred. Ultimately, all will see, hopefully before it is too late, that trees are our kin, that all life is *being* and must be respected, and that our true human role on this planet is not one of despoiler but steward."

April stood up and moved closer to Vas. As she grew in power, the High Priest shriveled.

"These truths I offer you for the sake of all life," She said. "And now," she continued, moving a step closer, fully herself and alive to her power, "lest you want me to break your mind, you will move aside so that I may leave."

Without standing up, a vacant-eyed Vas pushed his chair back, away from the door and April. Another step, another push. Her heart alive in her throat, she stepped out of the cage, slammed the door shut, turned the key in the lock and stuffed it in her pocket. Vas did not cry out or move. How long would this hold, she wondered? As weak as she was, she managed to exit his chambers, fly out a side door, and stumble into the street. Only when she was blocks away from the SPH fortress did she dare stop and catch her breath, exhausted, drained, but free.

And lost. She had no idea where she was or even how far she was from home. And what a fright she must look. How long had she been without a shower, hair uncombed, weak with hunger?

Be calm, daughter. The earth is your friend.

It wasn't hard to find a main road, street signs, buses, cabs. She fingered the key in her pocket. Was it worth anything? While she pondered her options, she watched a crow pecking at a crust on the pavement. Its feathers shone purple in the sunlight, its steady focus was calming. For a moment, she was lost in the simplicity of the crow's world and the discarded crust of bread until a horn blasted nearby, chasing away the bird and bringing April back to reality. She hailed a cab and when it stopped, she explained she had no money, but if he would get her to Glastonbury, her family would pay the fare.

"What's that you've got in your hand?" he asked.

April held out the key for him to see.

"Looks old. I'll take that for the fare if you're willing," the driver offered.

"It's yours," she said, relief flooding her as she slid into the cab and handed him the key, glad to be rid of it. Exhaustion threatened to overwhelm her, but she fought to stay vigilant.

When at last the cab stopped at Sirona's house, she used her last bit of energy to slide forward in her seat and attempt a thank you.

"It's nothing, ma'am," the driver said. "Whatever you've been through, I hope you're in good hands now. Cheers."

April nodded and stumbled out of the cab. Before she was halfway to the stoop, arms enfolded her and all but carried her into the house.

Sirona was beside herself with relief and joy. Getting April into the house and secure from whatever forces had captured her seemed of utmost importance. So bedraggled did April look that Sirona didn't know where to start, how best to comfort her, but there were some immediate concerns.

"Are you ok? Do you need medical attention?" Sirona asked.

"I'm not hurt. Not really." April managed.

"Were you released, or did you escape?"

April forced a poor excuse for a smile. "Both, really," she admitted. "It's a long story, but I'm too gross to be in company. I'm filthy and starved..."

"Have a shower then," Sirona said, already in motion. "I'm going to find you something beautiful to wear while Niall gets a meal together."

April nodded in gratitude. "But just tell me this," she asked her Auntie S. "How long has it been?"

Sirona turned to her, tears sprouting in her eyes despite herself. "Three days," she said, her voice catching. "It's been three days since the morning you went missing. We were planning a rescue attempt for tonight, but that is also a long story. Poppie and Tannen are planning to be here shortly. Should I hold them off for a while?"

Three days. April was struggling to process that information. "No, let them come" she said at last. "I long to see them."

Sirona nodded. "Feel free to run the tank dry," she said, as she turned to the bedroom, struggling to keep her mind clear of horrifying images of what April might have gone through. She is home, safe – shaken, but not destroyed. Focus on that, she told herself.

Poppie and Tannen arrived just as April emerged from Sirona's bedroom, dressed in loose white pants and a stunning tunic in swirling greens and blues, her feet bare and her wet hair pulled back on the sides, but cascading down her back in a mass of ringlets. She flowed into the room with a confidence at odds with what one might expect, given what she had gone through. After many hugs, they finally released her to the repast Niall had laid out for her. Then the stories began.

In the telling, she could see for herself the progression of what had changed in her. For now, all she could share were the events, of which she left out no detail that she could remember. The rest, however, the profound way in which she had been transformed, would have to come later.

"This Vas guy is a piece of work," Tannen said, gritting his teeth.

"He's a fool and a pompous ass," April countered.

"But he has followers..." Tannen protested.

"Some, but not that many that I could see. Yes, his ideas are dangerous, but they are ideas – beliefs – that have been around forever. They can be resisted, and must be. As for Vas, his dogmatism makes him brittle. He can be broken. I might have been able to do it today, but I was intent on escaping. Had I aimed too high I might have lost everything."

Sirona watched April with intensity. Her young friend had clearly undergone a sea-change she was curious to explore, but she knew that, sooner or later, the stress of what April had been through would catch up with her and she would crash. A good rest, and confidence in her security were well advised before exploring deeper things. Besides, Sirona wanted Rowan in on this.

Then it was April's turn to hear the tale of her would-be rescue which seemed to fall to Niall to recount, the others still too overcome by emotions to speak. So Niall told of the visit from Whitestone, the letter with the map and instructions, the assumed whistle-blower from the Brotherhood. April listened with great interest, wondering at Whitestone's involvement and the identity of the renegade Brother, but when Tannen suggested that maybe he and Niall ought to go through with the rescue plans enough to perhaps find some answers, April advised against it.

"For one thing," she offered, "that place is evil. Every inch of it reeks of the worst impulses men are capable of. Secondly, one might rightfully expect that what was offered to you as an escape plan might actually have been a trap. It fits the kind of deviousness Vas is capable of. Dangle me out as a prize to pull in my companions – co-conspirators in his mind – and imprison you as well."

"Damn, that never occurred to me," Tannen said. "I was too focused on getting to you."

"Exactly," April said. "And don't you think Vas would assume that's how you'd react? Finally," April continued, "I suggest we don't waste our time on Vas and his sick Brotherhood. They are merely the manifestation of a larger problem and it is that we need to spend our time and energy addressing."

"I don't disagree," Niall said, "and yet, I'm with Tannen, too. I'd like to know more about this Brotherhood."

"And so," Sirona said, an urgency growing in her, "it's time to convene the ladies of the Tor. We need their help."

That night, as Tannen drew April into the security of his arms. Burying his nose in the auburn sea of her hair, he asked, "You OK?" Just two words when there was so much he wanted to ask, but he'd let her decide what she was ready to share. At least she'd know he was ready to hear it.

It took April so long to answer, Tannen began to believe that she was very much not ok. So her answer stunned him.

"Better than ok," she said. "Now. Yes, I was terrified at first, but I wonder if we don't have to come close to our complete undoing before we are ready to be forged into something strong and clear. For some people, that might take a lifetime of experience, for others...but for me, it happened in the space of three days. But it's complicated."

"I'm listening," Tannen said, shifting his hold on her, but not letting go. How does one exist intertwined with another but give them space at the same time? He would figure that out if it was the last thing he did.

"For one thing," April continued, "it's now entirely clear what we're up against. Vas may be extreme in his views and quite ill psychologically, but in general, what he represents is the worldview that's killing the planet and the life it fosters. I have been seeing all this intellectually. Now I feel it in my gut and my spirit. There's a darkness there, like a black hole of lifelessness and unfeeling, which is terrifying. But it can't be ignored. It must be faced and healed."

"Any ideas on how?" Tannen asked.

"I'm working on it. But as Sirona said, we need the help of others..."

"You said, *for one thing.* There's more?" Tannen asked, sure that there was plenty more.

"Well," clearly April was a bit reluctant to continue. "I want to talk to Rowan about this, but it seems to me that Merlin came alive in me. Please don't think me crazy, but I heard him in my head; he guided me. But also more than that. It was both him and the him in me. I never thought I had the power to move people with words, although I've seen my mother do it, and she claims I can do it as well. Now that I think about it, my grandmother did it with my father, too, though I didn't see it that way at the time.

Tannen brought a hand to her head, weaving his fingers into her curls. "I don't think you're crazy at all. Isn't this what we've been leading up to?"

"I guess it is, but I didn't fully believe it until now. And," again April hesitated, "I'm seeing that I have to fully embrace whatever powers I might have, manifest them in a way that my mother and grandmother were reluctant to." At this, April pulled away from Tannen slightly so she could see his face. Now it was her turn to ask a question she wasn't sure she wanted to hear the answer to.

"Are you going to be alright with that?"

Tannen laughed like pressurized steam exploding through an open valve. "I put up with you going to a bee concert without me, didn't I?"

"Seriously," April admonished.

Tannen's face melted into an expression April had never seen before. "Let me tell you what *I* learned from these last three days. April, I couldn't bear to lose you. I was ready to storm the citadel to find you, as ill-advised as that would have been. Whatever it is you need to do, whatever you become, I won't leave your side."

"That may be a vow you'll regret..." April whispered.

"You forget who I am," Tannen said. "I'm of the lineage of the spirit of Merlin's owl. Once an owl makes a commitment, nothing short of death can break it."

"So we live out an old story in new forms..." April said, amazed at the wonder of her life. The incredible challenges they would face was a matter for another time. For now, they would spend the night intertwined in the joy of synchronicity realized.

Chapter 17

New Blood

Against his better judgement, Tannen agreed to let April go with Poppie and Sirona to visit Rowan while he stayed with Niall. To do otherwise would imply he didn't trust Sirona to protect April, which of course would be bad form.

"*By my side* doesn't have to mean literally, all the time," April had chided Tannen when she had first told him of her plans. "But I promise I will go nowhere alone, and I'll always tell you of my intentions." The truth was, however, that April was as reluctant to leave Tannen as he was to let her go, but Sirona was careful about "crowding" Rowan with too much variable energy, especially if she was going to be doing a soul ritual of any kind. And as part of their protection, Sirona explained that Tuttle's Time Tincture had the effect of deflecting unwanted attention. Logically, people operating at a slightly different time vibration were difficult to get a read on. Not invisible, just *elusive.*

Neither April nor Poppie had ever been to Tuttle's Time Emporium, so it pleased Sirona to watch their reactions as they approached the odd little shop. As they approached, the gold lettering above the door seemed to wink out at them, or maybe it was just a trick of the sunlight. Once inside, the three carefully threaded their way down the narrow aisle that seemed to barely part the sea of timepieces that crowded the shop. Not being much concerned with the passage of time, Poppie was amazed that so much human effort was put into measuring every little bit of it. Then again, perhaps the breaking down of time into minutes and hours was more of a mechanical construct than anything else. Certainly, the contents of Tuttle's emporium seemed to suggest such.

While Sirona spoke to Tuttle of their needs, the two stood as though in a trance, gazing around the shop, using only their eyes to pick out all the different clock faces, ornate hands, and stunning woodwork. To do otherwise was to risk upsetting the delicate arrangement of so much time in such a small space. When at last Tuttle emerged from his back rooms, a cobalt blue bottle between his fingers, it seemed he had eyes only for Poppie as he handed the bottle to Sirona but kept his gaze on the perky young lady.

"Go easy with this one," Tuttle advised, nodding at Poppie. "She's already barely operating at a typical human level." At Poppie's raised eyebrow, Tuttle chuckled and offered an explanation. "No offense Poppie. But you must know that you are eight tenths of a different realm, and entirely precious for being so. That you don't need my humble concoction is a compliment of the highest order, nothing otherwise." Putting a fatherly finger under her chin, raising her eyes to squarely meet his, he reiterated, "Just the tiniest spritz, ok? But know this, Rowan is going to be delighted to sit with you, of that I am certain."

Poppie blushed a rosy hue, but held Tuttle's gaze firmly in her own as a look of mutual fascination passed between them.

For her part, as they left the Time Emporium, April felt a pang of guilt. Tannen would have enjoyed seeing the place and chatting with Tuttle. That he was not experiencing this with her, she realized, was a loss. The more they shared, the more they could count on working together from the same information – two minds working as one. Then again, can two minds ever be as one? We can never truly know the mind of another, she realized. Still, she vowed that going forward, she would share as much with Tannen as was possible.

Rowan was delighted to see them. She ushered them into her leaf-draped rooms, her arms stretched out in welcome, her face creased into an over-sized grin, but Sirona, ever vigilant, sensed the slightest hitch in her step.

Once tea was poured and everyone settled in, Rowan opened the conversation.

"I sense that this is no casual visit. Despite my joy at seeing the three of you, I feel a depression of spirit, nor does the same trouble sit on each of you, but individually you each bring me a different challenge. Who wishes to begin?"

"I believe April's needs are most pressing," Sirona offered, at which Rowan nodded and readied herself.

"I've been...exposed...to profound evil. I feel...tainted. I need your help in cleansing myself of it, but also I need to understand the nature of evil more thoroughly." At that, April told Rowan the story of her captivity, to which Rowan listened intently and without comment. Once the tale was complete, April added what, so far, only Tannen had heard regarding her sense of Merlin's presence within her.

"I will say this," April concluded. "As horrible as the experience was, I believe it awakened the Merlinist spirit in me to the point where I am now beginning to feel comfortable in being integrated with it."

"A blessing, indeed," Rowan acknowledged. "And if I might say so, I felt that in you the moment I saw you. The truth is that there is evil in the world, and always will be, but most of the time it is diluted to the point where it can be explained away or ignored altogether, and so it does its work in a slow erosion of the good. It is rare to find it so concentrated and obvious in one individual as you experienced with this Ignatius Vas. But as you see, there is a blessing here. You now see the enemy clearly. Fortunately, you are strong, with an ancestry whose sole purpose was to stand as guardian for the good. Others, alas, crumble into paralysis under such trauma. Rest assured, as you requested, I can do a cleansing ceremony for you. It will clear away the contamination you feel, but not the anger and determination to counterbalance the disharmony.

"But now, I turn to Poppie," Rowan continued. "What discomfort do you carry with you?"

Poppie told of her experience at the Well, the strange singing that came out of her, unbidden, and her concern that she has no sense whether it is a force for good or otherwise.

"It is a power, to be sure," Rowan explained with no hesitation or surprise. "How you use it is up to you. Since we have opened our discussion today with a consideration of evil, it must be said that one of the greatest threats of evil is the ease with which it can encourage us to fall under its sway. The anger and fear it evokes can so easily be tipped into violence in the name of good, creating a liminal space in which too many well-intentioned people have lost their way."

Rowan reached out a gnarled finger to touch Poppie's cheek.

"You, my fairy friend, have a large dose of the fey in you. I don't even have to do a ritual to see that, so pronounced is it. And as fey, you already function at a vibration above that of pure humans, and so you are less vulnerable to their manipulations. But mind you, once aroused, the fey can grow furious and have been known to create havoc."

Poppie hung her head. "So, my singing could bring death and destruction."

"Not if you don't want it to," Rowan said, deeply sympathetic to the transformation Poppie now faced. "But you must shed the chrysalis of innocence and, like April, accept your powers. Back in the States, you were surrounded by people who were well rooted and kept themselves insulated from malevolent forces, and so you were well protected. I suspect that what is ahead for all of you will be altogether different, as is evidenced by what April has experienced. No doubt that is why the Well revealed your powers to you. You may need them, but you will also need to find new forms of protection, and restraint."

Poppie and April exchanged a glance in which there was an unspoken vow. Until now, they had been friends, frolicking in the joy of that friendship. Now they understood that they were at a decision point. If they were to remain friends, it must be a commitment of mutual support through the inevitable challenges they were destined to face. Not for the first time that day, April wished that Tannen was here as well.

"And you my dear Sirona," Rowan said, turning her attention to her friend.

"Well, you see what we are up against. That April has actually been kidnapped..."

"...suggests that things are afoot," Rowan said, finishing Sirona's thought. "As the powers of the old ways awaken, the fear of them likewise awakens in their enemies, and that fear makes them bold to the point of recklessness."

"And there's the issue of how Vas even found out about April," Sirona continued. "There must be a mole somewhere...and that's a discomforting thought."

"A Judas in our ranks," Rowan sighed. "But isn't there always?" What she didn't say was that in the grand scheme of things, betrayal often played a critical role in moving things forward. That's a larger view, however, that is best taken by those who come after rather than those immediately enmeshed in the conflict.

"Or perhaps it is not from someone inside," Rowan offered, "but rather a spy of some sort. As you well know, we are dealing with more than just the present material world. We'll never know for certain what was awakened in the cave as a result of your ritual, but I'm fairly certain the world of spirit is involved here."

"Nimue," Sirona said, shuddering.

"Perhaps," Rowan said, but there was doubt in her voice that Sirona did not hear.

"So," Rowan said, in the vocal equivalent of slapping one's thighs. "Clearly, we need a ritual of cleansing and rejuvenation. This I can do. April and Sirona, if you would go out to the grove and get comfortable. Poppie, if I may impose upon you, I'd like your assistance."

While April and Sirona made their way out the back door to Rowan's ceremonial grove, Rowan led Poppie into her inner chambers.

As Rowan set the altar, it seemed to April that the surrounding trees were leaning in, watching. On the wooden table at the center of the grove, Rowan spread a glimmering cloth woven in blues and greens that reminded April of the painting on the walls of the Mother Room, the cosmos and the earth as indistinguishable. Upon the cloth, she set a teapot, five cups, a shallow dish on which flower petals smoldered from the heat of a burning bit of charcoal beneath them, a sheathed knife with a wooden handle etched with runes, and a small, cauldron-shaped bowl filled with crystal clear water. Rowan began with the water, passing the cauldron around the circle, instructing each of the women to dip their fingers and anoint the one next to them on the forehead and throat. Next came the tea, an earthy blend that evoked lying in the grass under a cloud-studded sky. April wondered at the fifth cup that sat, filled, on the alter, untouched. As the ritual progressed, it seemed to April that the trees were edging forward, as though they would participate in the circle. Perhaps it was the sound of the wind in their leaves, or the effect of the tea that made April feel both feather light and thoroughly grounded at once, like anything was possible while nothing could shake her.

Then, creeping into her consciousness like a crystalline light came a quiet singing. *Fairy bells,* April thought. What else could it be?

"We are here to bring you cleansing and rejuvenation," Rowan intoned, as though part of the song. "Oak, ash, hawthorn, and rowan, under our protective canopy we give these blessings:

April, may you be free of the poison of evil's touch, but never afraid to look it in the eye and call it by name.

Poppie, may you feel your power as both sword and scabbard, the power of the blade, the restraint of the sheath. Know that your song is in harmony with the universe and heard by all things rooted, airborne, walking or mineral still.

Sirona, may your confidence be restored, your trust in your sight secure. Nothing is perfect, all things fluid. Unfurl your wings, see as from above, know that wrong can be brought right."

As Rowan's voice stilled, the fairy song continued, but grew fainter until it ended. Last to be heard was the wind in the trees, whispering its persistence. *We are always here for you* it seemed to say.

At the touch of cold steel upon their lips, the three awoke. As Rowan sheathed the knife, April stole a glance at the fifth cup. It was empty. Without a word, Rowan led the women back into the house. Savoring the comfort and sweetness of the ritual, the women sat in silence for some time before anyone spoke. The first to break the silence was April.

"The singing...Poppie, was that you?"

Poppie's cheeks blushed like a summer rose. "It was. Rowan coached me, said this would be the perfect place to test my new-found ability. Did it work?"

Sirona let out a hearty laugh. "My dear flower, it was perfect. I can't imagine the ceremony without it. I believe you could tame the most fearsome beast with your song."

April had another question, but was reluctant to ask it. She was certain the trees had moved, bent in and lent their calming essence to the ritual, but something kept her silent about that.

Instead, she asked, "Do you two mind if Poppie and I go outside for a bit?" Having Sirona to herself for a moment suited Rowan. There was something she needed to tell Sirona that she was certain her friend was not going to take well.

"Go out the side door and enjoy the arbor," Rowan suggested. "The grove needs time to clear the energy we raised." *And the trees need privacy in which to scuttle back to their places,* April thought.

Once the young women were out of earshot, Rowan spoke. "You will assemble a group and once more climb the Tor, I expect?"

"That was the plan," Sirona admitted. "I will let you know when we can assemble."

Rowan fixed Sirona with a steady gaze. "I'm afraid I've taken my last climb to the Tor dear friend," Rowan said, well aware of the blow this would be to Sirona, but it had to be so. "But I believe I have a useful substitute," Rowan hurried on before Sirona could protest. "I know a young man who is of Druid blood. He's particularly gifted and insightful, and, I believe, will bring a missing perspective to your work."

"Missing?" Sirona said, uncharacteristically testy in the face of moving ahead without Rowan. In truth, it was difficult for Sirona to imagine a project being successful without Rowan's unique abilities.

"We've been a bit off-balance in our perspective, drawing mainly from older folk and women..."

Sirona opened her mouth to object, but Rowan raised a gnarled hand to silence her.

"There are times when it is appropriate for women to do their work without the involvement of men, as is it necessary to make room for the elders to speak in this world that has lost its understanding of their value. When our project began, the make-up of our team was effective which is proved by our success. But now, we're moving into a different phase, one of bringing a new perspective to the world. To do so, we will have to undo centuries of ingrained bias and purposeful disinformation. Do you imagine that a coven of old women will be able to move that rock alone? You have already seen the importance of April, Tannen and Poppie to our project. We need to cast our net wide, to gather diversity as well as focus to our cause." Rowan paused a heartbeat, then, "Besides, balance on all levels is essential to our goal, is it not?"

Sirona's visage softened. Rowan was right. She thought about how April's youthful enthusiasm had invigorated her, and what happened to her when April and Raina left for the States...but her mind quickly skipped away from the memory of her breakdown.

"You're right, as always, dear friend. It is the younger folk who will carry this project forward and, after all, it is their world now. So tell me more of this Druid."

"His name is Wyn and he comes from Wales. I've only just begun to get to know him, but the power that emanates from him is astounding, unmistakable."

"I trust your judgement, Rowan, but the episode with Vas has me wary. We have a few weeks. Will you humor me and vet him thoroughly?"

"Look into his soul you mean?" Rowan said. "You know that I have to have his permission to do that..."

"If he's not willing to submit to it, then he's suspect." Sirona said, disinclined to relent.

"I understand your concerns," Rowan said kindly. "I'll do what I can."

Just what was it she hoped to accomplish on the Tor this time around? Sirona sat on her porch, St. Michael's Tower visible in the distance. Their first pilgrimage to that summit was in search of guidance about how to proceed with a ritual to release Merlin's spirit from where he had been ensorcelled by Nimue. In that instance, the clear purpose with which they undertook their task resulted in a rich store of insight that ultimately served them well.

Now their purpose was more amorphous, no more than a vague question about where to go from here. And hadn't they already addressed that with Lily's people and received some useful direction? *Circles, blood, a book* came out of their Solstice ceremony and then, after more consideration, the idea that the world needed a new myth and that April would, in some way, be at the center of that. Tapping her pen on the notebook that lay open on her lap, she let her mind drift back to that gathering at the Hedge and Hearth. She remembered now. It was Percy who suggested a new myth. But what would that look like? Perhaps that's what she hoped to glean some insight on by once more climbing the Tor.

But who would go this time? She thought it wise to confine their group to the sacred number of twelve. From the original group she had gotten positive responses from Muriel, Liselle, and Beatrice. Jemma, the keeper of the cauldron, also wished to attend and to bring her wife, Colleen. That made five. April, Poppie and herself brought it to eight. That Rowan would not be attending was a wound that had not yet healed, and although Rowan was sure that her replacement would be quite the prize, Sirona was not convinced. Still, with Wyn added to the mix, there would still only be nine. Sirona folded her hands across her list and closed her eyes. She may have dozed, for she saw Rowan plain as day admonishing her to open the circle, cast her net wider. It made sense. If they were to develop a new myth, they must seek beyond the usual. In that moment, Sirona realized with a start that she had kept her own circle fairly small and select, choosing to interact mostly with folks that were sympathetic to an outlook on life that allowed for the mystical. *Rowan, rooted or mobile, you never cease to instruct.* She would consult with the rest tonight at dinner, and trust that they would find three more trusted, insightful beings to assist them in their supplication.

"Where am I on that list?" Tannen protested around a mouth of food.

"I expect you'll stay here with me," Niall responded nonchalantly, as though there was no question about their roles. "We stay here and keep the home fires burning, tend the anchor line, guard the gate as it were, while our magical women get things sorted."

"I respect what you do Niall," Tannen said, "but I've made a vow to stay by April's side. As I see it, that's my rightful place. I'm not letting her climb up that hill without me."

Sirona watched the exchange with interest, particularly sensitive to Niall's feelings, realizing that he'd enjoyed the prospect of sharing his "watcher" role with Tannen. If the game was going to change, Sirona would have some mending to do. On the other hand, perhaps this was part of what Rowan sensed about how they should broaden their understanding of things going forward. They were indeed, Sirona realized, in new territory.

"But you're not...magical," Niall protested.

"How do we know that?" Tannen countered, all that he'd experienced in these past months suddenly erupting in a new thought. "Who's to say we don't all have gifts that just haven't been realized yet? What is *magical* anyway?'

"Cosmic awareness..." Sirona answered quietly, intrigued by where this was going.

Poppie folded her arms on the table, pushing her plate back an inch. "None of us is just who we are in this moment, in this skin. All of us carry multitudes..."

"I missed Tannen the whole time we were at Rowan's," April admitted. "Not that I didn't feel safe without him," she said, looking at Sirona, "rather it was that I wanted to be sharing the experience with him. Sometimes he sees things differently than I do, or notices things I miss, and that's valuable."

Sirona knew she had to come to Niall's rescue, at the same time that she saw the young people's position, clearly.

"We're in very new territory here," she began. "Rowan told me herself...we need a diversity of opinions, visions, and roles. Niall, your place has always been here and so it should continue to be, but I see the wisdom in having Tannen with us if he wishes to be."

"So that gives us ten," April hurried on. "We still need two more."

"What about Tuttle?" Poppie suggested.

"I don't know..." Sirona mused. "He keeps to himself."

"But this is no social gathering," Poppie persisted. "This is about saving the world!"

"Well, we could always put it to him that way," Sirona agreed with a chuckle.

"Just one more," April said.

Not yet sure of Wyn, Sirona held on to the number two, but did not share her more conservative math.

"We have a few days yet," Tannen observed. "I say we stay alert and perhaps just the right person will present themselves."

Niall rose to clear the dishes, effectively ending the discussion, his expression unreadable.

Tannen, Poppie and April all pushed to join Sirona on her trip to Tuttle's Time Emporium, but Sirona was firm in her refusal.

"I respect Tuttle deeply," she began. "As much as I'd like him to join us, I want to give him plenty of space to decline. If the three of you are there pleading, especially Poppie..."

"...then he might agree against his better judgement," April inserted, "and that would mitigate against him bringing his full energy to our ceremony."

"Exactly," Sirona said with a nod. What she didn't tell them was that when she saw Tuttle last, he seemed a tad diminished. *Thinned* was the word that came to mind. The Tor was a significant climb. There were others who could make up the twelve, but there was no one who could replace Tuttle's special brand of wisdom. Almost, she began to feel it ill-advised to ask him at all, but she didn't see a good way out of it now.

The door to the Time Emporium was locked and there was no sign saying *open, closed,* or otherwise. Strange. Sirona knocked and peered in the window of the darkened shop, her heart racing at the thought that there might be something wrong. Nothing but the usual scene, clocks faithfully measuring time in the dim light, but no Tuttle. She knocked again, to no avail, then walked around to the back of the store. There she saw Tuttle, slumped over in a chair amid the detritus of things discarded. But before she could reach him, he stirred, snorted, and looked up to see his friend speeding toward him, her face ashen with worry.

"Sirona my dear! Whatever is amiss?"

"You gave me a fright! What are you doing back here with the store all locked up?"

"It's early yet!" he said, calmly, failing completely to match Sirona's panic. "Just catching a little snooze in the morning air. I don't open the store until 10:00."

"It's half eleven," Sirona said, trying to hide her amazement that the wizard of time should be so considerably off.

"You don't say!" he replied, still unruffled. "My apologies, then. Let's get inside and get the lights on, shall we?"

Sirona followed Tuttle in through the back door and waited patiently while he turned on the lights, unlocked the front door and retrieved the door sign from behind a mantle clock crouched comfortably in the window.

"There now, that's better. The hordes should be arriving any minute," he said with a chuckle. "That gives us just enough time to put on the kettle and attend to your concerns."

It didn't escape Sirona that Tuttle was a bit off. It's not that he was without humor or light-heartedness when appropriate, but this off-handed nature wasn't typical of him, leaving Sirona even more disinclined to approach him with her request. It was with a great effort that she waited for him to brew them some tea and sit them down in the little kitchen just off the shop.

"Now then..." he said, inviting Sirona to begin at last.

As quickly as she could, she filled him in on their intentions for a ceremony on the Tor and Rowan's concern that they gather some differing perspectives.

"It appears," she concluded, "that Poppie and April are quite smitten with you and would like you to join us."

"I'm flattered," Tuttle said, acting a bit more like himself, "but what do you suppose I have to offer to this latest adventure of yours?"

In truth, Sirona had not given that much thought, differing to the inspirations of the others, or assuming Tuttle would know himself.

"I'm not really sure," she admitted. "Perhaps it's because you are so associated with time and our *adventure* as you call it has to do with bringing the wisdom of the distant past alive in the present, in the hopes of saving the future." As she said it, she realized just how much sense that made and, despite herself, now was fervently inclined to have Tuttle join them.

Tuttle stared into his tea, gently swirling its nearly exhausted contents.

"I know you don't tend to travel much," Sirona said, anxious to fill the silence, "and I warned the others that you were not likely to find this trek appealing, so there's no pressure. But something about what Rowan said made me compelled to ask, regardless."

Still, Tuttle sat silently, head bent toward his tea as though searching for something within its amber liquidity.

"I'll do it," he said looking up at last. "How much time do I have before we go?"

"A week or so," Sirona said, barely concealing her glee.

"I've not been up the Tor in years. Do me good to see it one more time," Tuttle said, setting his cup down decisively.

"I'll be in touch," Sirona said, hugging her friend. "The kids will be delighted."

Sirona flashed her most winning smile at her friend before she turned to leave, but as she closed the door of the Emporium, a worm of concern entered her heart. There was something in the way Tuttle had said the words *one more time.* Somewhere deep inside her, her intuition heard it as *one last time.*

Chapter 18

Ascent

"Get that, would you April?" Sirona called from the kitchen. "My hands are full of dough."

The first meeting of the group, still missing one, was scheduled for that afternoon, a few hours away. Who could be at the door at this hour Sirona had no clue, but someone else would have to deal with them if she was going to get the meat pies finished in time for the gathering. Tannen and Niall were out getting last minute supplies and Poppie was in the backyard singing, as she often was these days. April was the only one in the house beside herself.

The knock came again, unmet with the sound of a door opening or a greeting spoken. Frustrated, Sirona grabbed a towel and knocked off as much flour as she could, then, still working the towel through her encrusted fingers, made her way to the front door, where she saw April standing at the window, frozen.

"April, what is it?" Looking through the window, Sirona saw a figure wearing a black rain cape, the hood pulled low over the face against the weather.

"The Brotherhood..." April said, her voice trembling.

"I doubt it sweetie, it's just rain gear," Sirona tried to reassure April as she made her way to the door, but in deference to April's fear, rather than open it, spoke through it.

"Who is it please?"

"Wyn," came the answer. "Sorry to be here early..."

"It's Wyn, honey. Rowan's friend."

Reluctant to keep her guest waiting any longer in the inclement weather, Sirona opened the door, but kept an eye on April who apparently was not at all assured, as she stepped away from the door, her eyes round with terror.

"Wyn, do come in," Sirona said apologetically, admitting the Druid.

As he entered, Wyn pushed back his hood to reveal a pecan colored face with perfectly arranged features, though a hint of unease played around his eyes. Easily six feet tall with a confident bearing, nevertheless, he hovered in the doorway, dripping wet, well aware that there was some concern about his presence.

"Again, I apologize for coming early," he said, bringing his hands together respectfully and making a slight bow, "but I believe you will understand my reasoning in a moment." Having made his apologies to Sirona, his eyes slid toward April who was clearly, and inexplicably, more than a little upset by his arrival.

Sirona registered the glance at the same time that her whole body tingled with the awareness of his uncanny energy. It radiated from him like heat. His beauty and composed yet appropriately deferential manner caught her off guard, as did the fact that her hands were still caked with dough. Unable to offer a hand in greeting, she tucked the towel she was holding into the fold of her elbow and raised her hands in her own gesture of apology. "Well met, Wyn," she managed.

"I've caught you in the midst of something, I see," Wyn said generously, a smile breaking across his face, lighting up his attractive features with an endearing authenticity.

"Meat pies for this afternoon," Sirona explained, rather needlessly. "But do get your wet slicker off and come through." Then, turning to April who had not budged from the far corner of the room, "April, could you make our guest comfortable while I wash my hands?"

April edged forward with all the grace of the Tin Man, clearly reluctant to offer to take Wyn's cloak. Seeing that, Sirona suggested he hang his coat on the peg by the door, promised she would be back in a flash, and begged him to make himself at home, then gave April a look she hoped would break her out of her trance.

Obediently, Wyn removed his rain cape and hung it in the foyer, then turned to April, careful not to move toward her.

"I'm sorry if I make you uncomfortable."

April blinked as though waking, then, in the warmth of his gaze, found her voice.

"It is I who should apologize. Your cloak...it reminded me of...well, it's a long story. Very silly of me to be so overcome."

"Clearly not silly at all," Wyn said, his voice full of empathy. "I hope I have occasion to hear your story when you're ready to tell it."

Sirona's return saved April from having to find a response to Wyn's gentle offer.

"So," Sirona began, waving Wyn to a seat, "there is something we can do for you?"

"In a manner of speaking," Wyn said, drawing a note from his pocket and handing it to Sirona. "Rowan asked me to deliver this to you. I thought it best to give you some time to consider it before the meeting this afternoon."

Sirona recognized Rowan's scrawl.

My Dearest,

Wyn and I have spent time together in the grove. After sharing with him the reasons for your vigilance, he willingly allowed me inside. I see nothing of concern. If anything, I am more certain than ever that he has much to contribute to your endeavors, but it is not for me to be more specific than that. I will also say that should you still have doubts, he assures me he will not be offended.

In Harmony,
Rowan

Folding the note carefully, Sirona fixed Wyn's dark eyes with her own.

"I'm sorry to have asked for assurances, but this is no casual undertaking you may be included in."

"I understand," Wyn said evenly. "Had it been anyone other than Rowan, and any task less important than yours, I would not have allowed my soul to be searched."

Now it was Sirona's turn to make a slight bow to this young Druid. "It is no small thing to acquiesce to," she agreed. The healer in her wanted to know more. Was the experience instructive? Did it change anything for him? But such information cannot be asked for, only willingly volunteered.

"You see now why I imposed on you by coming early," Wyn said. "Now I will take my leave and should you be willing to have me back, send word." So saying, he pulled out a second slip of paper on which was written a phone number.

"No need," Sirona said, holding up her hand to refuse the number. "I trust Rowan implicitly. Had you anything to hide, I truly believe you would not have been able to accomplish that with her." *Then again,* she couldn't help thinking, *if you were able to, you would be a powerful Druid indeed. Even more powerful than either she or I have sensed. If that is so, perhaps better to keep you close than otherwise.* But the genuineness of his manner was not easily faked, Sirona concluded, no matter how powerful he might be. "You are welcome to abide here until the meeting if you like, or you can do otherwise. It's up to you. Tannen and Niall will be home presently and Poppie is out back. I trust they can provide diversion while I finish my pies. April?"

"Do stay, if you are willing," April said, having recovered herself sufficiently to move on to a curiosity about this young man. "We should get to know one another."

Apparently, it was a day for early arrivals. Beatrice arrived before April and Wyn had barely gotten past tentative introductions, with Jemma and Colleen coming shortly thereafter. Poppie came in from the yard just as Tannen and Niall arrived with Liselle in their wake. Once Niall was there, Sirona could leave the kitchen to him and join the gathering crowd in the living room. Muriel came shortly before the appointed hour, leaving only Tuttle to make his appearance. The hour came and went without him arriving, however, arousing Sirona's suspicion that everything was not quite as it should be with him. She was just about to begin the meeting without him when he arrived at the door, a bit disheveled, and full of apologies for having lost track of time.

Sirona opened the meeting with a "well met" and introductions where needed, then let April fill everyone in on what had happened since their last gathering. It was a long tale. Even April marveled at how much had happened in less than a year, but her audience listened with rapt attention. Sirona could tell from people's expressions that there were many questions, but those assembled were wise enough to seek only the most important information. It was what was to come next for which they were gathered.

"So," Sirona began, "you've heard the three elements that the folks in the States identified, and the conclusion that we need a new myth – one that provides a container for the ancient wisdom that will appeal to and influence the modern mind, while breaking through the sleepwalking routines most are living with. If we did indeed release Merlin's soul to find expression again in our time, we have no way of knowing what that will look like. In the meantime, we cannot wait. You've heard that April has experienced the quickening of Merlin's inheritance in her being and we trust that is just the beginning. How April deals with that is her personal journey, but she cannot do it alone. The power we raised last time we journeyed to the Tor was essential to our success in the forest. Now, it is my hope that calling on that power again will give us insight and direction for moving forward."

"We're honored to be called upon in this way," Muriel offered, as she smoothed the floral scarf around her wrinkled neck. "The cards this morning indicated a positive result, and if I may so suggest, while we planned our last ritual for evening, I believe this one should happen at sunrise."

"A new beginning," Liselle said. "Makes sense."

"That would have us beginning our climb in the dark," Sirona cautioned, well aware that at least a few of their fellowship were getting on in years.

"We can bring torches and take our time," Jemma said, "and as we near the pinnacle, we'll have the company of the pre-dawn light. Quite fitting!"

"And beautiful!" Poppie agreed.

"If there are no objections," Sirona acquiesced reluctantly, knowing she should trust to Muriel's message from the cards, "then dawn it is. We have just one more problem. We're still missing one person to make twelve."

"What about someone from the Chalice Gardens?" April suggested when no one else spoke. "Such a one might already be steeped in the power of the place and make a useful ally going forward."

"I believe I may have a candidate," Beatrice said, brightening. "He helps with the gardens and has a beautiful garden of his own, one might even say a magical garden. He has a relationship with plants that is uncanny."

Sirona hated to be negative, but her hypervigilance could not be silenced. "You all heard about April's run-in with the Society for the Preservation of Heaven. We can't always assume a person's alliances and the SPH is a secret society after all. How well do you know this person, Bea?"

"Fairly well, but I understand your caution. I think I know a way to test him. I can use the power of the Well to draw him out," she said, winking.

April saw Poppie bow her head, but not before April caught the cast of blush on her cheeks. "What is it Poppie?"

Poppie was all sixes and sevens about her new found talent. On the one hand she was delighted and spent hours practicing various tones and musical phrases. But on the other, the responsibility such power required was a weight she was not yet entirely comfortable with. It ran a bit counter to her habitual light-heartedness. In this case, however, she felt obliged to help if she could. "I believe I have a song that will help," she said, blushing more deeply. "While a good heart will find the song beautiful, a dark one will be distressed. To them it will sound like the scream of demons!"

"Beautiful," Beatrice cried, clapping her hands, eyeing Poppie with admiration. "My excuse for seeing him will be to introduce him to a special friend of mine. He loves all things fey and my dear Poppie, it seems you fit the bill."

All that remained was to set a date and hope for good weather.

"And if it's a day like this?" Colleen asked, mischief twinkling in her eyes as she voiced what everyone in the British Isles knew. Never trust to sunny days.

"Who's afraid of a little rain?" Muriel laughed. "We all know how to dress for it."

"And it will still be 'sunrise', " Jemma claimed, "even if we can't properly see it."

Niall had long since entered the room, waiting patiently for a break in the conversation to announce that food was laid out in the kitchen. Maneuvering so as to be at April's side in the food line, Wyn made a proposal.

"We have some time before the trip up the Tor. Could I interest you in a little outing? I thought we might go to Tintagel, enjoy the sea air as we get to know one another better."

Why was she still distrustful of this young man? Perhaps it was just the residue of her recent traumatic experience, or maybe it was something else. Did he have the power of persuasion she had found in herself and used on Vas? Increasingly, she was coming to understand Sirona's hypervigilance.

"Can we come too?" It was Poppie, who'd overheard, either coming to April's rescue, or dooming her to an outing with Wyn. April wasn't sure which, but now the die was cast. By "we" Poppie meant her and Tannen, of course, which at least made everything more appealing.

The tide was out, leaving the entrance to "Merlin's Cave" gaping like a tear in reality. Wyn had suggested that April and he explore the cave while Tannen and Poppie played in the surf. It was clear to April that he wanted her to himself. Why, she wasn't certain, but trying to avoid it was wearing her thin, so she might as well give in and get it over with.

"Do you mind if I cut to the chase?" Wyn began as they sat just inside the cave entrance. "I'm not much for small talk."

"I see that," April said, trying to keep her irritation out of her voice. "What is it you wish from me?" she said, exercising her own brand of directness.

"This thing about you having Merlin's DNA. Can you tell me more about it? How do you know this to be true?"

A much better question for my mother and Sirona, April thought. But they weren't here. She felt challenged. Up to this point, she had been around people who supported the notion of her connection to Merlin so she accepted it without question, resonating with her own experiences that seemed to verify the idea. But now that she was being challenged, would the story hold up under scrutiny? Uncomfortably aware of the possibility that it might not, she launched into every detail that had supported this idea on which she and her people had put so much store.

Wyn listened intently, interrupting only for clarification, giving no clue as to how he was receiving April's explanation.

"I cannot offer you proof," April concluded, realizing the truth of that statement for the first time. "I can only tell you what we believe and what we've experienced."

"And this experience you had when in captivity...can you tell me more about that? How was it that you knew you could control Vas?" Normally, April would have found the question indelicate, but after the gentle way Wyn had listened to her tale so far, she felt safe, relieved even, to be sharing this part of her story. Still, April hated reliving that day.

"I didn't know for sure," she said, a chill running down her spine at the memory. "I was desperate. It loomed as a possibility and I took it. I never felt safe until I was back at Sirona's. I still don't feel completely safe, as you've seen.

It hasn't escaped me that perhaps he let me go on purpose, drawing out a cat and mouse game. He was...is...like that."

"May I suggest," Wyn said, obviously choosing his words with care, "that you fully and completely believe in your power of persuasion. Not to suggest that you become reckless in its efficacy – whatever powers we might have can always be met with powers greater than our own – but believe that it exists in you, and it will be yours."

"Then you believe that I am of Merlin's lineage?" April asked, wondering how she would feel if he said "no."

"Unless we can retrieve a sample of Merlin's DNA from that tree in the cave and match it against yours, there is no way to prove it. On the other hand," Wyn hurried on, seeing the disappointment in April's face, "we all carry DNA from the very first of our kind. What is important here is the likelihood that the ancient wisdom, the ancient *experience* is latent in the DNA of contemporary people."

April stared at Wyn as one might look at the coveted horse or new car one might receive for their birthday. Here was a gift that was more than she dared hope for. Wyn had offered not just a rational explanation that solidified what had previously been based on dreams and assumptions, but he had suggested a powerful idea that just might be the key April had been looking for.

To think she had mistrusted him so thoroughly. Or was the caution she felt born of a sense that here was a depth of wonder in him that, once stepped into, could not be escaped?

"So you're saying that whether it is specifically Merlin's DNA that I carry or not, doesn't matter...that there are latent powers that anyone can access?"

"What do you know of Druids?" Wyn asked, seemingly changing the subject, but April was starting to fall into the rhythm of Wyn's incisive mind.

"I grew up in America," April said, as if it was an excuse for any number of failings. "Other than from fantasy novels, nothing, really."

Wyn smiled at her self-deprecation. "Put simply, as a Druid one studies and practices, inviting the power, the energy of the planet, inside the self. Perhaps DNA plays a role in one's success in the endeavor...to my knowledge that has not been studied. But whether it does or not, there are now and always have been people who connect with the energy that pervades the natural world. In a few, the ability just *is*. In others it requires study and practice."

"And in others, too many others," April said, "such connection is an alien concept, either ignored or actively avoided."

"So it would seem."

"At the risk of embarrassing you, Wyn, I have to say that you are the missing piece in our quest," April said, emboldened by the exciting possibilities Wyn's words were igniting for her.

"You have Rowan to thank for that," Wyn admitted. "But, April, let me say this. I know we are young and inclined to believe we must wait to take our place in the affairs of humankind, but we must get over that. It may well be that we are in the final hours of human life as we know it unless drastic changes are made. If we are the ones to do it, so be it. We must set aside our sense of place based on age and live into the power and knowledge we have. You are clearly gifted, child of Merlin or otherwise. Believe in it, act on it, and apologize for nothing!"

As Wyn uttered those words, a jagged shadow sliced into the light at the cave's mouth. Tannen and Poppie stood there, soaked to their waists.

"Tide's coming in you two," Tannen warned them. "If you don't want to be swept out to sea, we'd best get to the stairs."

Gaias Brightly was not your ordinary gardener. As local legend would have it, he routinely talked to his plants, praising their beauty, asking them what they needed, and, more often than not, in return getting inside information on weather, the lives of bees and the excretory habits of birds. His gardens were a wonder. Flowers and vegetables thrived while there was rarely a weed to be seen, the common explanation for which was that when a weed did appear, he would address it gently but firmly, explaining that he admired their role in the grand scheme of things but that their particular contribution was better appreciated along roadsides or on mountain slopes where their hardy roots helped protect against erosion, rather than in his garden which he had designated as a safe haven for more delicate flora. In nearly every case, the offending plant would be gone by the next morning and in its place some token of mutual respect – a charming pebble, an acorn, or a mystery seed which, when allowed to sprout, often resulted in a rare and beautiful plant.

In his person, Gaias so resembled the likes of fairytale elves that many had doubts about his parentage. His face was pleasingly spherical, punctuated by a modestly bulbous nose, above which sat eyes of such a piercing blue one might suspect the sky had bestowed a piece of itself on the face of its favorite gardener. But the ears...oh the ears! For peeking out from among a disarray of gray hairs, one could often spy just the slightest piece of pointy flesh. His similarity to the likes of elves and hobbits was enhanced by the fact that he made no bones about certain sections of his garden being reserved for the fair folk, and for them alone. Woe betide any human who violated those sanctuaries, despite their excuses that the charm of the place drew them in against their will.

So it was no surprise then, that when Beatrice and Poppie invited Gaias for a walk in the Chalice Gardens, he gleefully accepted. Nor, when, trudging up the incline, Poppie sang her song, as though casually humming to herself as people sometimes do, Gaias was moved to tears.

"Where did you learn that charming song?" he asked when he could recover his emotions sufficiently to speak.

"It just...came to me," Poppie admitted truthfully.

"You must come and sing it to my plants," he exclaimed, his eyes twinkling with anticipation. "What a lovely treat for them."

"I would be honored to," Poppie replied, then, waiting a beat, shyly countered, "and in return we would ask a favor of you."

At that, Poppie and Beatrice explained their need for a twelfth member of a ceremonial expedition to the summit of the Tor, to which Gaias agreed immediately. At the Chalice Well, Beatrice suggested they sit for a spell so that she and Poppie could fill Gaias in on the nature of their mission. As they did so, it seemed to Poppie that every leaf and bud surrounding the Well leaned in as though listening, and at certain points, without a wind to assist them, rustled and waved as though in approval of what was said.

Two by two, in pairs of one elder and one youth, the twelve found their way up the Tor in the early morning darkness. As their torchlight bobbed and skittered across the landscape, a gentle wind brought the smells and sounds of the earth before human rising. There was little talk, and that in hushed tones only, as though the band of twelve would pass through the sacred space unnoticed.

When the sky began to lighten and the birdsong became a chorus, the spirits of the twelve rose accordingly. Once on the summit, they instinctively arranged themselves in a circle to await the sun's arrival. As they did so, Poppie began a soothing and joyous song, an invocation that gained volume and momentum as the sky lifted. When at last the sun offered its first sliver of light, Poppie ended her song and every face became as a sunflower, turning in gratitude to the source of all life. Eyes closed against the growing brilliance, each person in turn made their own prayer of gratitude, then turned to the center of the circle and prepared to hear with open heart whatever insights should emerge, confident that the spiritual energy of the earth knew of their need. As sunlight spread across the hilltop, hearts and minds focused, thoughts were distilled to their essence, and the work of the ceremony began.

Muriel was the first to speak. "The cards are adamant," she said. "We must restore the balance. Young and old, woman and man, humankind and the *rest* of nature. As long as a piece of the whole is suppressed or oppressed, there is no health, no growth. Most particularly, the feminine has been degraded and silenced which is suicidal to human existence. From that willful perversion, all other toxic behavior stems. By oppressing the Mother, we oppress the earth itself and all life upon it. If humankind doesn't soon understand this, then our tenure here will end. That message was unequivocal."

"I've spoken to the plants," Gaias began tentatively, well aware of his newcomer status, "and they asked me to share this: each blossom has its own unique expression, filling the world with variety and inspiration, but the real truth is at the center. For regardless of the variability of shape and color, seasonal emergence or level of beneficence, they share the commonality of existing for their seeds, the guarantee of the future."

"A future with which humankind has, so far, been reckless." Tuttle said, seamlessly picking up the thread. As he spoke, it seemed to Sirona that his body flickered in and out, like a hologram. But his voice was firm. "There are those who, bless them, still cling to the ancient wisdom, but far too many live and function in a narcissistic irony, valuing glittery pleasures at the expense of what is fundamental to survival. They're so blinded by what they think they must have that they destroy what they truly need. Is there a way to wake them up, to take them to the center as you suggest, Gaias? I believe that is our mission."

Liselle looked up from where she had been studying her hands. "The circles are formed, April. Beatrice, Muriel, Jemma and Colleen and myself have all established story circles. For now we've been busy sharing our personal stories and building trust among ourselves. I believe we're ready to raise the energy at the center, but we need some guidance, something to work with..."

"That is the place for the new myth," Sirona said, feeling the voices coming together in a cohesiveness that sustained her hope that they were on the right track. "Hold fast to those circles, hold that space. As you've seen, April has been studying and seeking. I believe that a new myth will emerge..."

"There are women in Ireland who keep alive the tradition of the wise woman." Jemma smiled at April across the circle. "They are called *Seabhean*. Perhaps you could study with them, and," her smile exploding across her face, "stay with Colleen and I while you do."

Suddenly Poppie grew agitated. "Something's the matter with Wyn," she cried. All eyes turned to the young Druid. His eyes had rolled back in his head and his body trembled where he sat. Sirona flew across the circle, checked his pulse and put a hand to his forehead.

"His vitals seem fine as far as I can tell," she said. "I believe he may..."

The Spirits of Earth would have you know of this, he began, in a voice not quite his own. *Three things you must heed and not fear them, for they will come to pass whether you welcome them or not. But beware, in the wrong hands they will destroy you and all you hope to accomplish.*

Take note, first of all, that there will be children, twins, born of the one to whom all eyes will turn.

Secondly, a stone circle will appear where none has ever stood before.

And finally, heed the trinity, the interplay of the three. From it will emerge the blueprint you seek.

These things are given to you in trust. Guard them well.

At that, Wyn's head fell upon his chest and his body relaxed. Sirona continued to crouch before him, holding his shoulders until, at last, he looked up and his dark eyes met Sirona's own in recognition.

"You have prophesied," she said, looking at the young man with admiration and wonderment, but resisting the urge to smooth her hand across his moist forehead.

"I'm aware," came his reply, regaining his composure with practiced ease. "The veil is thin here, and the Earth Spirits restless. There is a sense of urgency they wish to convey. So far, they are committed to doing no harm, but time is running out. If you ever doubted the importance of what you are about here, doubt no longer." Then he turned his eyes to April who sat stone still, feeling the weight of the responsibility she could no longer doubt that she carried. "Lady, you have my unflinching devotion, and unbridled support of whatever power or wisdom I can offer."

Before April could respond in any way, if she could at all, the sun disappeared and a misty rain began. True to their lack of illusion about predictable weather, everyone had come prepared...rain gear was donned and tucked under them to protect against the damp, but no one moved to leave. Instead, as one they turned their faces heavenward. There was an unmistakable sweetness in the mist that covered their skin. Whatever it was washing away was personal to each of the twelve, but as a body, they were all refreshed, rejuvenated, and replenished for the work ahead.

Chapter 19

Sacred Alchemy

The scene looked more relaxed than it actually was. The heat of the day – unusual for late summer in England – held on even as the sun prepared to retire, promising an evening that would demand as little activity as possible and a stillness designed to catch the slightest breeze and hold on to it appreciatively in the hopes that it would last. Niall, Sirona, April, Poppie, Tannen and Wyn lounged in a loose semi-circle around a table strewn with cheese and biscuits and glasses of lemonade sweating into tiny lakes. Poppie had just finished singing her latest creation, a song of relaxation intended to bring the listener a serenity just short of sleep, in this case not quite as effective as she had hoped, for while the night demanded rest, urgency sat in the minds of the six like an itch. Plans needed to be made, but since the Tor, a kind of paralysis of enormity had set in.

Wyn had been invited to stay on after the ceremony, dividing his time between Percy's house and Sirona's, who used at least part of her time to share with him the vision she had had of Nimue in Arthur's court and the subsequent breakdown she had experienced. Wyn had been profoundly sympathetic, but had not as yet shared with the group some of the thoughts he'd been marinating. Perhaps tonight was a good time to offer the altered perspective he had on the whole Nimue and Merlin thing. Perhaps it would shake loose the inertia they seemed to be suffering from. At the very least, it would make a good story.

"If I may," Wyn began, "I'd like to offer a slightly different perspective on Nimue and her relationship with Merlin."

Despite the heat, his listeners stirred, leaning in with apparent eagerness, no one more eager than Sirona to hear his views. Heartened, Wyn continued.

"As I understand it, casting Nimue as an evil enchantress was more the product of recent tellings than the earlier, more original tales of the Arthuriad. In some tales, Nimue is also the Lady of the Lake and her relationship with Merlin not antagonistic, but one of genuine affection. So in that light, is there a way we might see his ensorcellment differently than we have been?"

"Not easily," Tannen replied, still caught in his own trauma from April's kidnapping. In his mind, there was nothing good about being trapped.

"Let's remember this," Wyn continued. "We know of the Roman slaughter of Druids on their Isle of Anglesey in the mid first century and continued genocidal attitude toward them throughout the ages. Merlin was among the last of his kind and it is given that even Arthur had at least a tolerance for Christianity if not sympathy. Could it be that Nimue was aware that Merlin was in danger? If he had met his death at the hand of the Christians, it may have been that his memory would have been erased from history. But ensorcellment...what a tale to be told! He would be free of pursuit, but not exactly dead and done with."

"My vision of Nimue and the monk," Sirona said, immediately catching the drift. "I read it that she was being *recruited* as it were, and no doubt that was the monk's intent, but he could have been inadvertently revealing to her Merlin's imminent peril."

"She might well have played along and seen how to use that as part of her plan to make it *look* like she was Merlin's enemy," April said, excited by the intrigue and possible use of misdirection. Brilliant.

"Still," Sirona said, her face a tableau of the agony she felt around Merlin's demise, "such a fate..."

"And yet look at the result," Wyn said kindly, touching her arm to signal that he was not discounting her feelings. "There are few more alive in the imagination of humanity than Merlin and the wizards who are patterned after him. And there is your experience of him in the cave...a presence that would have been impossible if he'd been killed outright."

It was an intriguing thought.

"But how does love do that to the beloved?" Niall asked, such behavior alien to him.

"Don't forget," Wyn replied, "this was a time of a worldview much different than ours. Personal sacrifice for a greater good was not uncommon. Modern western society is caught up in a fierce individualism at the expense of the community rather than the other way around. Indeed, it seems we've evolved to be blind, completely blind even to the *concept* of the greater good. We've set ourselves as more important than even the earth itself. *But,* by her ensorcellment of Merlin, Nimue has in effect put him on ice, preserved him, for this very time, this tipping point in the history. This is at the very heart of your endeavors and Nimue's actions have made it all possible."

"Your comments to me in the cave," April said, visibly connecting the dots. "You suggested it really didn't matter that much whether I was of Merlin's lineage or not. Because the idea of him was alive in my mind, I could access those powers in myself. Perhaps we all could."

"And that goes both ways," Poppie said. "The wizard, magician, Druid, whatever, is an archetype, an idea that came from us in the first place and then some of us live into it."

Tannen shot Poppie a look.

"My songs are showing me things," she admitted. "And Wyn has been teaching me as well."

"This is it then, isn't it?" April shot out of her chair and paced back and forth while the others waited for her pronouncement. "We all have it, we are all descendants of the indigenous people who could connect with the spirit of the planet. That knowledge has to still be in us somewhere!"

"But how do we get to it?" Tannen said, not meaning at all to challenge the idea, but to move it to the next step.

"That's what we've got to figure out, but first, I need to find more of it in myself," April said.

Tannen shot her a look to which she nodded in the affirmative.

"So," Tannen began, standing and moving to April's side, "we've decided we are going to take Jemma's offer to go to Ireland and live with her and Colleen while April studies with the Seabhean, if they'll have her."

Niall was the first to speak. "Sounds like a good plan. And you'll still be on this side of the pond which will make many people quite happy."

"True," Tannen agreed, "but there's more. We need to go back to the States first to...get married..."

Heat be damned, the lazy evening transformed into a mayhem of hugs, cheers and a few tears. Wyn hung back, but his smile was genuine as he watched in appreciation of not just two individuals finding their wholeness in one another, but the playing out of the archetypal marriage of masculine and feminine. Whether they were aware of it or not, their marriage would be part of the process of transfiguration they were seeking for themselves and for the world. Even knowing April and Tannen for so short a time, he was confident that their marriage would be one of equals.

Aries Lake, USA

"Don't tell me you've been up all night?" Art said from the doorway of Raina's studio. Once he'd announced himself, he moved into the room, his eyes wide at what he was seeing. "What are you about, woman?"

"If you can't tell," Raina chided, "then I've yet to be successful."

On the wheel, which Raina stopped as soon as Art appeared, sat a half-finished pot, no less than a foot and a half across, and scattered across the work tables were clay rings, obviously destined to become part of the pot Raina had been working on when he arrived.

"None of this was here yesterday," he observed.

"No it wasn't, but it's here now and don't you dare touch a thing," she said, hopping up from her stool to stand beside him, wiping her hands on a damp rag as she went. "They're still too wet to touch."

"So you did work all night," he said, half accusatory, half congratulating himself for his astuteness, but folding his arms across his chest to assure Raina that the wet clay would not be violated by a stray gesture.

"When the muse calls, one is wise to not just listen, but follow directions as well." Raina was laughing now, obviously full of creative energy despite her lack of sleep. Confident that Art had his body under control and posed no threat to her carefully measured and pulled pieces, Raina returned to her wheel, pulling Art with her.

"So you have no idea what this is, or rather will be?" She asked, holding out her hand as though to introduce Art to a new friend.

"Well, it looks for all the world like you are building a rather large pot, but it's too big to cook my stew in."

"You're so funny, Art Fisher, but I think you know what this is hoping to be."

"You've said from time to time that you would like to make a cauldron, but didn't think you could. I guess that has changed?"

Serious now, Raina said, "I hope so. I won't know until it's complete, but so far so good. And, even if this one fails, I've made a start at least. And besides, it's only clay."

"So why now?" Art asked. He rarely let Raina get away without sharing her processes. She was such a delightful puzzle to him – one he'd seen as a blessing in these later years. He knew from the first time he met her that suddenly, here was an opportunity for a whole new world to explore. That they didn't have a lifetime of years to accomplish it, however, he was well aware.

"Dreams," she answered, "what else? I don't remember the particulars, but I awoke in the middle of the night with an urgent sense that April would need a cauldron and that it was me who needed to make it. So here I am, trusting that if it's needed, I'm meant to be successful, sooner or later."

"Anything I can do to help?"

"It's going to get heavy," Raina admitted. "I'm not a good enough potter yet to make something this big and keep it thin and light as well. You can help me move it when the time comes."

"I'm at your service, lady," Art said with a bow. "Now, do you want breakfast or are you going to keep working?"

"Who can turn down a Fisher breakfast?" Raina replied. "Besides, I need to wait for the next ring to dry enough to put it in place."

At breakfast, talk turned to the gang in Glastonbury. They'd not heard much about what was going on. They wanted to assume that no news was good news, but Raina confessed to feeling trepidatious from time to time, admitting that a few days ago she had a nagging feeling that April was in distress. It was agreed that they would send an email after breakfast, take a refreshing swim, then Raina would return to her clay work, Art promising to leave her alone for as long as she needed. No surprise adventures, no marvelous displays of natural wonders he would call her to see. He would tend to his work and the beauty of the lake on his own...but nothing less than a magic cauldron could elicit such a vow from him.

For Raina's part, the itch was palpable. The clay called to her, literally making her palms tingle, the only cure for which was to coat them in the slip that sloughed off the wet clay as she worked it. The feel of the pot beneath her hands was infectious. Even after she had successfully bonded a ring to the base, she would wet her hands and with the lightest touch, hold them against the spinning vessel. As she did so, the face of her daughter would often float into her mind and more than once she found herself whispering to her. *May you be well, may you be strong, may you find a love that sustains you. Bless you for what you've taken on, bless you for forgiving me, bless you for being so unafraid.* Over and over she would speak the words, either in a whisper or silently in her head as her palms caressed the swirling clay, until all the elements – the blessings, the clay, her hands – became as one.

By late afternoon, she had successfully added three rings, bringing the pot nearly to the rim. As she sat back to assess her work, she noticed that the pot was not flawlessly round, despite the fact that it certainly felt that way when she worked it. Clay has a mind of its own, she had realized well before this, and though it submits to the will of the potter, it rarely if ever does so without making its own statement, its own minor (if one was lucky) oddity that kept the piece slightly imperfect and the potter consistently humble.

Raina's will wanted to throw what she hoped would be the final ring, but her back ached, her legs were beginning to tremble and she would have to find Art to take the pot off the wheel to make room to throw the next and final ring. She knew that to keep working would be asking for trouble. So far, so beautiful; tomorrow was another day.

She rinsed her hands in her bucket, slipped out of her apron, then took a plastic garbage bag and gently laid it across the pot where it sat, tucking the edges under the wheel head. On wobbly legs, she made her way out of the studio and onto the porch for a late afternoon nap. As her mind moved from wakefulness to sleep, she imagined designs encircling the finished cauldron. Geometric slashes like those on Neolithic pots, or Celtic-like swirls? Leaves, flowers, birds? Busy or plain? But exhaustion overcame her restless mind and soon she was oblivious to the world singing its summer song all around her.

When Art came upon her, he stopped with his foot on the bottom step of the porch, pleased to see that she was resting at last, and delighted at the beauty of her graceful repose. He'd had a reply email from Glastonbury, but he'd not wake her. He'd wait until she awoke on her own to tell her that their loved ones would be coming home in just a few days.

On the day the "Glastonbury Four" arrived home, all hell was about to break loose on Aries Lake. The sky had darkened and a sheet of moderate rain was clearly only a prelude to what was about to descend. With little time to get situated, the four scrambled into Art's cottage where Raina, Percy and Lily were eagerly awaiting them. As soon as all were safely inside, a double-pronged lightning bolt hit the center of the lake with a heart-stopping thunder clap directly on its heels. Then another strike and the power went out just as thunder rolled across the roof. When the rain came in earnest it obliterated any view of the lake and lashed against the windows. Art was ready with candles and oil lamps, setting them decoratively about the great room.

"Might as well get comfy," he said. "Looks like we're not going anywhere for a while. Let me get some munchies and stout and we'll just pass the storm hearing the tales I trust you are bringing us."

Sirona stood at a window, arms folded across her chest, watching the deluge with an unreadable look.

"We needed the rain," Raina said, approaching her friend. She had missed Sirona, missed the light-hearted and indomitable woman who had brought her out of a compromised state and into wholeness. As their shoulders touched, she felt the tension her friend was carrying.

"So," Raina said quietly, "not all the news you bring us is good, then?"

"Some of it will be hard to hear," Sirona said, tilting her head towards her friend, "but in the main, everything is ok for now. This storm. You're right. We needed it. So much has been building. It will clear the air."

Wordlessly, the two stood together and watched the rain etch tiny gullies in the dirt. Nothing remains unchanged, but some things cannot be eroded, despite the storms that assail them. Things like friendship.

There was a comfort in the room, as there often is when the weather rages and the roof holds. Amid the snacks and the stout, small talk fluttered among them as they worked their way toward sharing the more significant things that had taken place over the past few weeks. Finally, sensing that for some reason, the Glastonbury crew was struggling to begin their tale, Art's curiosity got the best of him.

"So," he began, looking from one to the other of them, "you've maintained a radio silence for these past few weeks. We assumed you were too busy to communicate?" He did his best to avoid sounding judgmental but the four knew full well the reason they had kept quiet about things and knew as well that there would be some consequences for that.

Sirona opened her mouth to speak, but April beat her to it.

"So," she said, drawing a long breath, "I was kidnapped by the members of a group that calls itself the Society for the Preservation of Heaven." As she expected, the room erupted in a storm of its own, but April took command, raised her hand and forged ahead with the story, leaving out few details. Raina was beside herself and casting a glance at Sirona flashed the thought to her – *so this is what you meant!* Art sat white-knuckled in his chair, while Percy hung his head, hiding the emotions that ripped through him. Lily, no stranger to the likes of Ignatius Vas, covered her pain with a practiced stoicism.

"Dear ones," April said, bringing her narrative to conclusion. "As horrible as this is to hear, know that I am ok. Supported by the love and goodness of all of you, I know my worth, and know as well that Ignatius Vas and those who believe as he does are part of our quest. We cannot hide from them, ignore their plots, or fight them on their own turf. If we are to be successful, the more we know about them, the more likely we are to find a way to overcome the effects of their worldview. And, most importantly, the event triggered the awakening of Merlin within me. Who knows if, how, or when that would have happened had I not undergone that duress. I imagine," she continued, looking at her mother, "that what I experienced has its parallel in childbirth. Wonderous things cannot be born without pain. It is the way of things and we can't expect it to be different."

"And," Raina said, her voice quivering, "the pain we forget, but the thing that is born is ours to cherish forever."

"Just so," April said, smiling, proud, as always, of her mother's bravery. "Just so."

Now that the worst was out in the open, the rest of their tale flooded forth. Lily was pleased but not particularly surprised to hear of Poppie's fairy singing; Percy was curious about Wyn; and all of them were transfixed by the events on the Tor, most particularly the prophecies. The hours flew and spirits rose as everyone realized they were even farther along in their goals than they would have thought.

As the thunder receded into the distance and the rain dwindled to a mist, Tannen rose and cleared his throat. All eyes were upon him as he made his pronouncement.

"And so," he said, clearing his throat before he could proceed, "we've saved the best for last. April?" he said as he motioned for her to join him standing. "We have decided that we are going to Ireland so April can study with the *Seabhean*...and... before that," putting his arm around April's waist and pulling her close, "we wish to be married, and soon." Another eruption, this one full of joy and suspicions realized.

"A wedding?" Raina was beside herself. She'd never had much doubt that April and Tannen would eventually tie the knot, but that they wanted to do it post haste was both thrilling news and cause for consternation. How to prepare on short notice? But the couple assured everyone that all they wanted was a simple, homespun event.

"We'd like our elders to bless us! Mom, Sirona, Art, Percy and Lily. Would you be willing to do that?" April asked.

Art rubbed his hands in glee while Percy grabbed Tannen in a bear hug and Lily nodded and let a wise smile escape her lips. For her part, Raina suddenly realized why she had been inspired to make the cauldron. It must be finished for the ceremony. Only the pleasure of being with her daughter kept her from fleeing to her studio on the spot to finish the project.

The date was set for early September, three weeks hence. The room was on fire with the excitement of plans to be made.

"Are you good with having it here, lakeside?" Art asked, pretty sure of what the answer would be.

"Where else?" April and Tannen answered as one.

"If you don't have plans for a dress yet, I'd like to make you one," Lily offered to everyone's surprise and delight.

Sirona had a special offering, but she kept to herself the information that Rowan had made a special tea for the couple, one blessed with a spell of protection against enchantment. Whether or not Rowan had discerned the coming marriage, Sirona had no clue, but married or not, Rowan planned for their protection.

Art called for a toast with his home brew, his most recent batch being something of an enchantment itself, his brewing skills having reached a level almost beyond perfection.

And so the day moved into the evening among hugs, well-wishes and more plans, until it was clearly time for folks to gather their things and settle in their respective homes for the night.

"Your daughter is looking for you," Art informed Raina from the door of her studio where Raina had been working diligently since early morning.

"Don't let her in!" Raina said, quickly rinsing her hands and reaching for the plastic to cover the pot, now nearly complete.

"I made her wait on the porch..." Art assured her.

"Sweetheart, what's up?" Raina said trying to sound casual but suddenly aware that there were smudges of clay on her arms.

"I might ask you the same, but I expect you won't tell me," April said, happy to let her mother have her secrets, although the fact that they had something to do with clay was obvious. "I'm wondering if we could take a walk?"

"Absolutely. We could try to get to the waterfall, but we'd best wear long sleeves."

"I've already packed a lunch, could we leave in an hour or so?"

"Of course." Raina gave her daughter a long hug. She had changed. Less innocent, but radiating a beauty and confidence Raina couldn't help marvel at. This was her daughter. Despite everything, she was here and thriving. A walk would be grand. Raina welcomed the time alone with her.

"I'll get cleaned up and be ready when you get here." Reluctantly, she let her daughter go as she wrestled with the urge to hold her close forever.

It wasn't an easy trek, but they laughed at the thorns grabbing at their shirts and the sweat rolling down their backs. At the falls at last they took off their shoes and plunged their feet into the cool water of the stream. There were so many things Raina wanted to ask, but she let April take the lead.

"I need to go see Dad," April said, pulling her feet out of the water and gathering her knees in her arms as she turned to face Raina. Raina felt the stinging in her eyes and throat as fear rose in her chest despite herself. But April wasn't asking for Raina's permission or admonition against getting anywhere near Malcolm.

"Before or after the wedding?" Raina asked, if nothing else, prepared to advise her to wait until she was safely married.

"I originally thought before..."

"Not to ask his permission I hope...." It was a criticism of Malcolm, loaded with all her distain for the man, but as she said it, she realized it sounded like a criticism of April. If that's the way she took it, she didn't let on.

"Of course not. But I want him to know I'm married and moreover I need to confront him. I can't get over the feeling that he had something to do with my kidnapping."

Raina raised her eyebrow.

"The spying here, knowing I was in Glastonbury. I can't figure how he knew *where*, but its more than that. When I was in their hall, being questioned by Vas, Dad just came into my mind for no logical reason. Then, when I was taken to Vas' rooms, one of the two men who held me, just seemed familiar and he held my arm more tenderly it seemed."

"And yet he was dragging you to a cage."

"I know. It seems contradictory and yet it doesn't. Dad always seemed to wrestle with his feelings about me. At times I believed he loved me, at other times he railed against me being *just like my mother.*" April bit her lip at the memory of the puzzle that was her father.

"Maybe he thought he was saving my soul or some such," April continued, "not knowing just how twisted Vas is. And then there's the fact that Whitestone brought a letter to Sirona explaining how to rescue me. It was clear to Sirona that the rescue plan was not Whitestone's. He said himself he was just the messenger, but Sirona now suspects him of being the one to give us away in the first place. He knew of our plans after all and he knew you and Sirona. You are the likely link between Whitestone and Dad. How Dad might have gotten mixed up with the Society is a mystery but philosophically, it makes sense. I believe one of their founding principles is a hatred of women...especially those who exercise their own sovereignty."

"I have no doubt," Raina said, her forehead a sea of wrinkles, "that your father was not finished with me. That would have been the case even if I hadn't 'stolen' you from him as I'm sure is the way he reads all that has happened. But you think that after going to all the trouble of spying on us and leading Vas' thugs to you, if indeed it was him, then Malcolm changed his mind and laid a half-assed plan for your escape?" Raina was intrigued by the possibility, but not surprised at any duplicity on Malcolm's part.

"That's my thinking, but I have to confront him to be sure."

"And you think he will be honest with you?" Raina asked, her distain for Malcolm now uncontrollable. "He'll lie through his teeth." Then Raina looked hard at her daughter, awareness dawning. "You think you can use your powers on him!"

"I do, yes." April admitted. "They worked on Vas, and Malcolm is my dad, after all. There's at least some connection there that will make him more vulnerable. I believe Vas is still a threat so I need to at least try to find out the truth of Dad's involvement...or not."

Raina opened her mouth to utter a warning, but April anticipated it.

"Don't worry Mom, I've got this. You know how swords are made strong by being heated and then plunged in cold water? Well, my experience with Vas did that to...or for...me. I now know the true meaning of the expression that *what doesn't break us...*"

"*...will make us stronger,*" Raina finished for her. "My heart, you have indeed grown. I wouldn't have wished that experience of captivity on you for the world..."

"...and yet, it broke open my powers, my connection to my birthright. Not all gifts come wrapped in shiny paper."

"No indeed," Raina agreed. "Some even come wrapped in nightmares. But now, tell me of this Wyn person."

"He's a fascinating individual. I was suspicious of him at first, my paranoia on high alert after my abduction. But it didn't take him long to prove himself. And, after all, it was Rowan who found him. I doubt hidden agendas or duplicity would get by her."

Raina laughed. "How I miss her...."

"She didn't go up the Tor with us. Maybe she was just making room for Wyn, but I'm worried that she is struggling some."

"Movement isn't her forte," Raina reminded April. "I was surprised she made the climb the first time. Still, she may be getting on and if she's taken on this Wyn in some way, that makes him all the more interesting. So, do go on."

"There is so much to say about him," April said, turning back to the stream and kicking her feet in the water like a little kid. "I really hope you can meet him. The most important thing now is that he's shown me some new ways of looking at things, most particularly how one cultivates a connection to spirit/life energy. We all have the potential, but it needs to be actively studied and practiced. That I'm a descendant of Merlin perhaps gives me an edge, but if anyone can do it..."

"...then perhaps that is part of the new narrative we want to bring to the world," Raina said, picking up on April's excitement.

"Actually, an old narrative," April said thoughtfully, "at least for some, but yes, *new* in our present age. It seems to me that it is central to our cause. If people learn, or re-learn, to connect with the energy that pervades and connects all living things, one might assume that they'll be less likely to thoughtlessly destroy the planet."

Raina stepped into the stream. Reaching down she scooped water onto her face then turned to the sky before she turned back to her daughter.

"And these are the things you hope to learn with the Seabhean and, I presume, from Wyn as well?"

"Yes."

"I will miss you," Raina said, her voice cracking. "It's been such a joy to find you at last. To have you with me the way I would like you to be would frustrate your destiny, which of course I will not do. But...I will miss you."

"When we get settled," April said, suddenly realizing her own desire to be with her mother, "you must come and visit. There may be some important work for you to do there as well that we're not even aware of yet."

"There may be," Raina said, but her tone of voice belied a lack of interest in taking on a new quest.

Lily's people arrived shortly before the service, decked out in their finest, their complex natures shining forth without disguise in honor of this most sacred of rituals, giving the impression that it was not just humans attending this wedding, but representatives of the creatures of the earth as well.

On the verge of the lake stood the arbor Art and Percy had built of rough-hewn lumber and deadfall branches and miraculously decorated with a hilarity of interwoven vines, alive and blossoming, both coloring and perfuming the air.

Below its living roof, on a small table sat Raina's cauldron, etched in curling vines and Celtic symbols that echoed the surrounding flora, while a blue/green glaze spoke of the marriage of heaven and earth. Perhaps it was the dappled sunlight descending through the vines that made the colors appear to swirl and the designs dance, or maybe it was the love Raina had put into it with every turn of the wheel, every careful movement of her hands as she etched sacred symbols. Whatever it was, to all who looked upon it, the cauldron seemed alive, another guest from the world of mystery and myth ready to confer its own mystical blessing on the couple.

Inside the cauldron sat a smaller bowl filled with a red liquid – Rowan's potion against enchantment. Sirona had mixed it that morning, repeating the blessing Rowan had taught her and adding some words of her own which bubbled up from deep in her psyche, never spoken by her before, reserved for this unique moment of hope. Her hands trembled as she stirred the liquid, this moment being the first time she realized the full significance of the ceremony that was about to take place. More than the marriage of two beloved individuals, this was a covenant by all involved to commit to the quest Tannen and April were undertaking, that being, not to just seek and articulate a new myth, but to live it and devote their lives to bringing it to others. Perhaps Sirona understood better than most what this could mean. For over two thousand years, the world has fought against the old ways, the knowing connection between the earth and humankind. April and Tannen would be going head-long into that battle. In some ways, this ceremony was a sacrifice. Sirona shuddered at the thought. *Let this be a day of joy,* Sirona pledged to herself. *For this day and all those to come.*

As the ceremony began, Art stood like the king he was beneath the arbor, with Tannen at his side, ready, as were all assembled, to receive the bride. When she appeared on Percy's arm, there was a collective gasp from the crowd. April looked like a new myth herself in Lily's otherworldly creation. An amalgam of indigenous and fairy inspiration, white lace and delicate fringe draped artfully to accent April's figure at the same time suggesting something ephemeral, as though a being from the land beyond the wave had come to grace mere mortals with her presence, and one lucky mortal in particular with her hand in marriage. Sirona and Raina clung to each other for support as they gazed upon April's transformation into everyone's dream of ultimate harmony and inspiration.

Once the couple was united beneath the arbor, the elders rose as one, circled the couple and, as each spoke their blessing, kissed both April and Tannen on each cheek. Then Raina and Percy wrapped the couple's hands in the manner of hand-fasting while the two spoke their vows. Art began the communal sipping of Rowan's tea by first serving the hand-fasted couple, then serving the assembly as each came up single file, sipped the potion, circled the couple, then returned to their seat.

It was Poppie who closed the service. As her voice filled the air everyone present felt a quickening in their chest, the flutter of love filling every cell of their being. Colors deepened, a gentle breeze caressed each face as the unity of creation took form in sound and entered into every heart. Suddenly, someone cried *look* and pointed to the lake. There, in the center, rose a water spout, shimmering like a fist full of crystals thrown into the air, swirling like so many winged elementals dancing in delight, a tiny rainbow in each drop. At the sight, Poppie faltered in her singing for a brief moment, then found new energy as her song and the water melded into one.

Never had two people been so thoroughly and joyfully wed, not just by human will, but by the spirits of the earth as well.

"Are you sure you don't want me to go with you?" Between the bags in the hallway, all packed and ready for Ireland, and April's announcement that she and Tannen would go to Malcolm's after lunch, Raina was thoroughly beside herself. Sending her daughter off to yet another distant shore was one thing, but letting her willingly walk into the enemy's camp was quite another.

"Mom, we agreed. Tannen and I will go. It would serve no good purpose for you to engage with Dad. This is between the two of us. Besides, I can keep better control of the situation if it's just us. No complications, just a direct confrontation on one issue."

Raina sank into a chair, anxiety rising in her like a taser to the heart. If she could change anything, she would change this determination of April's to confront her father. Best to stay as far away as possible. But deep down she knew April was right. Never turn your back on the Devil, but face him square and stand your ground.

"Tannen..." Raina croaked, struggling to articulate her fears to her new son-in-law.

"I know, Raina," Tannen said, anticipating her admonition to beware. "Trust me. In and out and I never leave her side."

If Malcolm was surprised to see his daughter at the door, he didn't show it.

"Come on in, honey," he said, as though such a visit was a common thing. "Drink?"

April and Tannen entered, but stood side by side in the foyer. From where she stood, April scanned the room, looking for any clues that might support her suspicions, but saw nothing unusual.

"We're not staying long Dad."

"Well, you can't stand in the doorway. Come in," he said, once again waving them inside, but to no avail. "Introduce me to your friend."

"We will stay right here, thanks," April said, drawing a deep breath for what she would say next. "This *friend*, is Tannen, my husband."

At that, Malcolm's mask of nonchalance slipped a centimeter.

"Nice to meet you...Tannen," Malcolm said, regaining his composure enough to hold out a hand that Tannen did not take. As Malcolm awkwardly pulled his hand back and put it in his pocket as though to brush away the insult, he turned to April, his eyes tightening, his pretense of civility fading. Malcolm unmasked.

"What's this about April?" he asked, his voice threatening.

April met his eyes squarely and called to mind the kidnapping, the ominous collection of robed and hooded men pressed around her as Vas leered at her from his seat of authority. All the indignation, fear, and disgust she had felt she now used as fuel to ignite her resolve.

"It was you, wasn't it?"

"Whatever do you mean?" Malcolm countered, trying to pull away and recover an air of nonchalance, but April's stare kept him pinned.

"It was you who spied on us at the lake, you who stole my notebook, you who gave me over to Vas as though I was nothing to you."

Still frozen in place, Malcolm's efforts to retreat from April's accusations resulted in his face bloating, reddening.

"What are you talking about?" Malcolm managed to ask, but while his words protested, his face gave him away, completely.

"Where's your hooded cloak, your proof of membership in the Society for the Preservation of Heaven? What did you gain by offering me up to Vas to keep *caged* as his plaything? Tell me the truth. Now." April struggled to keep her anger from breaking her focus. It was more difficult than she had imagined, but she clenched her fists and directed all her energy into her gaze, holding Malcolm in its grip.

"And you'd still be there if it wasn't for me!" Malcolm blurted out despite himself.

"And I'm supposed to be thankful for your flimsy escape plan that endangered my friends, when it was you who gave me to Vas in the first place?"

"Believe me, I had no idea what his intentions were..."

"Please!" April said, almost losing her concentration in her disgust at a father who could so horribly betray her. "Vas's sickness reeks like an infected wound. Don't think for a minute I'd believe you could be ignorant of it." She had planned to pull more out of Malcolm, intended to get a full confession of every last bit of it, but her anger was getting the best of her. If she lost her grip on him, no telling what might ensue. Turning to Tannen she said, "I think we're done here." But as the two turned to leave, Malcolm shouted at their backs.

"You chose your crazy, despicable mother over me! What did you expect me to do?"

Fury rose in April like vomit. Wheeling around to face her father, the anger in her eyes turning them black, she held out her hand, palm up, as though she were conjuring a fireball to aim at the center of his being.

"Someday," she began, her voice a low growl, "when the full weight of what you've done has worn you down to a shriveled shell of a man, I will come back to you and you will tell me how you could be so cruel to your daughter...and your wife. For these are things I would know. Or maybe," she continued, as she twisted her hand as though to demonstrate her intentions, "I will come and force the poison out of you, make you vomit until you are clean, and then we'll see if there is anything left of you, and whether any redemption is possible."

With that April waved her hand and released Malcolm from his bondage, then the two left without another word.

As Tannen opened the passenger door for April, she fell into the car like a rag doll. By the time Tannen had come around to his side and started the car, April was crying piteously.

"April!" Tannen exclaimed, more alarmed at her tears than the power and anger she had wielded toward her father.

When April could gather herself enough to speak, she whispered, "I had so hoped I was wrong..."

Never before had April been so grateful for Tannen's love. As they lay together in the cottage loft, alone and fully belonging to one another, the touch of his skin against hers worked like a balm pulling together the edges of the blistering wound left by her father's treachery. Full of a thankfulness she had no words for, she wrapped herself around him, imagining herself a vine finding its footing against a sturdy oak, weaving in and out of the grooves and crevices of another living thing, growing new tendrils to replace what had been broken.

Tomorrow they would leave for Ireland, the land of sacred wells and green beyond imagining. April shuddered and dug her fingers into Tannen's hair. In the morning, she would check her back to be certain she hadn't sprouted wings. For now, she would let sleep carry her wherever it willed, trusting completely in the ultimate rightness of the Universe. But if she had anticipated a deep and dreamless sleep, such was not to be.

Merlin approached the young woman, holding out his hand to her, gentleness radiating from him like a warm breeze. She came to him, beautiful beyond imagining. "You needn't hide your powers from me as you do with others, Carys," the wizard said as he drew her to him. "Indeed, you cannot, for I can see all of you and cherish every inch."

"Then I will be open with you and it will be a pleasure to be so...a welcome respite from all that I keep hidden. But if you care for me as you claim, you must promise to keep my secret. With you I will shine brightly, but to all others I must remain simple and plain."

Merlin wrapped himself around her and whispered in her ear as they fell together in sacred union beneath the oaks.

As though born of the towering trees, a figure drifted down from their heights, covered in leaves and wearing a necklace of acorns, her hair alive with birds, her toes long and gnarled like roots. As she hovered over the couple, the rustle of leaves took on the quality of speech and so a declaration was made. "From this union is born the child to carry forth the best of the old ways, male and female essence alike, safe throughout the ages until such time as humankind has reached the height of foolishness. Then shall she arise and lead them back to the wisdom of the earth."

Epilogue

Ireland/Eriu
c. 525

As Annwyl sat outside Brigid's room, awaiting her turn to bid goodbye to the dying bishop, her mind travelled back through the trials and joys of the past years.

Ten seasons since Annwyl had left her babe on Abertha's stoop, terrified of what Nimue's curse would mean for the child. How those horrible words had echoed through her mind all these years. "Just as Merlin is not dead, but trapped in limbo, so too your spawn will carry this torment through the ages," Nimue had pledged, her eyes sparking with the fire of jealousy. Reeling with the news that she was pregnant, but carrying a cursed child, and with nowhere else to turn, Annwyl had returned to Merlin's cave on the Cornish coast, there to struggle with her fate as the child grew within her.

Alone she bore the child and alone she made the decision to leave it with the woman who had raised her. Precious Abertha. Only then did Annwyl fully realize what that woman had given her of love, tolerance, and eventually a hope for her future. But that hope was ensorcelled in the Forest of Broceliande, unable to be freed despite Annwyl's attempts to do so. Failure weighed heavily in Annwyl's heart as she swaddled the babe and made for Wales.

Well aware of Abertha's keen hearing, Annwyl had ridden hard out of the yard, away from her baby daughter and into a desolation of spirit from which she could imagine no respite. As she rode along the seacoast, the crashing surf called to her from below. A step off the cliff would be all it would take for the blessed sea to eat her, carry her into oblivion, wash over her for eternity as it did so many other beings, living and dead. But although the thought haunted her, she rode on to where the path turned away from the coast and into the heart of the land, and the dark interior of a life at odds with itself.

She had found work where she could, on farms and in taverns, enough to keep her physically alive and some manner of roof over her head, but never anything that would bring her back to herself. Persistent was the ache at the center of her being, the place where her babe would have slept against her heart. But what good was a cursed heart, tormented by loss and failure, to her or anyone else? And so she would stay on only as long as she was a stranger and move on at the first sign that someone might open their heart to her, however slightly.

It went on that way, through the country and through the seasons until at last, she had found herself in the far north at a tavern called the Goat and Gull. She begged for work as she was accustomed to doing and was granted food and rough lodging in return for tending the gardens and helping the brew master. But there was something different here, something in the way certain folk looked at her. Whereas she was generally given little if any mind, here there seemed to be some kind of interest in her. She would have left at the first sign of it, but she'd ridden a long way and was tired and hungry and, though she could not explain it, there was something about the place and the mountains in the near distance that drew her. And so she stayed and suffered the looks pregnant with curiosity and tight with words unspoken.

Until the day, on her knees in the garden, Annwyl was approached by a cloaked and hooded figure, strands of white hair blown free by the wind the only indication of what lurked within. Annwyl's heart quickened in fear as the figure knelt beside her in the dirt and turned its hidden visage toward her, staring for what to Annwyl seemed a very long and fraught time.

"It is you, then," the cloaked figure said at last, so quietly Annwyl barely heard it. Pushing the hood back only enough to reveal

the stunningly beautiful face within, framed by snow white hair, eyes like the stars that blink blue-white in the midnight sky, the figure spoke urgently. "I am Abertha's sister, Snow. I bid you come with me, quickly and quietly. I know of your birth and I know of your babe. Abertha brought her to us to bless, and so we have. You must trust me, for I can say no more here, nor might I tarry. Please, come."

For all her years of longing, there was no refusing Snow's request. Should this stranger have evil intent against her, what of it? What she promised was more than Annwyl dared imagine would ever be offered her. As Snow rose from the dirt and offered Annwyl her hand, Annwyl put all caution behind her and prepared to follow Snow into the mountains beyond.

The time she spent behind the Falls passed in a blur of joy and well-being. In all her life, Annwyl had never felt so at home. At first, her days with Snow were full of life's comforts: scented baths, simple but elegant gowns, nourishing food and soothing music. But once Annwyl was settled into a luxury she had never known, Snow began to share with her the story of her birth. She told Annwyl of her birth mother, Carys, and the love she shared with Merlin, and at Carys' death how Abertha had been chosen to rear Annwyl in anonymity and safety. Annwyl questioned Snow freely, and in return Snow held nothing back. And so, at long last, Annwyl's life took on form, the foundations of her being built up beneath her, so that who she was began to take shape for her. She began to imagine a life among these people, her people as she now knew. But as that dream ripened within her, she learned the nature of Snow's sense of urgency.

"The time has come for us to leave this place and travel beyond the nineth wave," Snow had explained. "It is no longer safe for us here, even hidden as we are here behind the falls. The Old Ways are no longer tolerated. Those who practice them are being rooted out."

"Was it not dangerous, then, for you to come to me at the Goat and Gull?" Annwyl had asked.

"Indeed it was," Snow had replied, "but it was worth the risk to reclaim you, to us and to yourself."

"Then let me go with you," Annwyl had begged, the thought of leaving her true family so soon after finding them tearing her apart, threatening to return her to her previous sense of worthlessness.

"Dear Annwyl," Snow had replied, her starry eyes full of cosmic tears, "what a waste that would be! What a loss. Your path will not be an easy one, but it is an honorable one, a heroic one. You are an emissary to the future. It is not your destiny to abandon this present world. You carry the heritage of two powerful beings. Like it or not, you are the vehicle of humankind's future survival. You must persist and resist, carry the seed forward."

"But Nimue's curse!" Annwyl had cried.

"Believe that you can overcome it with vigilance and love," Snow had told her. "Your powers and the wisdom of the old folk are alive in you and will persist, whether you openly employ them or not. I regret that we aren't able to teach you more, but perhaps that will work to your advantage. If you knew too much, it would likely shine forth from you and make you a target, resulting in the death of your line. As it is, you are well suited to hiding in plain sight.

"Go west to the Emerald Isle," Snow had continued. "The Romans have less influence there, and so you might find some peace. Sink your soul into the land; it will teach you, but you must listen carefully, though I suspect it will recognize you and readily open its secrets to one of its own."

"And my babe, Buddug, what of her?"

"Your path back to her lies through the green land, Eriu, I'm sure of it."

Within days, Snow's people had left their Keep behind the Falls and Annwyl found herself once again on the road, loss and sadness a poor tailwind for what lay ahead.

And so it was that she had eventually found her way to Cill Dara and the saintly Brigid. Though even had Brigid lived longer, would she have stayed? She doubted it. As Snow had predicted, the enchanted land of Eriu did indeed open its wisdom to Annwyl. Slowly but surely it spoke, in a language it took Annwyl great concentration to discern, but learn it she did, bit by bit. Still, Annwyl's heart did not fully open until she met Brigid, and when it did open it burst like a ripe fruit, spilling out years of love withheld in the face of loss. To her credit, Brigid was fierce in her responsibility for her own actions. Having been the instrument of Annwyl's awakening, she then set herself to Annwyl's healing. In the inexhaustible font of Brigid's love, Annwyl did in fact heal.

Now, as Brigid lay dying, her followers had begged Annwyl to stay, to help them carry on Brigid's work, but it was Brigid herself, not the church she had founded, that had kept Annwyl in Cill Dara. While the new religion felt benign in Brigid's hands, Annwyl well knew the other side of it. Hadn't it been a struggle to have Brigid ordained, despite the obvious power of her calling? Devoted as they were, the women of the Brigidine order could claim no such gifts. Sooner or later, Brigid's vision of Christianity would be overshadowed by the male hierarchy and the religion that had forced her people to go into hiding. No. Wherever she was destined to go next, she would not stay here.

As she was beckoned, she rose to enter the room and, for the last time, sat beside the woman who had unlocked her heart.

The Characters

500 AD

Abertha -- Foster mother to Annwyl
Annwyl -- Merlin's daughter by Carys
Brigid -- St. Brigid of Kildare
Buddug *("bee-thig")* -- Annwyl's daughter
Carys -- Annwyl's birth mother, died in childbirth
Derwen -- Foster father to Annwyl
Nesta -- The herbalist and Abertha's friend
Snow -- Abertha's Sister
Ysbail -- Abertha's Mother
(Gawen – Annwyl's lover and son of the Duke of Cornwall)
(Tanan – Cornish Knight that accompanied Annwyl to Forest of Broceliande)

Present Day

Abernathy Whitestone -- Merlin scholar
April Quinn -- Raina's daughter
Art Fisher -- avatar of King Arthur
Eudora -- the "Bee Witch"
Ignatius Vas -- High Priest of the Society for the Preservation of Heaven
Lily -- Keeper of the Hedge and Hearth
Malcolm Holtz -- April's father/Raina's ex-husband
Niall -- Sirona's lover
Percy Smith -- reincarnated spirit of Merlin's Owl
Raina Quinn -- Retired college professor, scion of Merlin
Rowan -- Tree woman, reader of soul lives
Sirona Fisher -- Art's sister, avatar of Morgan le Fay

Tannen -- Percy's son
Tuttle -- Keeper of the Time Emporium

Lily's people:
Ben -- wolf spirit
Chet -- Chipmunk spirit
Darla -- Tree spirit
Gladys -- Swan spirit
John -- Bear spirit
Poppie -- Elemental

Glastonbury group:
Beatrice -- denizen of Glastonbury
Colleen -- Jemma's wife and computer expert
Gaias Brightly -- Magical gardener
Jemma -- the keeper of the cauldron
Liselle -- from France
Muriel -- Tarot reader
Wyn -- Young Welsh Druid

Acknowledgements

Self-publishing gives an author almost complete control over their work which is especially valuable to those who resist conforming to popular trends or altering their vision to enhance marketability. But it also means relying on friends and relatives for the things that would otherwise be done by professionals. On that score, I've been profoundly fortunate to have people in my life who support my work not just with words, but with their time and considerable talent as well.

Granted, my partner, Dave Street, is captive to my enthusiasms, but he unfailingly and unselfishly listens to every word I write, usually right off my fingertips, and gives me the support I need to persist.

Then there's the gang of four: Gail Grow, Karen Kaufman, Amy Lent and Jenny Schmonsky who, with their varying talents, edited copy and gave helpful suggestions, without which *The Book of April* would have gone to press embarrassingly unprofessional.

The list of relatives and friends who have given me their support, not just by buying, reading, and commenting on my work, but with marketing as well, is gloriously long. Heartfelt thanks to all of you.

A special thanks to Paul Block for taking the time to read *The Wizard's Return* and giving me a professional opinion, without which I may not have had the confidence to continue the trilogy.

Finally, of course, great appreciation for Troy Book Makers just for being there and making self-publication a welcoming possibility for people. They are supportive, reasonable, and easy to work with. Meradith, senior author liaison, is attentive, knowledgeable and patient.

To all those I don't have room to name, thank you for being the kind of people who support others in their creative/spirit journeys, doing your part to keep art alive.